MAIGRET AND MONSIEUR CHARLES

AND

MAIGRET AND THE DOSSER

Superintendent Maigret is presented with what appears to be a quite baffling mystery when Nathalie Sabin-Levesque reports the disappearance of her husband, Gérard, a prosperous lawyer of the Boulevard Saint-Germain. Maigret soon discovers that Gérard has been leading a double life as Monsieur Charles, a well-known playboy of the night-clubs with a penchant for having affairs with selected hostesses. Nathalie herself is a nerve-racked alcoholic who is not at all co-operative, but who at first arouses Maigret's sympathy. He soon finds, however, that his inquiries must begin with her mysterious past. . . .

*   *   *

Maigret is summoned to investigate what proves to be a case of attempted murder when a drowning tramp is fished out of the Seine after being violently attacked and thrown in. The victim turns out to be no ordinary tramp, but is a doctor who has dropped out of society and who has been 'dossing' beside the bridges on the river bank. He is strangely unwilling to give any information, and Maigret suspects that the 'tramp' knows the identity of his attacker. Although the investigation subsequently reveals the truth, Maigret is unable to prove anything as the victim steadfastly refuses to give evidence.

Also by
GEORGES SIMENON

★

MAIGRET AND MONSIEUR CHARLES

and

MAIGRET AND THE DOSSER

*

GEORGES SIMENON

THE
COMPANION BOOK CLUB
LONDON AND SYDNEY

---

*Made and printed in Great Britain
for the Companion Book Club
by Odhams (Watford) Ltd.*
600871835
12.74/283

CONTENTS

★

MAIGRET AND MONSIEUR CHARLES

★

Translated from the French by
MARIANNE ALEXANDRE SINCLAIR

CHAPTER ONE

MAIGRET WAS PLAYING in the tepid rays of a March
sun. It was not with his childhood bricks he was playing
but with his pipes.

He kept five or six pipes on his desk and he invariably
selected with care the one which suited his mood.

His gaze was vacant and he was slumped in his chair.
He had just made a decision which would affect the remaining years of his career. He had no regrets, but even
so he could not help feeling a touch of melancholy.

Mechanically and with great solemnity, he rearranged
the pipes on his blotting paper in more or less geometric
patterns, or else into shapes that reminded him of various
animals.

His morning's post lay in a pile on the right-hand side
of his desk and he did not feel like dealing with it.

On his arrival at the Police Judiciaire just before nine
o'clock, he had found a summons from the chief of police.
This in itself was unusual and as he went to the Rue du
Palais he wondered what it could mean.

The chief of police saw him immediately and was extremely affable and well-disposed.

'Can you guess why I wanted to see you?'

'I must admit I can't.'

'Do sit down and light your pipe.'

The chief of police was a youngish man, hardly more
than forty. The product of a good university, he was a
stylish dresser, perhaps a little too much so.

'You know that the head of the Police Judiciaire is
retiring next month after twelve years in office . . . I discussed the question of his successor with the Minister of

the Interior yesterday and we both agreed to offer you the post.'

The chief of police undoubtedly expected Maigret's face to light up with joy. Instead of which the latter's expression grew sombre.

'Is it an order?' he asked, almost abruptly.

'No, of course it isn't. But as you know it's an important promotion; there's no higher position in the Police Judiciaire . . .'

'I know that. Yet I'd still prefer to remain at the head of the Criminal Division. Please don't be offended at my reaction. I've had forty years of active police service. It would be hard for me to spend my days cooped up in an office, looking through files and occupying myself with administration . . .'

The chief of police could not conceal his astonishment.

'Shouldn't you think it over for a few days before giving me your answer? Perhaps you'd like to talk it over with Madame Maigret?'

'She would understand how I feel.'

'So do I and I don't want to insist . . .'

Nevertheless his expression was one of slight annoyance. He understood without understanding. Maigret needed the human contact which he got from his investigations. People had often disapproved of his not directing his inquiries from his office and of his becoming actively involved, carrying out routine tasks usually considered the duty of ordinary inspectors.

Maigret was playing, his mind a blank. He had now arranged his pipes in a pattern which reminded him of a crane.

The sun poured in through the window. The chief of police had accompanied him to the door and had shaken hands in a friendly way. Yet Maigret knew that his decision would be resented in high places.

Slowly, he lit one of his pipes and began to smoke it, taking short puffs.

It had taken him a few minutes to decide about a future which of itself would not be very long, since he would retire in three years' time. Good God, they could at least allow him to spend those three remaining years as he wished!

He needed to escape from his office, to be out and about in all weathers, to discover a whole new world with each enquiry. He needed those long hours spent waiting at the counter of some *bistrot*, drinking calvados or beer, depending on the circumstances. He needed the long, patient struggle in his office with a suspect who, after refusing to say anything for several hours, would often break down and make a dramatic confession.

He was uneasy. What he feared was that they would reconsider and somehow oblige him to accept the promotion. And he did not want that at any price, even though it was as good as a field-marshal's baton.

He continued to rearrange his pipes, occasionally moving one like a chess piece. A discreet knock on the door which communicated with the inspectors' duty room made him jump.

Before he could reply, Lapointe walked in.

'Sorry to disturb you, *patron* . . .'

'You're not disturbing me in the least.'

It was now almost ten years since Lapointe had joined the Police Judiciaire, and he had been known as 'little Lapointe'. In those days, he had been tall and lanky. He had since grown stouter. He had got married and had two children.

Yet he was still known as 'little Lapointe', and some would have added: 'Maigret's pet'.

'There's a woman in my office who insists on seeing you personally. She won't tell me anything. She's sitting bolt upright on her chair and is very much determined to have her way.'

That often happened. People would read about Maigret in newspaper articles and would insist on seeing him in person. It was often difficult to make them change their minds. Some of them even managed, God knows how, to discover his home address and would come and ring his doorbell in the Boulevard Richard-Lenoir.

'Did she give you her name?'

'Here's her card:'

Madame Sabin-Levesque
207 bis, Boulevard Saint-Germain

'She seems peculiar to me,' Lapointe added. 'She stares right at you and she's got a sort of nervous twitch that makes the right-hand side of her mouth droop. She hasn't taken her gloves off, but you can see that her fingers never stop clenching.'

'Ask her to come in, and stay with us. Bring your shorthand pad just in case.'

Maigret looked at his pipes with a sigh of regret. His little break was over.

He stood up when the woman came into the room.

'Please sit down, Madame. . . .'

She was staring at him.

'Are you really Superintendent Maigret?'

'I am.'

'I imagined you fatter.'

She was wearing a fur coat with a matching hat. Was it mink? Maigret had no idea; the wife of a divisional superintendent usually had to make do with rabbit fur or, at best, musquash and racoon.

Madame Sabin-Levesque's gaze travelled slowly round the office, as though making an inventory. When Lapointe sat down at one end of the desk with his pencil and pad, she asked:

'Is this young man going to stay here?'

'Yes, he is.'

'He's going to take down our conversation?'

'It's the regulations.'

She frowned and her fingers clasped her crocodile handbag more firmly.

'I thought I could speak to you in private.'

Maigret did not answer. He was watching her and he had to agree with Lapointe that there was something extremely odd about her. At some moments, her stare was so intense as to be embarrassing, while at others she seemed far away.

'I suppose you know who I am?'

'I've read the name on your card.'

'Do you know who my husband is?'

'I expect he has the same name as you.'

'He's one of the best-known solicitors in Paris.'

The corners of her lips twitched constantly. She seemed to find it difficult to keep calm.

'Please go on.'

'He's disappeared.'

'In that case, you shouldn't have come to me. There's a special department which concerns itself with missing persons.'

She gave a sad, ironic smile and did not bother to answer.

It was difficult to decide how old she was. Probably in her early forties, at most forty-five; but her face was lined and there were bags under her eyes.

'Had you been drinking before you came here?' Maigret suddenly asked her.

'Do you really want to know?'

'Yes, I do. It was you who insisted on coming to see

me, wasn't it? You must expect me to ask questions you might consider indiscreet.'

'I expected you to be different, more understanding.'

'It's precisely because I'm trying to understand that I must know certain things.'

'I had two glasses of cognac, to give me courage.'

'Only two?'

She looked at him without replying.

'When did your husband disappear?'

'Over a month ago. On February 18th. It's now the 21st of March . . .'

'Did he tell you he was going off on a journey?'

'He didn't tell me anything.'

'And you've waited until now to tell us that he's disappeared?'

'I'm used to it.'

'To what?'

'To his going away for several days at a time.'

'How long has this been going on?'

'For years. It began shortly after our marriage, fifteen years ago.'

'Doesn't he give you any explanation when he goes away?'

'I don't think he does go away.'

'I don't understand.'

'He stays in Paris or in the suburbs.'

'How do you know?'

'Because in the beginning I had him followed by a private detective. Then I stopped it, because it was always the same thing.'

She spoke with some difficulty; she had certainly drunk more than two glasses of cognac. And it wasn't simply to give herself courage that she had drunk them, for it was obvious from her raddled face and from the effort she had to make to keep her composure that she often got drunk.

14

'I'm waiting for you to tell me the details.'

'My husband's like that.'

'Like what?'

'He has these fancies all of a sudden. He meets a woman he likes and he feels the need to live with her for a few days. So far, his longest romance, if you could call it that, has lasted two weeks.'

'Do you mean to tell me that he picks up these women in the street?'

'Almost. He usually finds them in nightclubs.'

'Does he go out by himself?'

'Always, yes.'

'He never took you with him?'

'We have meant nothing to each other for years.'

'Yet you're worried.'

'I am, for his sake.'

'Not for your own sake?'

She gave him a hard, defiant look.

'No.'

'You don't love him any more?'

'No.'

'Does he love you?'

'Even less so.'

'But you still live together.'

'We have a big flat. We keep different hours, so we don't meet often.'

With astonishment across his face, Lapointe continued to take his shorthand notes.

'Why did you come here?'

'So that you'd find him.'

'This is the first time you've been worried?'

'A month is a long time. He didn't take anything with him, not even a small suitcase, no spare clothes, nothing. He didn't even take one of the cars.'

'Have you several cars?'

15

'Two. A Bentley, which he usually takes, and a Fiat, which I normally use.'

'Do you drive?'

'Our chauffeur, Vittorio, drives me when I go out.'

'Do you get out a lot?'

'Nearly every afternoon.'

'Do you go and see friends?'

'I don't have any friends. . . .'

Maigret had seldom met such a bitter, disconcerting woman before.

'Do you go shopping?'

'I loathe going into shops.'

'Do you go for walks in the Bois de Boulogne, or anywhere else?'

'I go to the cinema.'

'Every day?'

'Almost every day. When I don't feel too tired.'

As with all addicts, the moment had come when she needed a drink to give herself a lift. Maigret could see that she would have given anything for a brandy, but he did not intend to offer her one, even though he kept a bottle in his cupboard for special occasions. He felt slightly sorry for her.

'I'm trying to understand, Madame Sabin.'

'Madame Sabin-Levesque,' she said, correcting him.

'As you wish. And so your husband disappears regularly?'

'Never for as long as a month.'

'So you've told me already.'

'I have a foreboding.'

'What kind of foreboding?'

'I'm afraid that something may have happened to him.'

'Do you have any reasons for supposing that?'

'No. You don't need a reason to have a foreboding.'

'According to you, your husband is a prominent solicitor.'

'Let's say that he has one of the most successful practices in Paris.'

'How does he manage to go away so regularly?'

'Gérard isn't at all like the usual solicitor. He inherited his father's firm, but it's the head clerk who handles everything. . . .'

'You seem tired . . .'

'I'm always tired. My health isn't good.'

'What about your husband's health?'

'He's forty-eight, but he's as fit as a young man.'

'From what you tell me, we'd be most likely to pick up his trail around the nightclubs . . .'

'That's right.'

Maigret was thoughtful. He felt that he was on the wrong track and that her answers were not getting them anywhere.

He wondered for a moment if the woman were mad or at least unbalanced. Quite a few of that sort had sat in his office and he was always at a loss to know how to deal with them.

Her actual words made sense and sounded normal enough, but at the same time one could sense a divorce between her and reality.

'Do you know if he had a lot of money on him?'

'As far as I know, he nearly always used his cheque-book.'

'Have you discussed this with the head clerk?'

'We're not on speaking terms.'

'Why not?'

'Because about three years ago my husband forbade me to go down to the office.'

'Why was that?'

'I don't know.'

17

'You must know the head clerk, even if you're not on good terms with him.'

'His name is Lecureur; he's never liked me much.'

'Did he work in the firm before your father-in-law died?'

'He's been there since he was twenty-two.'

'He màmay know more about your husband's whereabouts.'

'Perhaps. But if I went to ask him he wouldn't tell me anything . . .'

Maigret was beginning to find that twitch of hers exasperating. He realized that the interview was becoming more and more of an ordeal for her, but in that case why had she come?

'Was there a marriage contract between you?'

'No.'

'Have you any money of your own?'

'No.'

'Does your husband give you all the money you need?'

'Yes, he does. He's not at all mean. I couldn't swear to it, but I think he is very rich.'

Maigret was questioning her in no particular order. He had investigated a number of avenues at random and, so far, he had got nowhere.

'Listen, you're tired. That's understandable. If you don't mind, I'll come and see you at your flat this afternoon. . . .'

'As you wish.' She did not get up, but still fidgeted with her handbag.

'What do you think of me?' she finally asked him, in a lower voice.

'I don't think anything yet.'

'You find me complicated, don't you?'

'Not necessarily.'

'The girls at school used to find me complicated and I've never really had any friends.'

'Yet you're very intelligent.'

'Do you think so?' She smiled, her lips quivering as she did so. 'It hasn't done me any good.'

'Have you ever been happy?'

'Never. I don't know the meaning of the word.'

She pointed to Lapointe, who was still taking notes in shorthand.

'Does this conversation really have to be recorded? It's difficult to talk freely when someone's writing down every word you say.'

'If there's something confidential you want to tell me, we'll stop taking notes.'

'I have nothing more to say just now. . . .'

She got up with some effort. Her shoulders drooped, her back was slightly hunched, and she was hollow-chested.

'Does he have to come with you this afternoon?'

Maigret hesitated, wanting to give her a chance.

'I'll come alone.'

'What time?'

'The time which suits you best.'

'I usually have a nap. What about four o'clock?'

'Fine.'

'It's on the first floor. You take the right-hand door under the arch.' Without offering her hand, she walked stiffly to the door, as if afraid of losing her balance.

'Thank you all the same for agreeing to see me,' she said, in a remote voice.

And, throwing Maigret one last glance, she made her way towards the large staircase.

The two men stared at each other, as though to postpone the moment when both would open their mouths to begin asking questions. The difference was that Lapointe seemed dumbfounded, while the chief superintendent's expression still remained solemn, although there was a malicious gleam in his eye.

He went over to open the window and began to fill a heavy pipe which he had chosen. Lapointe could no longer contain himself.

'What do you think, *patron*?'

Those who worked with him rarely ventured to ask such a question, since he usually replied by grunting, in a now familiar way: 'I don't think.'

Instead, it was now he who asked a question:

'About this vanished husband story?'

'About her particularly . . .'

Maigret was lighting his pipe as he stood by the window, contemplating the Quais. He gave a sigh.

'She's a strange woman. . . .''

Nothing more. He did not try to analyse his impressions, still less put them into words. Lapointe could see that he was troubled and regretted having thoughtlessly asked the question. Nevertheless, he murmured:

'Perhaps she's mad?'

The chief superintendent looked at him searchingly, without speaking. He remained a long while by the window, then asked:

'Will you have lunch with me?'

'Certainly, *patron*, especially since my wife's gone to see her sister at Saint-Cloud.'

'Shall we say in fifteen minutes?'

When Lapointe had left, Maigret picked up the phone and rang the Boulevard Richard-Lenoir.

'Is that you?' his wife's voice asked, even before he had opened his mouth.

'It's me.'

'I bet you're going to tell me you're not coming home for lunch.'

'You win your bet.'

'At the Brasserie Dauphine?'

'With Lapointe.'

'A new case?'

His last important case had ended three weeks earlier; this wish of his to have lunch at the Place Dauphine was, in fact, his way of celebrating his return to active duty. It was also partly his way of cocking a snook at the chief of police and the Minister of the Interior, who had wanted to lock him up in a luxurious office.

'Yes.'

'I haven't read anything in the papers.'

'The papers haven't mentioned it yet; perhaps they never will.'

'Have a good lunch—I only had grilled herrings for you.'

He remained in thought for a few minutes, then picked up the phone again, staring at the armchair where his visitor had sat.

He could almost picture her sitting there again, so edgy, with those staring eyes and nervous tic.

'May I speak to Maître Demaison, please?'

He knew that Maître Demaison would be at home at this hour.

'Maigret speaking.'

'How are you? Got some poor old murderer you want me to defend?'

'Not yet. I only want some information. Do you know a solicitor on the Boulevard Saint-Germain by the name of Sabin-Levesque?'

'Gérard? I'll say I do! We read law together.'

'What do you think of him?'

'Has he gone off again?'

'You know about that?'

'All his friends know. He falls for a pretty woman now and then and vanishes for the night, or for a few days.

He's got a taste for what you might call semi-professionals, such as strippers or nightclub hostesses.'

'Does this happen often?'

'As far as I know, about ten times a year. . . .'

'What's he like as a solicitor?'

'He inherited one of the best practices in Paris, practically the whole of the Faubourg Saint-Germain, but he's nothing like the conventional type of solicitor. He wears light-coloured suits and sometimes check tweed jackets.

'He's a very cheerful, easygoing fellow who looks on the bright side of life, but that doesn't prevent him from managing his clients' affairs very astutely. . . . I've known several men and women who are clients of his; they think the world of him. . . .'

'Do you know his wife?'

There was a pause.

'Yes.'

'Well?'

'She's an odd woman. *I* wouldn't like to live with her, and I dare say Gérard feels the same way, since he makes a point of avoiding her.'

'Does she ever go out with him?'

'Not as far as I know.'

'Does she have any men or women friends?'

'I don't know of any.'

'Any lovers?'

'I've never heard any gossip about her. Most people think she's either neurotic or mad. She's a heavy drinker.'

'I've noticed that.'

'I've told you all I know.'

'It seems the husband disappeared a month ago.'

'And no one's heard from him?'

'Apparently not. She was worried and so she came to see me this morning.'

'Why you and not the Bureau of Missing Persons?'

'I pointed that out to her. She didn't answer.'

'Usually, when he's away for several days, he keeps in touch by phone with his head clerk, whose name I've forgotten. . . . Have you spoken to him?'

'I'll probably be seeing him this afternoon.'

A few minutes later, Maigret opened the door of the inspectors' duty room and motioned to Lapointe. The latter darted forward with a clumsiness he could not conceal in Maigret's presence. For Maigret was his god.

'We don't need our overcoats,' the chief superintendent said in a low voice. 'We're not going far.'

That morning he had only taken a light overcoat, which he had found hanging up on a hook.

The pavement echoed under their footsteps. It was good to be in the atmosphere of the Brasserie Dauphine again, with its mingled smells of cooking and drink. At the bar there were several police officers, to whom Maigret waved.

They went straight into the cosy dining-room, which overlooked the Seine.

The proprietor shook hands with them.

'A little glass of *pastis* to greet the Spring?'

Maigret hesitated, then finally agreed, and so did Lapointe. The proprietor brought the drinks.

'An inquiry?'

'Probably.'

'Mind you, I'm not asking any questions. . . . We're discretion personified here and our lips are sealed. . . . How would you like some sweetbreads with mushrooms?'

Maigret sipped his *pastis*, his first for a long time. The *hors d'œuvres* was set out before them.

'I wonder if she'll be more talkative this afternoon when I'm not there.'

'I wonder, too. . . .'

They took their time over the meal, and the proprietress

23

insisted on their trying her home-made almond cake with which, after wiping her hands on her apron, she now served them.

It was not quite two o'clock when the two men climbed the vast staircase of the Police Judiciaire.

'They've modernized the buildings but it never occurred to them to put in a lift,' Maigret grumbled, out of breath.

He went into his office, lit a pipe and began to sort through his mail in a desultory fashion. It consisted mainly of administrative forms which needed filling out and reports to be countersigned. The time passed slowly. Occasionally, he would look out of the window and let his mind wander far away from the office.

For once, spring was on time. The air was crystal-clear, the sky a delicate blue, and the buds on the trees were already swelling. In a few days, the first leaves would begin to show their pale green shoots.

As he passed the door of the inspectors' duty room, he called out:

'I don't know when I'll be back.'

He had decided to walk to the Boulevard Saint-Germain, but he soon regretted the idea, for it seemed a long way to number 207 *bis*, and he had to mop his forehead several times during the journey.

The huge stone building, which had turned grey with age, looked like most of the other houses along the Boulevard. He went in through a highly-polished oak door and found himself in the vaulted entrance, at the end of which he could see a paved courtyard with old stables which had been converted into garages.

On the left-hand door there was a solicitor's gilded escutcheon and a brass plaque which stated:

Maître G. Sabin-Levesque
Solicitor

Across the way, to the right of the other entrance, a man was peering at him through the window of the concierge's lodge.

Madame Sabin-Levesque had told him that the flat was on the first floor. On the same side, there was another brass plaque which read:

> *Professor Arthur Rollin*
> *Pediatrician*
> *Third Floor—By appointment only*

That doctor's fees must have been high. The lift was vast. Since the flat was only on the first floor, Maigret decided to walk up the elegant staircase, with its thickly-carpeted steps.

When he reached the first floor, he rang the bell. Almost instantly, an attractive young maid opened the door and took his hat.

'Will you please come in? Madame is expecting you.'

He found himself in a panelled hallway. The large drawing-room into which he was next ushered was also panelled, with nineteenth-century portraits hung on the walls.

He did not sit down. The furniture was massive, mostly in the Louis-Philippe style, and though the total effect was of luxury and comfort, all gaiety was absent.

'Madame is waiting for you in her boudoir. I'll take you there. . . .'

They went through two or three more rooms, which Maigret did not have time to take in, until they at last came to the boudoir, hung with blue silk, where Madame Sabin-Levesque lay reclining on a chaise-longue. She was wearing a *peignoir* of darker blue and held out a hand loaded with rings to Maigret, who, not knowing whether to kiss or to shake it, merely touched it with his finger-tips.

'Please sit down. I'm sorry to be receiving you in this fashion, but I'm not feeling well and I think I'll go back to bed after our talk.'

'I'll try not to keep you long.'

'What's your impression of me?'

'I told you this morning that you're a very intelligent person.'

'You're wrong about that. I only follow my instincts, nothing more.'

'First of all, let me ask you a question. Before you came to tell me your husband had disappeared, did you check with the head clerk to find out if he had any news of him?'

'I rang him several times during the last month. . . . There's a private line between the flat and the office . . . I ought to tell you that my husband owns this building. He inherited it from his father. . . .'

'Monsieur Lecureur . . . that's his name, isn't it? . . . Monsieur Lecureur hasn't heard from him either?'

'Not once.'

'Did he on previous occasions?'

'I didn't ask him. I think I told you that I'm not on very good terms with him.'

She hesitated.

'Would you care for a brandy or anything else to drink?'

'No, thank you.'

'I'm going to have a brandy. You see, I'm not ashamed to drink in front of you. Anyway, everyone will tell you I'm an alcoholic, which is true. . . . They'll probably also tell you I'm mad . . .'

She rang a bell and the butler arrived a few moments later.

'Bring me the brandy and a glass, Honoré.'

'Only one glass, Madame?'

'Yes, just one. Superintendent Maigret doesn't want a drink . . .'

26

Her manner had become rather aggressive. She stared at him defiantly, a smile hovering painfully on her bitter lips.

'Did you share a bedroom with your husband?'

'We did for about three months, immediately after we were married. Now the rooms on this side of the main drawing-room are mine. My husband's domain is those on the other side.'

'Do you usually have your meals together?'

'You've asked me that already. . . . Yes, we do, once in a while, but we don't keep the same hours and we have different tastes . . .'

'What do you do during the holidays?'

'We have . . . Sorry, I mean Gérard was left a big villa near Cannes. . . . We go there. . . . He bought a yacht recently and I see even less of him than I do in Paris.'

'Does he have any enemies that you know of?'

'None that I can think of . . . except for me. . . .'

'Do you hate him?'

'Not really. I don't even resent him. It's just his character.'

'Are you his heir?'

'Yes, his sole heir.'

'Is he very wealthy?'

'Enough to make quite a few women wish they were in my place. But, you see, it so happens that I'm not interested in money, and I'd be happier living in a garret. . . .'

'Why don't you ask for a divorce?'

'Too lazy. Or too indifferent. There comes a time when one doesn't feel like anything any more; one just goes on repeating the same gestures, day after day, without thinking.'

She picked up her glass with a shaking hand.

'Cheers . . .'

She emptied it to the last drop.

'There, you see? I suppose I ought to blush with shame . . .'

'Who said you ought to? Your husband?'

'Yes, when I began drinking. That was many years ago . . .'

'And now?'

'He doesn't care.'

'Would you be relieved to discover he was dead?'

'Not really. He means so little to me, alive or dead.'

'You think some misfortune's happened to him, don't you?'

'I think it may have; that's why I came to see you.'

'What do you think could have happened?'

'He usually picks up his . . . shall we call them his girl-friends? . . . in nightclubs, where one meets all sorts of people . . .'

'Do you know any of these clubs?'

'I know of about two or three, from finding some matchboxes with the names printed on them. . . .'

'What were they?'

'The *Chat Botté* . . . the *Belle Hélène* . . . let me see . . . the *Cric-Crac* . . .'

'Have you ever felt tempted to go and see one of them for yourself?'

'I'm not curious.'

'So I see.'

She was helping herself to more brandy and her lips had begun to twitch again. Her gaze was blank and un-seeing; Maigret had the feeling that at any moment she might look up and demand to know what he was doing there.

'In other words, you think there may have been a crime?'

'Don't you?'

28

'Couldn't he have fallen ill?'

'He's as strong as a horse.'

'An accident . . . ?'

'I'd have seen it in the papers.'

'Did you ring up the hospitals?'

'I did, yesterday.'

If she was capable of doing that, then despite appearances she was keeping her wits about her. There was a photograph in a silver frame on the white marble mantelpiece, and Maigret got up to have a closer look at it. It was a posed portrait of Madame Sabin-Levesque when much younger, probably before her marriage. She had been very pretty in those days, with something rather waif-like about her face.

'Yes, it's me . . . I've changed, haven't I?'

'Was this photograph taken before or after your wedding?'

'A few weeks after. Gérard insisted on having it done by a well-known photographer in the Boulevard Haussman.'

'He must have been in love with you in those days.'

'I don't know. He seemed to be.'

'Did you grow apart suddenly?'

'No. The first time, he went off for twenty-four hours and I didn't say anything. He told me he'd gone to see one of his clients in the provinces. . . . Later on, he began to do more or less as he pleased. He stopped telling me in advance. He'd go out after dinner and I'd never know when he'd be back.'

'What sort of man is he?'

'Everyone will tell you that he was a very cheerful person, who got on well with everybody and who was always ready to do others a favour. Some people found him rather childish . . .'

'And you?'

29

'I can't really complain. Either I simply didn't know how to handle him, or else he was mistaken about me . . .'

'In what way?'

'He took me for a different kind of person than I am.'

'What did you do before you met him?'

'I was a secretary in a law firm . . . Maitre Bernard d'Argens, Rue de Rivoli. . . . Gérard knew my boss . . . he came to his office several times . . . and then one day he asked me to go out with him. . . .'

'Were you born in Paris?'

'No. In Quimper.'

'What makes you think he's been murdered?'

'Because there's no other explanation . . .'

'Is your mother still alive?'

'Yes. My father's dead. His name was Louis Frassier. He was an accountant. My mother's maiden name was Countess Outchevka . . .'

'Do you send her any money?'

'Of course I do. Gérard doesn't care about money. He used to give me as much as I wanted, with no questions asked. . . .' She emptied her glass and raised her handkerchief to her lips.

'Will you allow me to look around the flat?'

'I'll come with you . . .'

She got up from her chaise-longue and, walking carefully, made for the door.

CHAPTER TWO

THERE WAS AN ATMOSPHERE of wealth, the grand families of the last century, austerity even, about the apartment, which occupied a whole floor of the building. Madame Sabin-Levesque, still unsteady on her feet, began by showing Maigret round her rooms.

The boudoir gave on to a vast bedroom, also lined in blue silk, which seemed to be her favourite colour. The bed was unmade, though she did not seem bothered at giving Maigret this intimate glimpse of her life. The furniture was white. There was a half-empty bottle of brandy on the chest-of-drawers.

'What's your first name?' Maigret asked her.

'Nathalie. I suppose because of my Russian blood.'

The bathroom walls and floor were covered with grey-blue marble; it was as untidy as the bedroom.

There was another room, completely lined with cupboards, and a kind of small sitting-room not unlike the boudoir.

'This is where I take my meals when I don't wish to eat in the dining-room.' Her manner was detached, like that of a museum guide.

'Now we're going into the servants' quarters.'

They first entered a very large room containing glass cabinets full of silverware, then a small white-painted dining-room, and finally into the kitchen with its old-fashioned stove and copper saucepans. There was an old woman at work in the kitchen.

'That's Marie Jalon. She was already here when my father-in-law was still alive.'

'When did he die?'

'Ten years ago.'

'So you lived here with him?'

'For five years . . .'

'Did you get along well with him?'

'He was completely indifferent to me. I used to eat in the dining-room in those days and I could easily count the number of times he spoke to me.'

'How did he get on with his son?'

'At nine o'clock, Gérard would go down to the office, where he had a room of his own. I don't really know what he did there.'

'Was he already in the habit of disappearing in those days?'

'Yes, for two or three days at a time.'

'What did his father say?'

'He'd pretend not to notice anything . . .'

Maigret felt as though he had stumbled on a different world, a decayed world, turned in upon itself.

They must have given balls and soirées here in the last century or the beginning of this one, for there were not one but two drawing-rooms, of which the second was nearly as enormous as the first.

The panelling which covered the walls had grown dark with age.

The pictures hanging everywhere, portraits of gentlemen with side-whiskers and very high starched collars, also spoke of a bygone era.

It was as though at a given moment time had stopped.

'We're going into my husband's domain now . . .'

They went into a book-lined study. There were walnut library steps to get to the higher shelves, which reached the ceiling. The desk, placed at an angle near the window, was topped in brown leather, with leather accessories. Everything was tidy, as though no one lived there.

'Does he stay here in the evenings?'

'When he's at home.'

'I see he has a television.'

'So do I, but I never watch it.'

'Have you ever spent an evening in this room?'

'Yes, just after we were married.'

She spoke with some difficulty and seemed totally indifferent to what words she was uttering. Those once more down-turned lips of hers gave her face a bitter expression.

'His bedroom . . .'

Maigret had had just enough time to establish that the drawers of the desk were locked. What did they contain?

The ceilings everywhere in the flat were extremely high. The windows were also high, though the dark red velvet curtains prevented much light from coming in.

The walls of the bedroom were not panelled but lined with light brown leather. It contained a double bed and some armchairs which showed signs of wear.

'Did you ever sleep here?'

'A few times during the first three months . . .'

He wondered if he could detect any hatred in her voice or her face.

She went on showing him round like a museum guide.

'His bathroom . . .'

He observed the toothbrush, the razor, the hairbrush and the comb.

'He never took anything with him?'

'Not as far as I know.'

A room lined with cupboards, like the one in Nathalie's suite, then an exercise room.

'Did he use it?'

'Hardly ever. He's grown rather plump; not exactly fat, but overweight.'

She was opening a door.

'Here's the library . . .'

It contained thousands of books, mostly old ones, with very few modern works.

'Did he read a great deal?'

'I didn't come to check on what he did in the evenings. We've reached the far side of the building, so these stairs will take you straight down to the office. Do you still need me?'

She was going off to her bottle again.

'I suppose you're going down to the office now?'

'As a matter of fact, I'd like to ask Monsieur Lecureur a few questions. I'm sorry to have disturbed you.'

She left him. Maigret felt sorry for her, but also found her irritating. He began filling his pipe as he went downstairs, for he had refrained from smoking in the flat.

When he entered the large office, where six typists were working busily, they looked up at him in surprise.

'Monsieur Lecureur, please.'

In the filing cabinet were hundreds of green-backed dossiers, of the type used by civil servants and most solicitors. A small dark-haired woman led him through a room which was quite bare except for one long table and a large old-fashioned safe.

'This way . . .'

In the next room, an elderly man sat alone, poring over a huge ledger. He glanced up without curiosity as Maigret went through into the next room where five more people were working.

'Is Monsieur Lecureur alone?'

'Yes, I think so.'

'Will you please ring through and ask him if Chief Superintendent Maigret can see him?'

They stood waiting for a moment, then a padded door opened.

'Come in, please . . . I must admit I'm rather glad you've come.'

Lecureur was younger than Maigret had imagined, after hearing that he had worked for Monsieur Sabin-Levesque's father; he did not seem more than fifty. He was dark, with a small moustache, and wore a very dark grey suit, which seemed almost black.

'Please sit down.'

More panelling. The firm's founder must have had an exaggerated passion for walls that were covered in dark wood.

'I imagine you've been notified by Madame Sabin-Levesque?'

'Yes. In fact, she came to see me in my office this morning.'

The mahogany furniture was in the Empire style.

'I assume you take over Monsieur Sabin-Levesque's work when he's away?'

'It's my duty, as his head clerk. However, there are certain deeds I can't sign, so it's rather awkward.'

He was a self-assured man and, like many men who constantly deal with important people, there was something not exactly servile but perhaps slightly deferential about his manner.

'Was he in the habit of warning you when he went off like that?'

'No. It was never planned in advance. Of course, I know nothing about his private life . . . I'm only guessing. He often went out in the evening . . . almost every evening, in fact . . .'

'Just a moment. Did he play an active rôle in the running of this practice?'

'He spent most of the day in his office and he saw nearly all the clients personally. He never gave the impression of being a busy man and yet he worked harder than I did. . . . Especially at anything which concerned the handling of private fortunes or buying and selling country houses and estates. . . . He was incredibly shrewd and I couldn't have done the same in his place.'

'Is his office next to yours?'

Lecureur went over to a door and opened it.

'Here it is. . . . You see, it's just like this one except that it's got three more armchairs.'

The spotlessly tidy office overlooked the Boulevard Saint-Germain and the monotonous rumbling of the traffic could be heard outside.

The two men went back into Monsieur Lecureur's office.

'I gather he usually appeared again after two or three days . . .'

'There have been times recently when he stayed away for as long as a week.'

'But he kept in touch with you?'

'He nearly always rang me up to find out if he was needed.'

'Do you know where he rang you from?'

'No.'

'Do you have any idea if he had another flat in Paris?'

'I've thought about that possibility. He never had much money on him and he paid for nearly everything by cheque . . . I saw the cheque stubs before they went to the accountant . . .'

He stopped talking and frowned.

'I wonder if I have the right to go into these matters. I am still bound by professional etiquette.'

'Not if, say, he's been murdered . . .'

'Do you really think something like that may have happened?'

'His wife seems to think so.'

Monsieur Lecureur shrugged, as if to imply that anything she said was of no account.

'To tell you the truth, the idea's crossed my mind, too.

It's the first time he's been away for so long and hasn't telephoned me. He had an appointment here more than a week ago with one of our clients, one of the largest, if not the largest landowner in France.

'He knew about it . . . he may have seemed absent-minded or rather frivolous, but in point of fact he never forgot anything and he was if anything over-conscientious as far as his professional life was concerned.'

'What did you do?'

'I postponed the appointment and pretended he was ill.'

'Why didn't you warn the police if you were worried?'

'It was up to his wife, not me, to do that.'

'She tells me she never comes down here.'

'That's true. . . . She came in once or twice, years ago, but she didn't stay for long. . . .'

'Did she get a chilly reception?'

'No one was exactly delighted to see her, not even her husband.'

'How come?'

Once again, Lecureur stopped, even more embarrassed this time than previously.

'Please excuse me, Monsieur Maigret, but you're placing me in an awkward position. My employer's relations with his wife are no business of mine. . . .'

'Not even if a crime's been committed?'

'Naturally, that would be a different matter. . . . We all love Monsieur Gérard . . . I call him that because I've known him almost since his student days. . . . Everyone who works for him admires him. . . . They don't presume to judge his private life.'

'I gather they don't feel the same way about his wife.'

'It's as though she were a discordant element in the house. I'm not saying she's mad, but the fact is that she gets under everyone's skin.'

'Because of her drinking?'

'There's that, too.'

'Was your employer unhappy with her?'

'He never complained. Over the years, he's made another life for himself. . . .'

'A moment ago you spoke about those cheque stubs that would pass through your hands. I imagine some of those cheques were made out to the women he stayed with now and again. . . .'

'I suppose so, but there's nothing to prove it . . . the cheques weren't made out to specific people but to the bearer. . . . Some of them were for five thousand francs, anything up to twenty thousand. . . .'

'Were any of the cheques made out for the same sum every month?'

'No. Which is why I don't think he did rent another flat.'

The two men looked at each other in silence. Eventually, the head clerk continued, with a sigh:

'Some of our employees saw him now and again going into a nightclub. . . . On those occasions, he nearly always vanished for a time. . . .'

'Do you believe something's happened to him?'

'I'm afraid it may be so. What do you think, Superintendent?'

'Judging by the little I know so far, I think something may have happened to him, too. . . . Did he ever receive calls from women in his office? . . . I'm assuming all incoming calls go through a switchboard . . .'

'I've asked our operator about that, of course. There's no record of any calls of that kind. . . .'

'Which leads one to suppose that he took an assumed name whenever he disappeared like that.'

'I think I ought to mention one thing . . . I began to get worried two weeks ago . . . I rang up Madame Sabin-

Levesque to tell her so and advised her to get in touch with the police. . . .'

'What did she say?'

'That there was nothing to worry about yet and that she would take care of the matter in due course. . . .'

'Didn't she ask you to come upstairs or else come down here herself to talk it over with you?'

'No.'

'I haven't any more questions to ask you for the time being. If you have anything new to tell me, will you please ring me up at the Police Judiciaire? Oh yes, I just wanted to know one more thing. . . . Do the servants upstairs feel the same way about Madame Sabin-Levesque as the staff do down here?'

'Yes, they do. Particularly the cook, Marie Jalon, who's been there for forty years and who knew Monsieur Gérard when he was a child. She absolutely loathes her.'

'What about the others?'

'They just put up with her. Only the maid, Claire Marelle, is devoted to her. It's she who undresses her and puts her to bed when she collapses on the floor. . . .'

'Thank you.'

'Are you going to open an inquiry?'

'Yes, though I haven't much to go on. I'll keep in touch.'

Maigret left the building and went into a café next to the Métro Solferino. He did not order a brandy, for Madame Sabin-Levesque had put him off that drink for some time; instead he had a big glass of ice-cold beer.

'I want a *jeton* for the telephone.'

He went into the phone-booth and looked up the number of the lawyer Nathalie claimed to have worked for before her marriage.

The name Bernard d'Argens was not listed in the directory.

He drank his beer and then took a taxi, asking the driver to take him to the Rue de Rivoli.

'Wait for me. I shan't be long.'

He went to the concierge's lodge, which was like a little parlour. The concierge was not a woman but a white-haired man.

'Where can I find Maître d'Argens, please?'

'He's been dead for over ten years.'

'Were you here in those days?'

'I've been here for thirty years.'

'Who took over his practice?'

'No one. There's an architect there now.'

'Is all his staff gone, too?'

'Maître d'Argens only had one old secretary, who retired to the country.'

'You don't remember someone called Mademoiselle Frassier?'

'A very lively, pretty brunette? . . . She worked for Maître d'Argens over twenty years ago. . . . She only stayed for a year because the job didn't suit her. I don't know what became of her . . .'

Maigret went back to his taxi, his brow clouded over. Of course, the inquiry had only just been opened, but it had got off to a bad start. There was almost nothing to go on, and they would also have to be very discreet, just in case the solicitor turned up suddenly without warning.

The sun had vanished behind the houses and it had grown cooler. Maigret was sorry to have left his overcoat at the office.

He felt like another beer, so he asked the taxi to stop at the corner of the Quai des Orfèvres and the Rue du Palais.

He kept on thinking of Nathalie, that strange Madame Sabin-Levesque, and he had a feeling she knew a great deal more than she was giving away.

He went back to his office, filled one of his pipes, then walked over to the door of the inspectors' duty room. Lapointe was typing and Janvier was looking out of the window. Lucas was on the phone.

'Janvier . . . Lapointe. . . . Will you both come into my office?'

Janvier was not getting any younger either; he now had a promising pot-belly.

'Are you free, Janvier?'

'Nothing important right now. I've finished with the young car-thief.'

'Can you face spending the night out?'

'Why not?'

'I'd like you to go to the Boulevard Saint-Germain as soon as you can, to keep a watch on number 207 *bis* . . . I'll give you the particulars of a woman. . . . If she leaves the house, you're to follow her. . . . You'd better have a car handy. . . .

'She's rather tall, dark and extremely thin, with staring eyes and a nervous twitch. If she goes out, she'll probably be walking, but she does have a chauffeur and two cars . . . a Bentley and a Fiat. . . .

'Ask Lourtie to come and take over from you tomorrow morning and tell him what I've told you.'

'What is she wearing?'

'When she came here, she had a fur coat on, mink I think.'

'O.K., *patron*.'

Janvier went out and Maigret turned to Lapointe.

'How about you? Anything new?'

Lapointe blushed and stammered without looking at Maigret:

'Yes . . . a few minutes ago. . . . There was a call. . . .'

'Who from?'

'The woman this morning.'

'What did she want?'

'First she asked if you were there. . . . I told her you weren't. She sounded dead drunk:

' "Who is it speaking then?" she asked.

' "Inspector Lapointe."

' "What, the young nincompoop who was writing down everything I said this morning?"

' "That's right."

' "Well, could you kindly tell your boss from me to go to hell . . . and the same goes for you, too. . . ." '

Lapointe, still embarrassed, went on: 'Then it sounded as if she were struggling with someone.

' "Leave me alone, for Christ's sake! . . ."

'Then someone must have snatched the phone out of her hand because the line went dead.'

Just before he left the Police Judiciaire, Maigret said to Lapointe:

'Could you please come and collect me at my flat in one of the cars at eleven o'clock?'

'Tomorrow morning?'

'Tonight. I feel like going to take a look at a few night-clubs.'

Madame Maigret had kept the herrings for him, since it was one of his favourite dishes. He ate while watching the news on television in an absent-minded way. Madame Maigret could guess, just by looking at her husband, that his new case was a rather unusual one and that he was taking a special interest in it, almost treating it as if it concerned him personally.

And indeed, this was true. On that mild, clear first day of spring, Maigret had been plunged into a world which was foreign to him; moreover, he had met a type of woman quite disconcertingly unlike any he had ever come across before.

'Will you get a dark suit out for me? My best one.'

'What's happening?'

'Lapointe is coming to fetch me at eleven. We're going to visit a few nightclubs.'

'That'll make a change for you, won't it?'

'If only it can help me to clear up a few problems . . .'

He dozed in his armchair in front of the television set. At ten-thirty, his wife brought him a cup of coffee.

'You'll be staying up late . . .'

He lit a pipe, then started to sip the coffee; for him, a pipe always went well with coffee.

He had a wash in the bathroom and changed his clothes. Not that it mattered what he wore, but he belonged to a generation which had always changed into tails to go to the opera and into a dinner jacket for going out to a nightclub.

At five minutes to eleven, he thought he heard a car stopping outside. He opened the window and saw the small black police car drawn up at the kerb below, with a tall silhouette standing next to it.

He gave Madame Maigret a kiss and walked across to the door, grumbling, but at bottom delighted not to be the head of the Police Judiciaire.

'Now you're not to wait up for me . . .'

'I won't, don't worry. I'm sleepy.'

It was not too cold outside and the moon was rising over the roof-tops. Many windows were still lit up and some of them were open.

'Where are we going, *patron*?'

He took out an old envelope from his pocket. On it he had jotted down the addresses which he had found in the phone-book.

'Do you know the *Chat Botté*?'

'No.'

'It's in the Rue du Colisée. . . .'

43

They went down the Champs-Elysées, with its double stream of car headlamps and its neon signs blazing on either side. A doorman stood in front of the nightclub entrance. He was wearing as much gold braid as an admiral and he gave them a military salute as he opened the swing doors for them.

They went through a heavy red curtain and left their hats and coats in the cloakroom.

The pianist was allowing his fingers to wander the keyboard at random, while the guitarist was tuning his instrument. There was also a double-bass, but the musician who played it had not yet arrived.

The room was entirely decorated in red. The walls, the ceiling, the seats, everything was red, a rather orangey red which seemed cheerful rather than garish. The bar, by way of contrast, was of stark white stucco. Behind it, the barman was wiping glasses and putting them away.

The *maître d'hôtel* came up to them, without much enthusiasm. He had perhaps recognized Maigret, or else it was just that the two men did not look like serious customers.

Maigret shook his head and went towards the bar. Three women sat at separate tables and, at another table, a couple seemed to be arguing.

It was still too early; the club would not come to life until midnight.

'Good evening, gentlemen. . . . What can I get you?'

The barman had white hair and looked distinguished. He was watching them with a show of unconcern.

'I don't suppose you serve beer?'

'No, Monsieur Maigret.'

'Give us whatever you like . . .'

'Dry Martini?'

'That'll do.'

One of the women came over to sit at the bar, but the

44

white-haired barman made a slight gesture in her direction and she went back to her table.

When he had filled their glasses, he asked: 'Well?'

Maigret smiled.

'You're right,' he admitted. 'We're not just here to have a good time. We're not here to make trouble for you either . . . I need some information.'

'If I can help, it'll be a pleasure.'

A kind of complicity had been established between the two men. Maigret found it hard, however, to describe someone he had never seen.

'Medium height, if anything a little on the short side. Between forty and forty-five years old. . . . Plumpish . . . a pot-belly already. . . . Fair hair which is thinning . . . a chubby face. . . . He dresses very smartly, usually wears beige.'

'Are you looking for him?'

'I'd like to know where he is.'

'Has he disappeared?'

'Yes.'

'Has he committed any crime?'

'None.'

'It could be Monsieur Charles. . . .'

'Does the description fit?'

'More or less. . . . A very jolly sort, wasn't he? . . . Always in a good mood?'

'I think so.'

'Haven't you met him?'

'No.'

'He comes here from time to time and sits at the bar. He orders a bottle of champagne . . . then he takes a look around the room and goes over each hostess one by one. When he finds one to his liking, he has her sent over . . .'

'Does he stay late?'

'It depends. Sometimes he leaves with the girl. At other times he just slips her five hundred francs and goes away . . . probably to go and look elsewhere. . . .'

'When did you last see him?'

'Quite a long time ago. . . . Let me see, about six weeks . . . perhaps two months.'

'When he went off with one of the girls, did she stay away for a few days?'

'Not so loud. The proprietor doesn't like that kind of thing. There he is, over by those tables . . .'

A man in a dinner jacket was watching them from a distance. He looked like an Italian, with brilliantined hair and a small moustache. He too had probably recognized the chief superintendent.

'In theory, the hostesses aren't allowed to leave before we shut.'

'I know . . . I also know that, in practice, the rule isn't too strictly enforced. Have any of the young women here ever gone out with him?'

'I think Martine has. . . . You'd better go to her table if you want to speak to her . . . I'll have a bottle sent over.'

The young woman, whose long hair fell loosely down over her shoulders, was looking at them, intrigued.

A few customers had arrived, some with their wives, and the trio was now playing a blues.

'Did you order something to drink?' she asked.

'The barman ordered it for us,' Maigret grunted, wondering how he would manage to charge this to expenses.

'Have you ever been here before?'

'No.'

'Would you like me to call one of my friends over?'

The proprietor, who was standing near the table, said to her:

'Watch out, Martine, they're cops.'

46

'Is that true?' she asked Maigret.

'Yes it is.'

'Why do you want to talk to me in particular?'

'Because you've been out with Monsieur Charles.'

'What's wrong with that?'

She did not ask the question defiantly. Her voice remained gentle and friendly and she seemed amused by the whole incident.

'Nothing, but it so happens that Monsieur Charles disappeared a month ago. On February 18th, to be precise. Have you seen him since that date?'

'I wondered why he wasn't coming here any more. I mentioned it to some friends of mine. . . .'

'What do you think of him?'

'I'm sure his real name isn't Charles. He must be an important man who has to conceal his identity when he wants a bit of fun. He's very well-groomed and neat. I told him he had hands like a woman, they were so beautifully manicured . . .'

'Where did you go with him?'

'I thought we'd go to a hotel, but he asked me to take him back to my place . . . I've got a nice little flat on the Avenue de la Grande-Armée . . . I don't usually take anyone there. . . . Mind you, I hardly ever go out with clients. Some people think that's what hostesses are there for, but it isn't true.'

The champagne had been poured out and she raised her glass.

'Here's to Monsieur Charles then, as it's thanks to him you're here. I do hope nothing's happened to him.'

'We have no idea. He just disappeared. . . .'

'Did that crazy wife of his get worried?'

'He told you about her?'

'We spent four days together. . . . He was funny; you know, he insisted on helping me do the cooking and the washing up. . . . Sometimes he spoke about himself in a vague sort of way. . . .

'I won't ask you who he is. . . .'

'An important man . . . as you guessed.'

'Does he live in Paris?'

'Yes.'

'I suppose he has a little fling from time to time?'

'That's right. . . . Four or five days, maybe a week. . . .'

'I rang my boss, Monsieur Mazotti, and told him I was ill, but I don't suppose he believed me. . . . He gave me a dirty look when I came back to the *Chat Botté*.'

'When did all this happen?'

'About two months ago. Perhaps a bit longer . . .'

'Was it the first time he had come to this nightclub?'

'I'd seen him here a few times before, sitting at the bar . . . I suppose he didn't find what he was looking for, because he left by himself.'

'Did he go to other nightclubs?'

'He didn't tell me, but I'm sure he must have done.'

'Did he have a car?'

'No. We walked back to my place, arm in arm. He was in such a good mood.'

'Had he drunk a lot?'

'Not what you'd call a lot; just enough to be feeling merry.'

'Did he say anything about having a bachelor flat in town?'

'Why, did he have one?'

'I don't know.'

'No. He wanted to come back to my flat. . . . We were like a couple of newlyweds during those four days. He would watch me having a bath or getting dressed. . . . He'd lean out of the window to see me leave when I went out shopping. Then, when I'd return, I'd find the table laid. . . .'

'Can you think of anything else which would help me to find him?'

'No. I'm trying to think. . . . We went for a walk in the Bois de Boulogne but it looked like rain, so we came home again quite soon. He was very . . .'

She stopped, grown suddenly shy.

'Go on.'

'You're going to laugh at me. . . . He was very affectionate and considerate, just like a real sweetheart. When he left, he slipped a cheque in my hand. . . . You're going already?'

Mazotti, the proprietor, was waiting for them by the red curtain which hung in front of the entrance.

'Did you find out what you wanted to know, Superintendent?'

'Martine will tell you. Good night.'

Maigret was beginning to get a clearer picture of Gérard Sabin-Levesque's character. He had just learned more about the solicitor than either Madame Sabin-Levesque or the head clerk had been able to tell him.

'Shall we go on?' he asked Lapointe.

'Why not, while we're at it? . . . *La Belle Hélène*, Rue de Castiglione.'

The atmosphere of this nightclub was more genteel. Pastel shades everywhere and violins playing a slow waltz. Once again Maigret walked up to the bar, followed by Lapointe. He frowned when he saw the barman.

'Have they released you?' he asked.

'I'm on parole for good conduct.'

It was Maurice Mocco, a Corsican criminal who had a long record.

'What will you have to drink, Superintendent? . . . And what about you, young fellow? . . . Is this your son, Monsieur Maigret?'

'One of my inspectors.'

49

'I hope it's not me you're after?'

'No.'

'What will you have to drink?'

'Two beers.'

'I'm afraid we don't serve beer.'

'Then some water.'

'You must be joking!'

'No, I'm not. Do you know Monsieur Charles?'

'Which one? We've got at least two. The first one is completely bald and must be at least seventy. He's from Bordeaux; he comes to Paris once a week on business, then on to us for pleasure. . . . The other one doesn't come so regularly. He's on the small side, very well-dressed, extremely friendly, always wears light colours.'

'Rather plump?'

'I suppose you could say that. . . .'

'Has he ever gone off with one of the hostesses?'

'He usually leaves alone, but there was one girl who caught his eye once. Her name was Leila and she's been gone a long time. . . . This happened last summer. . . . They were sitting over at that table, having a chat . . . Leila kept on shaking her head and he kept on insisting. . . . After he left, I called her over. . . .

' "What sort of guy is he?" she asked me.

' "A real gent."

' "He asked me to go to a country hotel with him for a few days . . . the simple life . . . fresh air . . . all that jazz!"

' "How much was he offering you?"

' "Ten thousand to start with. . . . Then, when I refused, he put the price up to fifteen, then twenty thousand. . . . He just couldn't believe it when I still refused. . . .

' "The country, my eye! . . . With all the perverts you meet these days! . . ." '

'What became of Leila?'

'I think she got married to an engineer from Toulouse. She never came back here.'

Maigret needed fresh air himself, for it was terribly stuffy in the nightclubs and the perfume used by the women made him feel giddy. The two men walked down the deserted street.

'That old scoundrel, Mocco, gave us one precious piece of information, which is that Monsieur Charles sometimes took his conquests off to the country. . . .'

'I think I know what you're getting at.'

'Those women come from every sort of background . . . I once met one who had a Ph.D. in sociology . . . some of them have lovers . . . and some of their lovers can be rather unsavoury characters.'

It was two in the morning, but Maigret felt wide awake.

Ten minutes later, the two men got out of the car in the Rue Clément Marot, in front of the *Cric-Crac* nightclub, where pop music spilled out into the street. The exterior of the club was painted in rainbow colours, just like the interior, where couples were dancing on the tightly packed dance-floor.

Once again the two men headed for the bar. But this time the proprietor, a fair young man called Ziffer, went over to greet them instantly.

'What can I do for you, gentlemen?'

Maigret waved his badge under his nose.

'I beg your pardon, Superintendent . . . I didn't recognize you. It's so dark in here. . . .'

The room, which was quite small, had only one lamp, a slowly revolving globe entirely covered with tiny reflecting mirrors.

'You won't find anything irregular here, I assure you.'

'Do you know a Monsieur Charles?'

Ziffer frowned, like a man trying hard to remember something.

The barman, a very fat man with bushy eyebrows, called out:

'He always used to come and sit at the bar. . . .'

'When did you see him last?'

'Not for weeks.'

'Did you see him on the 18th of February?'

'What day was that?'

'A Tuesday.'

'I can't remember off-hand. . . . All I know is that he was sitting up at the bar with Zoé the last time he came here. . . .'

'Did she go off with him?'

'That isn't allowed, Superintendent,' the proprietor interrupted.

'I know . . . I know. Did she go off with him?'

'No. But he jotted down something in a little note-book; it must have been an address Zoé gave him. . . .'

'Is the girl here?'

'She's dancing just now. . . . The platinum blonde over there . . . the one with the gorgeous breasts. . . .'

'I'll go and fetch her for you,' Ziffer offered eagerly.

And Maigret, mopping his forehead, once again asked the barman:

'I don't suppose you serve beer? . . .'

CHAPTER THREE

ZÓE HAD BIG, INNOCENT, BLUE EYES, just like a little girl. She fluttered her eyelashes and stared curiously at this unknown man, while the proprietor whispered in her ear:

'It's Maigret, the famous Police Superintendent. You can be frank with him.'

She had obviously never heard of the superintendent, and she waited patiently for him to start asking her questions, like a schoolgirl in class.

'Do you know Monsieur Charles?'

'I know him by sight, of course. He comes here once in a while.'

'What do you mean by once in a while?'

'Nearly every week.'

'Does he go off with one of the hostesses every time he comes?'

'Oh no! In fact, he practically never does. He takes a good look at us all and occasionally treats one of us to a bottle of champagne.'

'Does he dance?'

'Yes. He's a rotten dancer.'

'How long has it been since you saw him?'

She looked up at the ceiling, exactly like a schoolgirl answering her teacher.

'Let me see . . . quite a long time. . . . Last time, we drank a bottle of champagne together.'

'You don't happen to remember what date that was?'

'Yes I do. It was the 18th of February . . .'

'How can you remember that?'

'Because it was my birthday. . . . He even bought some

flowers for me from Joséphine, the old flower-seller who comes in every night.'

'Did he ask you to spend the night with him?'

'Yes he did. . . . I told him the truth, that I had a boy-friend waiting for me at home and that made him sad. I was sorry because he's very nice. . . .'

'Did anything else happen?'

'I told him that if he wanted a nice girl I had a friend who wasn't a hostess but who had men to visit her some-times . . . only high-class ones, mind you. . . . I said I'd go and ring her up to find out if she was free. . . . I spoke to Dorine. She agreed to see him.'

'Did you give Monsieur Charles her address?'

'Yes, it's in the Avenue de Ternes.'

'What time was it?'

'About one in the morning. . . .'

'Did he set off right away?'

'Yes.'

'Have you seen Dorine since?'

'I rang her up that same night at about three in the morning, just to see if everything had gone well. . . . She told me Monsieur Charles had not arrived yet and that she was still waiting for him. . . . When I next saw her, she told me he never turned up. . . .'

'And since then what happened?'

'What do you mean?'

'Have you seen Monsieur Charles again?'

'No. Actually I'm surprised he's stayed away so long.'

'Thank you, Zoé.'

'Is that all?'

'Yes, for the time being.'

He watched her return to her table; the proprietor came over and asked:

'Are you satisfied?'

'Fairly.'

So far, Zoé was the last person to have seen the solicitor. He had left her at one o'clock in the morning to go to the Avenue de Ternes and had never arrived there.

'Where now, chief?' Lapointe asked him, once again at the wheel of the little car.

'Back home . . . I've had enough for today and you must be tired too.'

'Funny kind of chap, wasn't he?'

'Yes, funny kind of chap. Either he had a soft spot for nightclub hostesses, or else it was just that he didn't want to complicate his life by having a regular mistress. . . .'

When Maigret got home, he began to undress; Madame Maigret, who was in bed, asked him in a friendly voice:

'Did you enjoy yourself?'

'I think I've made a little discovery . . . we'll soon see if it's worth anything.'

'Not too tired?'

'I'm all right. Wake me up tomorrow at the usual time.'

He took a long time to fall asleep. He was feeling a bit edgy and his head still buzzed with the din of the nightclubs.

This did not stop him, however, from being in his office at nine o'clock on the following morning; the first person he saw in the inspectors' duty room was Janvier.

'Come in here.'

The sun was a little warmer than on the previous day; he had a slight headache, so he went to open the window.

'What sort of night did you have?'

'Quiet. Except for one odd incident.'

'Tell me about it.'

'I parked the car a hundred yards from the house . . . I was sitting at the wheel, watching number 207 *bis*. . . . A few minutes after eleven, the door opened and I saw the woman coming out . . .'

'Madame Sabin-Levesque?'

'Yes. She was walking stiffly, as though she was finding it hard not to stagger. . . . I let her go on a bit, then I started up the car. . . . She didn't go far . . . less than two hundred yards. . . . She went into a phone-box. . . .'

Maigret frowned.

'She put a coin in but she probably couldn't get through because she hung up again almost at once. She did the same thing a second time. . . . The third time, she got through. She spoke for a long time and she twice had to put more money in. . . .'

'Strange she didn't call from her own flat . . . I suppose she thought her line was being tapped.'

'I imagine so. . . . When she came out of the phone-box, her coat fell open for a second and I could see she was only wearing a nightdress underneath. . . . She went straight back to 207 *bis*, rang the bell, and the door opened immediately. . . . Nothing else happened all night. I passed on your instructions to Lourtie, and Bonfils will take over from him at about mid-day.'

'Get her phone tapped as soon as possible.'

Janvier was about to leave the room.

'Ask them to tap the office phones too. . . . After that you can go to bed.'

'Thanks, *patron*.'

Maigret glanced rapidly at his mail, signed a few forms and went in to tell the director of his progress.

'Are you going back there?'

'Yes. I don't think you'll see me at the office much during the next few days.'

Did the director know that Maigret had been offered his job? He did not mention it, but Maigret had the feeling that he was being unusually courteous today.

Lapointe had arrived, looking rather frail. He drove Maigret to the Boulevard Saint-Germain.

'Shall I come up with you?'

'Do. You may have to take some notes.'

'I've brought my notebook.'

Maigret almost stopped on the ground floor, but then he changed his mind and went up to the flat. Claire Marelle, the young maid, opened the door; she seemed far from delighted to see them.

'If it's Madame you've come to see, I can tell you straight away she's asleep.'

This information did not stop Maigret from walking into the flat, with Lapointe at his heels.

'Sit down,' he said to the young woman, pointing to a chair.

'I'm not supposed to sit down in here . . .'

'You're supposed to do as I tell you.'

She finally sat down on the very edge of a leather-covered chair.

Some people disapproved of Maigret's methods. A police officer of his rank was supposed to summon witnesses to his office, and he should have sent an inspector on that tour around the nightclubs.

Maigret lit his pipe. Claire Marelle watched him disapprovingly; she obviously found his behaviour uncouth.

'What time did your Mistress come home last night?'

'She would have had to leave before she could return.'

'All right, let's put it this way, what time did she go out?'

'I don't know.'

'Were you asleep?'

'I told you, she didn't go out.'

'I'm sure you're much too devoted to her not to stay up until you can put her to bed considering the state she's usually in. . . .'

The maid was quite pretty, but the sullen look she always wore did not suit her. She looked at Maigret, pretending to be indifferent.

57

'So what?'

'I can tell you that she came back around eleven-thirty.'

'She has the right to go for a breath of fresh air, doesn't she?'

'Didn't you feel worried when you saw her going out? She could barely stand on her feet . . .'

'You saw her?'

'One of my inspectors saw her. And do you know why she was going out at that time of night?'

'No.'

'To make a call from a public phone-box. . . . Whom did she call up usually?'

'No one. . . . Her hairdresser. . . . Tradesmen . . .'

'I mean private calls. You don't ring up a hairdresser at eleven in the evening, or a dressmaker, or a shoe-maker . . .'

'I don't know anything.'

'Do you feel sorry for her?'

'Yes.'

'Why?'

'Because she's been pretty unlucky with her husband. . . . She ought to be leading the kind of life to which she's entitled . . . society, parties, friends . . .'

'Does her husband prevent her?'

'He never pays any attention to her. Besides, he goes off for whole weeks on end. This time he's been away for over a month. . . .'

'Where do you think he is?'

'With some woman or other. . . . He only fancies the women he picks up God knows where . . .'

'Has he ever asked you to go to bed with him?'

'I'd like to see him try. . . .'

'Very well. Could you go and fetch the cook? While I'm talking to her, wake your mistress up and tell her I want to see her for just a few minutes.'

She obeyed him reluctantly, darting him angry looks as she left the room.

Maigret winked at Lapointe.

Marie Jalon, the cook, was a short, stocky woman; she stared curiously at the chief superintendent and seemed delighted to be meeting him in the flesh.

'Please sit down, Madame. I already know you've been in this household a long time. . . .'

'Forty years . . . I used to work for Monsieur's father.'

'Has anything changed since those days?'

She gave a deep sigh.

'Everything's changed, sir. . . . Ever since that woman came here, I just don't know where to turn. . . . No regular hours any more. . . . Meals served when she decides she's hungry. Sometimes she doesn't eat a thing all day, then I hear a noise in the kitchen in the middle of the night and I find her raiding the fridge . . .'

'Do you think your employer is unhappy about the situation?'

'I most certainly do. He doesn't say so . . . I've never heard him complain. He's not the complaining sort . . . I've known him since he was a little boy, forever playing about my feet. . . . He was shy then. . . .'

'Do you find him shy?'

'And how! You can't imagine what dreadful scenes he puts up with without ever daring to raise a finger to her. . . .'

'Aren't you worried about his absence?'

'I wasn't to start with. . . . We're used to it. . . . He has to have his little treat now and again.'

Maigret smiled to hear her use that expression.

'I'm wondering who could have warned you. . . . Would it be Monsieur Lecureur? . . .'

'No. It was Madame Sabin-Levesque who came and told us she was worried.'

59

'Worried? Her? . . . I see you don't know her. She wouldn't lift her little finger if he fell dead at her feet . . .'

'Do you think she's mad?'

'Drunk, more likely. She starts on the bottle the moment she's had her morning coffee. . . .'

'Have you seen your employer since the 18th of February?'

'No.'

'Have you had any news of him?'

'None. . . . I must say, I'm worried about it.'

Madame Sabin-Levesque was standing motionless in the doorway. She was wearing the same dressing-gown as on the previous day and had not even bothered to comb her hair.

'Was it to me or to my cook you wanted to speak?'

'To both of you . . .'

'Whenever you wish. . . .'

She led the two men to the boudoir where she had first received Maigret. There was a bottle of brandy and a glass on a silver tray.

'I don't suppose you'd care for one?'

Maigret shook his head.

'What do you want this time?'

'First of all to ask you one question. Where did you go last night?'

'Yes, my maid told me you were having me watched. It'll save me telling you a lie. I didn't feel well so I went out to get a breath of fresh air. I saw a phone-box and all of a sudden I felt like calling up one of my girl-friends. . . .'

'Do you have any girl-friends?'

'Does it surprise you? Yes, I do.'

'May I know the name of the friend you rang up?'

'It's none of your business, so I won't tell you.'

'Your friend was out?'

'How did you know?'

'You had to dial three different numbers. . . .'

She did not answer but swallowed her drink. She was not feeling well and it was obvious that she always woke with a hangover, for which liquor was the only cure. Her face was swollen and this made her nose look longer and more pointed.

'Right, then I'll ask you another question. The drawers of your husband's desk are locked. Can you tell me where the keys are?'

'They must be in his pocket. I didn't search his rooms.'

'Who was his best friend?'

'In the early days of our marriage, a lawyer called Auboineau and his wife often used to come here for dinner. . . . They went to law-school together. . . .'

'Do they still see each other?'

'I don't know. . . . All I know is that Auboineau doesn't come here any more. . . . I never liked him. He's very pompous and never stops talking as though he were pleading in court. . . . As for his wife . . .'

'What about her?'

'Never mind. She's just so haughty because she's inherited her parents' chateau.'

She had another drink.

'Are you going to stay much longer?'

Maigret realized that she was exhausted and he felt sorry for her.

'I suppose you'll go on having me watched by one of your men?'

'Yes, I will. That's all for today. . . .' Maigret nodded to Lapointe, who got up to follow him.

'Good-bye, Madame.'

She did not answer; the maid was waiting in the drawing-room to show them to the door.

On the ground floor, Maigret went through the archway to the solicitor's office and asked to speak to Lecureur. The head clerk came to meet the two police officers and ushered them into his private office.

'Any news?' he asked.

'Not really what you'd call news. As far as I know, the very last person to see your employer was a night-club hostess who works at the *Cric-Crac* in the Rue Clément Marot; when he left her, he was on his way to visit another young woman in the Avenue de Ternes, who was expecting him. . . . This was in the middle of the night of February 18th. . . . He never reached his destination. . . .'

'Did he perhaps change his mind on the way there?'

'Perhaps. . . . Are you quite sure he hasn't telephoned you even once during this last month?'

'Not once.'

'Whereas during all his previous absences he kept in touch with you by ringing up regularly?'

'That's right, every two or three days. He was extremely conscientious. Two years ago, he came rushing back on one occasion because we needed his signature . . .'

'What sort of terms were you on?'

'Very friendly. He had complete trust in me.'

'Did you know what he kept in the drawers in his desk upstairs?'

'No, I didn't know. I seldom went up there and I never saw those drawers open. . . .'

'Have you seen his keys?'

'Many times. He had a set of keys which he always carried with him. One of the keys was for the big safe you probably saw in the typists' room.'

'What's in it?'

'Confidential documents concerning our clients' affairs, particularly their wills. . . .'

'Have you also got a key to it?'

'Naturally.'

62

'Who else?'

'No one.'

'Did he ever deal personally with certain matters which he would not discuss with you?'

'Sometimes he saw a client privately in his office, but he nearly always took notes and, when the client was gone, he would give me a full account.'

'Who controls the financial side while your employer is away?'

'I do. I have power of attorney.'

'Is he very wealthy?'

'Yes, he's wealthy.'

'Has he increased his fortune since his father's death?'

'He certainly has.'

'And is his wife his sole heir?'

'One of the employees and I acted as witnesses when he signed his will, but I didn't read it. I assume he made quite a number of other large legacies.'

'What would happen to the practice?'

'That would depend entirely on Madame Sabin-Levesque.'

'Thank you.'

It suddenly occurred to Maigret that, ever since Nathalie's first visit to the Police Judiciaire, they all spoke of the missing solicitor both in the present tense and in the past.

Mostly in the past.

'If you wish to see me today, you'll have to come right away. I'm performing an operation at one o'clock.'

Maigret noticed that Doctor Florian, like most society doctors, affected a solemn tone of voice. He lived in the Avenue Foch, which presupposed a select clientele.

'I'll be there in a few minutes.'

Maigret and Lapointe had gone into a bar on the

Boulevard Saint-Germain to have a beer and to make a phone-call.

'He's waiting for us . . . the Avenue Foch.'

Soon afterwards, the small black car was making its way up the Champs-Elysées. Lapointe was silent, a trifle gloomy, as though something was troubling him.

'What's the matter?'

'That woman . . . I can't help feeling sorry for her.'

Maigret did not answer but he probably felt the same way as Lapointe; yet as they drove round the Arc de Triomphe, he muttered:

'We'll have to know her better before we can feel sorry for her. . . .'

The doctor's house was luxurious and more modern than the one on the Boulevard Saint-Germain. They glided up to the sixth floor in a spacious lift and a butler in a striped waistcoat opened the door for them.

'This way . . . Professor Florian is expecting you.'

The butler took their hats and coats, then opened the swing doors to let them through. Two Greek statues in almost flawless condition stood on either side of the door.

The surgeon was tall, even taller and stouter than Maigret. He shook hands with the two men energetically.

'This is Inspector Lapointe,' Maigret said, introducing his young colleague.

'Please forgive me for sounding so rushed, but I have a very busy schedule. I've been wondering why you want to see me ever since you rang fifteen minutes ago.'

His consulting room was huge, very luxurious and sunny. The french windows, which opened on to a terrace, were ajar and from time to time the curtains billowed in the breeze.

'Please sit down.'

His greying hair made him look older than his age; he was dressed severely in striped trousers and a black jacket.

64

'I believe you're a friend of Gérard Sabin-Levesque.'

'We're the same age and we were at university together. He studied law, I did medicine. He was the ringleader of a rather fast set to which I belonged.'

'Has he changed a lot?'

'I haven't seen much of him since his marriage.'

Doctor Florian frowned.

'I really must ask you for what reason you question me in this way. As a doctor, I'm bound by the Hippocratic oath, while as a friend, I naturally wish to be discreet . . .'

'I do understand. Sabin-Levesque has been missing for over a month. . . . He didn't tell anyone he was going away, neither his wife nor his head clerk. . . .

'He left the house one evening, the 18th of February, without taking any luggage. We now know that on the evening, or rather the night, of the 18th, he went to a nightclub called the *Cric-Crac* in the Rue Clément Marot. He left the club alone, to go to an address in the Avenue de Ternes which he had been given, but he never reached his destination. . . .'

'What does his wife have to say?'

'Do you know her?'

'I used to go and visit them sometimes in the early days of their marriage.'

'In those early days, was he already going off on those —what shall we call them—escapades?'

'You know about those? He was always attracted to women and to the atmosphere of nightclubs, even in his student days. He never outgrew the attraction, but there's nothing abnormal about it and I don't think the term "escapade" is appropriate.'

'I'm only using it for lack of a better word.'

'He never actually told me so when I went for dinner there, but I had the feeling he never really stopped leading a bachelor life, if I may put it that way.'

'How well did you know his wife?'

'I met her perhaps a dozen times.'

'Do you know how they met?'

'He's always kept rather quiet about that. . . . I have the feeling she doesn't come from his sort of background. I seem to remember that, at one time, she worked as a secretary for a lawyer. . . . At least I think so.'

'That's correct. What impression did she make on you?'

'She seldom spoke to me. During those dinners, she was either morose or aggressive; at times she would leave the table, mumbling some excuse.'

'Would you say she was unbalanced?'

'I couldn't tell you. I'm a surgeon, not a psychiatrist. I think the main problem was her drinking. . . .'

'She's drinking more than ever. She was drunk when she came to the Quai des Orfèvres to tell us that her husband was missing.'

'When was that?'

'The day before yesterday.'

'And he's been missing since February?'

'Yes. She waited for over a month. After the first week, the head clerk told her she ought to tell the police but she told him it was none of his business. . . .'

'Strange. . . .'

'And worrying too.'

The doctor lit a cigarette with a gold lighter. He said to Maigret:

'Go ahead, please light your pipe. . . . I'm disturbed by what you tell me. All I can say is that Gérard was, and I am sure still is, an extremely brilliant man. When I knew him, he was what you would call a playboy. He loved sports-cars and amusing places. I gather that he often didn't turn up at lectures, but that didn't stop him from passing exams with the greatest of ease. I don't know if he's changed. . . .'

'Your account fits in with what we've been told already by others. I imagine he got married on the spur of the moment and that he soon realized it was a mistake.'

'I would think so. . . . His friends stopped seeing him because of his wife. . . . She was always humiliating him in front of them . . . I never heard him answer back. He would carry on with the conversation as if nothing had happened . . .

'Later, he still went on living with her but he completely ignored her existence.'

'Do you think he was unhappy about the situation?'

'It's hard to tell with someone who is always joking. . . . It wasn't a normal life, of course . . . I understand why he had to have those flings. . . . But his going away like this for a whole month is a more serious matter. Hasn't he even been in touch with his office?'

'No, though he usually kept in touch. This time he hasn't bothered to find out if they needed him at his work.'

'You seem very interested in the wife. . . .'

'She lived in the same apartment as him and they were presumably fond of each other once.'

'Poor old Gérard . . .'

The doctor got up.

'Please excuse me but duty calls. . . . Come to think of it, we had a mutual friend who is a psychiatrist; he works at Sainte-Anne. He's called Doctor Amadieu and lives in the Latin Quarter. He attended some of those dinners at the Boulevard Saint-Germain. . . .'

He escorted them to the door. The butler was waiting with their hats and coats.

'Ten past twelve,' Maigret said when they got into the little car. 'Let's try and find out if Doctor Amadieu goes home for lunch.'

Ringing up the psychiatrist gave him an excuse to go

into a café and drink an aperitif; this time, he chose a *pastis*.

'I'll have the same,' Lapointe said.

Amadieu was at home. This week he would not be on duty at Sainte-Anne until two in the afternoon.

'I suppose it's urgent?'

'Yes, I think it could be described as urgent.'

The psychiatrist lived in a rather untidy flat; he was probably a bachelor, for he was eating alone at table. A maid was clearing up the dishes. Amadieu had bushy red hair and freckles; his rumpled tweed suit looked as though it had been slept in.

Maigret found out later that Amadieu was one of the most eminent psychiatrists in France, if not the whole of Europe.

'Do sit down. Light your pipe and tell me what you'd like to drink.'

'Nothing for the moment. I know your time is valuable. You used to be on close terms with Sabin-Levesque.'

'Yes, I think you could say that, after all those nights on the town we had when we were students together. . . . Don't tell me he's in trouble with the law? . . .'

'He vanished over a month ago.'

'Without telling anyone?'

'No one. He used to go away, but never for more than a week, and he would always keep in touch with his head clerk. This time, he hasn't. . . .'

'I wonder what's happened to him?' Amadieu muttered to himself.

Then he added, puzzled: 'But how can I help you?'

'I'm looking for a man I've never met, whom I knew nothing about until yesterday; I'm trying to get some kind of picture of him.'

'I see.'

'I've just been to see your friend, Doctor Florian. He's

the one who gave me your address. He says that Sabin-Levesque was actually a very reliable sort of person.'

'I agree with that.'

'Do you think the sort of life he's been leading all these years could have driven him to suicide?'

'It wouldn't be like him. Besides, his life had its consolations . . .'

'I know about that. I've met several of his girl-friends.'

'I had dinner at the Boulevard Saint-Germain quite a few times soon after his marriage. . . .'

'Just as a friend?'

'I think I can tell you the truth, despite professional etiquette. . . . Gérard asked me to come and observe his wife. . . . He wondered if she was quite sane. . . . I found her extremely intelligent; she seemed to see right through me from the very first. She would look at me coolly, as though challenging me . . . and she would deliberately drink like a fish. . . .'

'She still does.'

'I know, but when I was present she drank twice as much. She would glance at me every time she poured herself another drink.

'"It's a disease, isn't it, doctor?" she would say to me. "I'm what you call an incurable alcoholic . . ."

' "Practically no disease is incurable," I would reply, "if the patient really wants to be cured. . . ."

'"How can I want to be cured when I can't face life? . . . I'm all alone in the world; my husband despises me and doesn't give a damn about me . . ."

'"I'm sure you're mistaken. I know Gérard. If he didn't love you, he wouldn't have married you.'

'"He thought he loved me once. . . . I never was in love with him but I thought I might be in time. . . . He's the most selfish and cynical human being I've ever met . . ."'

Amadieu relit his pipe and blew a puff of smoke up towards the ceiling. The room in which they were sitting was a cross between a living room, a consulting room and a study, without quite being any of the three; books and magazines lay scattered everywhere.

'You can imagine what a spot I was in. Poor Gérard would just sit there and listen while all this went on, never saying a word.

'The sixth or seventh time I went there, she came up to me in the big drawing-room and, before I could even say hello, she announced in a slurred voice:

'"Please don't bother taking off your coat, Monsieur Amadieu. We won't be having dinner. From now on, you're *persona non grata* in this house. I'll choose my own psychiatrist when I need one . . ."

'And she turned her back on me and staggered off to her rooms.

'The next day, my friend Gérard came here to apologize. He told me she was becoming more impossible every day and that he now just did his best to avoid her. Incidentally, he added that she was trying just as hard to avoid him. . . .'

'Why didn't your friend ask for a divorce?'

'Because he was a Catholic and, in spite of the life he led, he was quite religious. Besides, those escapades of his would have been held against him in any divorce court.'

Maigret puffed on his pipe thoughtfully, gazing at the big red-headed man with the light blue eyes. He sighed and rose to his feet:

'In other words, you don't think she's mad?'

'Not at first sight. Mind you, I've only ever seen her when she was drunk. I'd have to study her case far more thoroughly before I could establish a diagnosis. . . . I'm sorry I can't help you more.'

They shook hands and Amadieu watched the two men walk down the stairs; there was no lift in his house.

'The Brasserie Dauphine?'

'With pleasure, chief.'

'Pity we can't send her to Sainte-Anne to be looked after by a man like that . . .'

'There must be times when her husband finds it hellish to live with her, even though they don't see much of each other. Just to know she's there under the same roof and feeling as she does . . . I think I'd be frightened. . . .'

Maigret looked at Lapointe, dead serious:

'Do you believe she'd be capable of . . . ?'

'I told you a while ago I felt sorry for her . . . I still do feel sorry for her, because she must be terribly unhappy, but even so she scares me.'

'Anyway, he's got to be somewhere, dead or alive . . .'

'More likely dead,' Lapointe sighed under his breath.

As soon as they reached the Brasserie Dauphine, Maigret went to the phone and rang up his wife.

'I know, you're not coming home for lunch,' Madame Maigret said before he could open his mouth. 'In fact, I was so sure you wouldn't that I only got a bit of ham and some salad for you.'

He would have liked another *pastis*, but he remembered his friend Pardon's advice and decided against it. Nor was he supposed to eat the *Tripes à la Mode de Cäen* which were on the menu, but he did, anyway, enjoying them thoroughly.

'I can't decide whether or not to ask for a search warrant. I'd have trouble getting one anyway, since there's no proof of any crime.'

'What would you be looking for?'

'A weapon. . . . Did the solicitor own a gun? . . . Did his wife? . . .'

'Do you think she would be capable of killing him?'

'She'd be capable of anything. She could just as well have killed him with a poker or a bottle. . . .'

'And what would she have done with the body?'

'I know. I don't see her waiting to murder him outside the *Cric-Crac* either. No shots were heard, so she would have had to knock him out first and then get rid of the body.'

'Perhaps she had an accomplice . . .'

'Or else we're just on the wrong track and our man was mugged. . . . It happens every night. . . .'

'If he was mugged, why should the killer go to the trouble of getting rid of the body?'

'I know . . . I know. . . . I can't make it out. . . . One moment I think I'm near the answer, and the next moment I feel I'm going round in circles.'

Maigret gave a strained laugh.

'The big joke would be if our solicitor reappeared suddenly, fit and smiling, and demanding to know what we were up to.'

'What do you think of Lecureur?'

'The head clerk? I don't like him much, though I couldn't say why. He's a cold fish; nothing ever troubles him and he's always too self-controlled. . . .'

'You spoke about what would happen to the practice if Sabin-Levesque turned out to be dead. . . . Lecureur's been working there for over twenty years. . . . He can't help but feel a little as though the business belonged to him. . . .'

'The widow would have to agree to keep him on and I don't think that's very likely. . . . There certainly doesn't seem to be much love lost between the two. . . .'

'Well, naturally they wouldn't kiss in front of us. . . .'

Maigret stared at Lapointe.

'Do you really think that might be so?'

'Yes I do, ever since this morning. . . . I may well be wrong but . . .'

'Isn't that explanation too facile? They're both intelligent people. Nathalie is as cunning as they come. . . . You heard what the psychiatrist said. It reminded me of some phrase I read recently: "Frenzied and utterly amoral . . ." '

'You think that description fits her?'

'It does when she's drunk. And since she drinks from morning to night that makes her a dangerous woman.'

'Dangerous enough to murder her husband?'

'Who knows? . . . She's got quite a temper. . . . I'm going back there to see her, just to provoke her.'

'Perhaps she was frightened?'

'Of whom?'

'Of her husband. . . . There must also have been times when he wished she was dead. He put up with her for fifteen years, I agree, but there can come a moment when a man just can't take any more. . . .'

Maigret laughed uneasily.

'We must sound rather foolish, the two of us, constructing our fine theories around a subject we don't know the first thing about.'

He did not order a brandy with his coffee. He was sick of it and would be for a long time to come, having seen the solicitor's wife gulp it down like water.

CHAPTER FOUR

MAIGRET SAT AT HIS DESK, with an apparently blank look in his eyes. He was watching the man who sat opposite him, who was wearing a smartly-cut chauffeur's uniform and twisting his cap round and round in obvious embarrassment.

As usual, Lapointe sat at one end of the desk with his shorthand pad.

It was he who had gone to fetch the Sabin-Levesques' chauffeur at the Boulevard Saint-Germain, finding him in a room over the garages.

At first the chauffeur was too nervous to sit down and Maigret had to insist.

'Your name is Vittorio Petrini?'

'Yes, sir.'

He was so smart that Maigret expected him to salute when he replied.

'Where were you born?'

'In Patino, a small village south of Naples.'

'Are you married?'

'No, sir.'

'How long have you been in France?'

'Ten years, sir.'

'Have you been working for your present employer all that time?'

'No, sir. I worked for the Marquis d'Orcel for four years.'

'Why did you leave that job?'

'Because he died, sir.'

'Tell me about the work you do for Monsieur and Madame Sabin-Levesque.'

'I don't have much to do, sir. In the morning I go shopping for Mademoiselle Jalon . . .'

'Is that the cook?'

'Yes, sir. She has trouble getting around, as she's quite old. Then I used to clean the car, unless Monsieur needed me.'

'You're talking in the past tense.'

'Excuse me, sir?'

'You talk as though it were in the past.'

'I haven't seen Monsieur for a long time.'

'Which car did he use?'

'Sometimes the Fiat, sometimes the Bentley, it all depended on which client he was going to see. Sometimes we drove as far as fifty, or even a hundred kilometres out of Paris. Many of Monsieur's clients are very old and don't come into town any more. Some of them live in beautiful châteaux. . . .'

'Did your employer talk to you on those journeys?'

'Sometimes, sir. He's a very good employer, not at all stuck-up and nearly always in a good mood.'

'Did Madame ever go out in the mornings?'

'Practically never. Her maid, Claire, told me that she gets up very late. Sometimes even after lunch.'

'What about the afternoon?'

'Monsieur almost never needed me. He stayed in his office.'

'Didn't he drive himself?'

'Sometimes. But then he preferred to take the Fiat.'

'What about Madame?'

'She went out sometimes at about four or five o'clock. Without me or the car. It seems she would go to the cinema, usually to one of the local ones, and then she would take a taxi home.'

'Didn't you find it odd that she never asked you to take her there or to come and fetch her afterwards?'

75

'Yes, sir. But it's none of my business.'

'Does she ever go out in the car with you?'

'Yes, once or twice a week.'

'Where does she go?'

'Not far. To the Rue de Ponthieu. She goes to a little English pub and stays there quite a long time.'

'Do you know the name of the pub?'

'Yes, sir. It's called the Pickwick . . .'

'What state is she in when she comes out?'

The chauffeur hesitated, reluctant to answer the question.

'Is she drunk?' Maigret insisted.

'Sometimes I have to help her get into the car.'

'Does she go straight home?'

'Not always. Occasionally, she would ask me to take her to another bar, the one at the Hôtel George V.'

'Was she alone when she came out of there too?'

'Yes, sir.'

'Was she able to get back into the car?'

'I helped her, sir.'

'What about the evening?'

'She never went out in the evenings.'

'Did your employer?'

'He went out, but he didn't use the cars. I think he preferred to go by taxi.'

'Did he go out every night?'

'Oh no. Sometimes he didn't go out for eight or ten days.'

'And did he stay away for a few days sometimes without coming home?'

'Yes, sir.'

'Did you ever drive them anywhere together?'

'Never, sir. Except once, to a funeral. That was three or four years ago. . . .'

He continued to play nervously with his cap, which had

a leather peak. His blue uniform was impeccably cut and his shoes shone like mirrors.

'What do you think of your employer's wife?'

He gave a faint smile, obviously embarrassed.

'Do I have to tell you? It's not my business to discuss her . . . I'm only the chauffeur. . . .'

'How did she behave towards you?'

'It varied. Sometimes she never said a word and she would purse her lips as if she were furious with me. At other times, she would call me her little Vito and chat the whole time.'

'What about?'

'It's hard to say. Maybe she'd say:

' "I wonder if I shall be able to bear this sort of life very much longer . . ."

'Or else, when she wanted me to drive her home, she would say:

' "Back to the prison, Vito . . ." '

'Is that what she called the flat in the Boulevard Saint-Germain?'

'Yes, when she'd been to a few bars:

' "You know, it's only because of this pig of a boss of yours that I drink the way I do. Any woman would do the same in my place. . . ."

'That sort of thing, you know. . . . I listened to her but I never said anything. I'm very fond of Monsieur. . . .'

'What about her?'

'I prefer not to answer that.'

'Do you remember the 18th of February?'

'No, sir.'

'That was the day your employer left the house for the last time.'

'He must have gone out by himself because he didn't ask for the car.'

'What do you do in the evenings?'

77

'I read or else I watch television. I try to get rid of my accent but I never manage to . . .'

The telephone rang, interrupting the conversation. Maigret motioned to Lapointe to answer it.

'Yes. . . . He's here. . . . Just a moment . . .'

Lapointe turned to Maigret: 'It's the Police Commissioner for the XVth *arrondissement* . . .'

'Hello, Jadot. . . .'

Maigret knew him and liked him very much.

'I'm sorry to disturb you, Superintendent. . . . But I thought you'd be particularly interested in what I have to tell you. . . . A Belgian bargeman called Jef Van Roeten was testing the motor of his boat at the Quai de Grenelle when the wash brought a body floating up to the surface. It gave him quite a shock.'

'Did you identify the body?'

'His wallet was still in his trouser pocket. . . . Gérard Sabin-Levesque. Does the name mean anything to you?'

'I'll say it does! Are you on the spot?'

'Not yet. I wanted to tell you first. Who is he?'

'A Boulevard Saint-Germain solicitor. He's been missing for over a month. I'll see you there. . . . Thanks.'

Maigret put a second pipe in his pocket and turned to the chauffeur.

'I won't be needing you any more for the time being. You can go. Thank you for your co-operation.'

As soon as the chauffeur was gone, Maigret turned to Lapointe.

'He's dead all right.'

'Sabin-Levesque?'

'They've just fished his body out of the Seine at the Quai de Grenelle. . . . Come with me . . . but tell the Criminal Identity Laboratory first.'

The little car threaded its way through a traffic jam and got to the Pont de Grenelle in record time. Below street level was the river wharf with its barrels and piles of timber and brick. Two or three barges were being unloaded.

A crowd of fifty people jostled around an inert shape in the centre. A policeman was doing his best to keep them back.

Jadot had already arrived.

'The deputy officer will be along soon.'

'Have you got the wallet?'

'Here it is.'

He handed the wallet to Maigret; it was limp, slimy and water-logged, not surprisingly. There were three five-hundred franc notes and a few hundreds in it, an identity card and a driving licence. The ink had almost completely faded, but certain words were still legible.

'Anything else?'

'Yes. A cheque-book.'

'In his name?'

'Yes.'

Maigret had been throwing a few covert glances at the sodden corpse lying stretched out on the ground. As always in such cases, he had to make a real effort of will to go any closer.

The corpse's belly was bloated, like a distended wineskin. There was a gaping hole in the chest, leaving horrid whitish viscera exposed. The face had lost almost all human resemblance.

'Lapointe, go and ring up Lecureur. Tell him to come immediately.'

He could not inflict such a sight on Nathalie.

'Where's the bargeman?'

Someone answered with a thick Flemish accent:

'I'm right here, Monsieur.'

'How long ago did you moor your boat on this spot?'

'Almost two weeks. I only meant to stay for two days

to unload my bricks, but my motor broke down. Some mechanics came to repair it and it was a long job. They only finished this morning. . . .'

His flaxen-haired wife stood by his side, holding a blond baby in her arms; she did not seem to understand French and was looking anxiously at the two men while they spoke.

'At about three o'clock, I decided to try out the motor because I want to return to Belgium tomorrow morning when I've picked up a cargo of wine at Bercy. . . . Something seemed to be obstructing the motor . . . then, when it started up, the body suddenly shot up to the surface. . . . It must have got caught in the anchor or in the propeller, which explains why it's all cut open like that. . . . Not my lucky day, sir.'

Oron, the deputy officer, couldn't have been more than thirty years old. He was very smartly dressed and distinguished-looking.

'Who is it?' he asked, after shaking hands with Maigret.

'Someone who disappeared over a month ago. Sabin-Levesque, a Boulevard Saint-Germain solicitor.'

'Had he swindled his clients?'

'It would seem not.'

'Did he have any reason for wanting to kill himself?'

'I don't think so. The last person to see him alive was a nightclub hostess. . . .'

'Murder then?'

'Very likely.'

'Committed right here?'

'I don't think he'd have let anyone bring him to the banks of the Seine alive. He was no fool. . . . Hello, Grenier, I've some dirty work for you to do. . . .'

'I've seen it. . . .'

Doctor Grenier belonged to the new breed of forensic experts.

'I can't do anything here. Not much use in my giving a coroner's verdict of death, since it's fairly obvious.'

The Forensic Institute had sent a special van to collect the body, but it had to wait until the Criminal Identity photographers had done their work. Lecureur soon arrived and walked down the stone steps which led to the wharf.

Maigret pointed to the shapeless heap, which gave off a nauseating smell.

'Will you confirm that it really is him?'

The head clerk approached reluctantly. He walked stiffly, holding a handkerchief to his nose and mouth.

'It's him all right,' he said as soon as he came back.

'What makes you recognize him?'

'His face. It may be disfigured, but you can still tell it's him. Do you think he threw himself in?'

'Why should he have done that?'

Lecureur moved still further back, trying to get as far away from the corpse as possible.

'I don't know. A lot of people drown themselves. . . .'

'I've got his wallet and his cheque-book.'

'That proves it then. It is him.'

'You'll be summoned to the Quai des Orfèvres to-morrow morning to make a sworn statement.'

'At what time?'

'Nine o'clock. . . . Have you got a taxi waiting?'

'Vito had just returned. . . . I asked him to bring me here. . . . He's up there with the Fiat.'

'Then can you give me a lift? . . . Come on, Lapointe.'

He walked up to Grenier, who seemed to be the only one not to mind the presence of the corpse.

'Can you tell me by this evening whether he was murdered before he was thrown into the water?'

'I'll try to. It won't be too easy, because of the condition he's in. . . .'

The three men made their way through the crowd of onlookers. Jef Van Roeten ran after Maigret.

'You're the boss, aren't you?'

'Yes.'

'Can I leave tomorrow morning? I've told you everything I know.'

'You'll have to go to the police station first to make a statement and then sign it.'

'Which police station?'

'That gentleman over there will explain. The one with the little moustache and the black overcoat; he's the chief of police for this district and he'll tell you what to do.'

They got into the small Fiat which Vito drove very smoothly, like all expert chauffeurs.

'Monsieur Maigret, will you excuse me,' the head clerk whispered, 'but if I don't stop at a bar and swallow something strong, I may vomit. . . .'

The three men got out again and went into a bar, empty except for two lightermen. Lecureur, who was white as a sheet, ordered a double brandy. Maigret asked for a beer, but Lapointe had a brandy also.

'I never thought they'd find him in the Seine.'

'Why not?'

'I don't know. Sometimes I thought he might have gone off with a woman . . . he could have gone to the Riviera or anywhere. . . . The only thing which really worried me, though, was that he didn't ring up. . . .'

They soon reached the Boulevard Saint-Germain.

'Will you please look up all recent transactions and get in touch with the bank?'

'Perhaps you could give me the cheque-book so that I can look through the stubs. . . .'

Maigret gave it to him and went in by the right-hand door under the arch, while the head clerk went into the office on the left.

'What! You again!' the maid exclaimed when she opened the door. She seemed furious.

'Yes, mademoiselle, it's me again. And I'd be grateful if you would go and tell your mistress right away that I'm here, waiting for her.'

He started walking towards the boudoir, keeping his pipe in his mouth just to annoy her.

Ten minutes later, Nathalie entered the room; she was not wearing a dressing-gown today but a very elegant suit.

'I was just going out.'

'Which bar were you going to?'

'It's none of your business.'

'I've some important news for you. Your husband's been found.'

She did not ask if he was dead or alive.

'Where?' was her only question.

'In the Seine, by the Pont de Grenelle.'

'I knew something had happened to him. . . .'

The corners of her lips twitched, but her gaze remained steady. She had been drinking, but she was in fairly good shape, for once.

'I suppose I must go and identify the body. Where is he? In the morgue?'

'We don't have morgues any longer. It's called the Forensic Institute now.'

'Will you take me there?'

'You won't have to identify him. Monsieur Lecureur has done so already. However, if you wish to see him . . .'

'Are you trying to insult me?'

'What do you mean?'

'Do you really think I'd be so morbid?'

'One can never tell with you.'

The precious bottle of brandy was on a small table, with some glasses. She helped herself to a drink, without offering one to her guests.

83

'Well, what now?'

'The press will know about it by tonight and they'll be sending reporters and photographers around to see you.'

'Can't you stop them?'

'You can refuse to let them in.'

'What will happen if I do?'

'They'll start ferreting around for other sources and they'll be pretty tough on you, you can be sure of that. They're a susceptible lot. They may well find out certain things . . .'

'I've got nothing to hide.'

'Do as you wish, but if I were you I'd see them and try to put up a good show. The first ones will be here in an hour, at the latest.'

This piece of information did not stop her from gulping down another glass of cognac.

'They keep in touch with the police . . .'

'You enjoy speaking to me like this, don't you?'

'Believe me, I don't.'

'You hate me. . . .'

'I hate no one.'

'Is that all you had to say to me?'

'Yes, that's all. We'll be meeting again soon, I have no doubt.'

'It won't be a pleasure. I despise you, Monsieur Maigret. And now, push off . . . Claire! Throw these characters out! . . .'

Maigret wondered whether to call off the inspector who still stood on the pavement opposite 207 *bis*, waiting to tail Madame Sabin-Levesque. He finally decided to leave him there; after all, they had got nowhere so far by tapping the phones, which was not surprising as Nathalie had not hesitated to go out at night, wearing only a nightgown under her fur coat, just to find a public phone-box.

'What do you make of it all, Lapointe?' Maigret asked, getting into the car.

'If she behaves like that with the press, she's in for a real caning in the papers tomorrow.'

'I've got nothing more to do at the office today. Drop me off at my flat.'

Madame Maigret gave him a sly smile when he came in. 'Happy?'

'Why should I be happy?'

'You found your body, didn't you?'

'Did you hear about it on the radio?'

'Yes, in a news bulletin at six o'clock. . . . Are you hungry?'

'Not really. Not after the afternoon I've just spent.'

He went over to the drinks cabinet, wondering what he might drink to get rid of the queasy feeling in his stomach. He finally chose a small glass of gin, an unusual choice for him; the bottle had not been touched for a year.

'Want some?' he asked.

'No, thanks. Sit down for a moment and read the papers. I'll make you something light.'

The soup was ready. After that, she gave him some ham, salad and diced cold potatoes.

'You're worried, aren't you?' she asked him in an undertone, while they were eating.

'I don't understand certain things and I never like that.'

'Who are you working with?'

She knew that he always worked with one or another of his closest colleagues. Sometimes it was Janvier, or else Lucas, although the latter usually took over from him in his absence. This time, it happened to be Lapointe.

'Would you like me to turn on the television?'

'No, thanks. I'm feeling too lazy to watch it.'

He sat down in his armchair and began to look through the papers. But his thoughts were elsewhere, chiefly with

85

Nathalie, who had turned them out of her house with such rude comments.

At nine o'clock he was dozing, and his wife was about to wake him up so that he could go to bed when the telephone rang and roused him with a start.

'Hello. . . . Yes, it's me. . . . Is it you, Grenier? . . . Did you find out anything?'

'I'd like to ask you one question first. Did the gentleman usually wear a hat or not?'

Maigret thought it over.

'I never met him and I didn't think of asking his wife or his staff. . . . Wait a moment. . . . He was a smart dresser and liked wearing youthful-looking clothes. . . . I imagine he went bare-headed. . . .'

'Or else someone took his hat off before hitting him over the head. . . . Not just one but I'd say at least a dozen very heavy blows. . . . The skull is in little pieces, like a jig-saw puzzle.'

'No bullets?'

'None in the head or in the body either. . . . I couldn't tell you exactly what the weapon was; a hammer, a spanner, a car-jack. . . . Probably a car-jack. Two blows would have killed him, but the murderer was really determined to finish him off. . . .'

'What about that hole in his chest?'

'That's more recent. The body was already in a state of decomposition when it must have got caught on an anchor or something of that sort. . . .

'There's one detail which may interest you. . . . His ankles have been bound very tightly, with wire probably. So tightly that one of the feet was almost severed. . . . The wire must have been used to tie him to something heavy, like a block of stone or a weight of some kind.'

'How long would you say he's been in the water?'

'It's hard to tell. . . . Several weeks. . . .'

'Four or five weeks?'

'About that. By the way, I examined the clothes. There was a set of keys in one of his pockets . . . I'll have them delivered to you first thing tomorrow morning.'

'I'm eager to see them.'

'Then send someone over for them. . . . You've more men than I have. . . .'

'Right. Leave them with the concierge.'

'I'm going to take a nice warm bath now and eat a big dinner. . . . I wouldn't like to do this sort of work every day. . . . Goodnight, Maigret.'

'Goodnight, Grenier. . . . And thanks.'

He was at his office before nine o'clock on the following morning. The first thing he did was to send an inspector to fetch the keys from the Forensic Institute.

There was a knock on the door. It was Lapointe, who instantly guessed that Maigret had some fresh news.

'Grenier rang me. . . . Sabin-Levesque was murdered with a blunt, or what the reports call a contusing, instrument. Ten or so very violent blows . . . the murderer tied a stone or some sort of weight around his ankles before throwing him into the water. . . .

'Incidentally, Grenier found a set of keys in one of the dead man's pockets. . . .'

'Have you seen the papers?'

'Not yet.'

Lapointe went to fetch them from the inspectors' duty room, and when he brought them back to Maigret's office there was a smile on his face.

'Look . . .'

On the front page of one daily, Maigret read the headlines:

WELL-KNOWN SOLICITOR MURDERED

The photograph which illustrated the item would have astonished anyone who had seen Madame Sabin-Levesque about an hour before the picture was taken. She did not look in the least bit drunk and had gone to the trouble of changing into a black suit with a white lace blouse.

Her brown hair was meticulously groomed. Her face, which seemed longer, wore a sad expression which was both appropriate and photogenic. She was holding a handkerchief in her hand, as though she had just been weeping and was afraid of breaking down again.

HIS GRIEF-STRUCK WIDOW CANNOT UNDERSTAND

There followed quite a long interview with Nathalie with all the questions and answers. She had received the reporters in the big drawing-room, not in her boudoir.

"When did your husband disappear?"

"About a month ago. At first, I didn't worry because he sometimes had to go and visit a client out of town."

"Who was left in charge of the practice?"

"His head clerk. A most competent man. My husband trusted him implicitly and had given him power of attorney."

"Did you go out a lot?"

"Not much. We saw a few friends at home, but we led a quiet life."

"Was it you who warned the police?"

"I decided to go and see Superintendent Maigret and to let him know I was worried. . . ."

"Why Maigret?"

"I don't know. . . . I've read accounts of several inquiries he's conducted and it made me trust him. . . ."

There was another, shorter interview with Jean Lecureur.

"I have nothing to tell you."

"Did he leave you a message?"

"No. He never left messages, but he usually rang me every two or three days."

"Did he do so this time?"

"No."

"Weren't you worried?"

"I was after about ten days."

"Why didn't you get in touch with the police?"

"I preferred to let Madame Sabin-Levesque know I was worried."

Another paper carried a photograph of Nathalie sitting in the main drawing-room.

MYSTERIOUS DEATH OF A SOLICITOR

The text was more or less identical, but it stressed the fact that the police had not been warned initially. The article ended with the words: "Apparently, Madame Sabin-Levesque was used to these mysterious absences."

'What's incredible,' Lapointe said with grudging admiration, 'is the way she managed to pull herself together so quickly. . . .'

An inspector came in with the set of keys. It contained half a dozen small keys and a safe key, most probably the key to the big safe in the office.

Bonfils brought in a list of all the Paris nightclubs and cabarets. Maigret was surprised to see how many there were: the list was three closely-typed pages long.

He slipped it into a drawer, got up and said with a sigh:

'Boulevard Saint-Germain.'

'Do you think she'll let us in?'

'I'm not going there to see her. I'll have to go up to the Magistrates' Court first. . . .'

He found out that Coindet was the examining magistrate who had been put in charge of the case. Coindet was an affable, good-natured old soul; Maigret had known him ever since the beginning of his career. He went down the long corridor of examining magistrates' rooms until he came to Coindet's office.

Coindet shook hands with him.

'I was expecting you. Sit down.'

A clerk of the court was sitting at the typewriter; he was at least as old as Coindet.

'You didn't send me a report, so I only know what I've read in the newspapers.'

'I didn't because there's nothing to report,' Maigret replied, smiling. 'You forget we only found the body yesterday.'

'Yet I hear rumours that you've been investigating this case for three days.'

'Without results. I need a search warrant this morning.'

'For the Boulevard Saint-Germain?'

'Yes. I'm not very popular with Madame Sabin-Levesque. . . .'

'That's not the impression she gives in the interviews.'

'What she tells the journalists is another matter. . . . I want to go over the solicitor's flat thoroughly; I've only glanced at it so far.'

'You won't leave me without news for too long?'

Coindet was alluding to Maigret's reputation for conducting investigations in his own good time, without worrying too much about keeping the magistrates informed.

Twenty minutes later, Maigret and Lapointe were going into the by now familiar gateway on the Boulevard Saint-Germain. It suddenly occurred to Maigret to go and talk to the concierge, a dignified-looking old man.

'I was wondering when you'd come and see me, Superintendent. . . .'

'I've been so busy.'

'I understand. . . . I'm an ex-policeman myself; I used to walk the beat. . . . I suppose you're particularly interested in the lady?'

'She's an unusual sort of woman.'

'And a pretty unusual pair they both are, or I should say were, now that he's dead. They had two cars and a chauffeur, yet when they went out, they nearly always went on foot. I've never seen them leave the house together and I hear they even ate separately.'

'Nearly always.'

'She told the reporters they received friends but in fact they never had visitors. From time to time, the solicitor would go off, his hands in his pockets, whistling a little tune, just like a young man, never taking anything with him. I suppose he must have had another woman, or at least another flat somewhere. . . .'

'I'll come back and see you when I have a moment. You seem like a man who keeps his eyes open.'

'Habit, you know. . . .'

A moment later, Maigret was ringing the doorbell of the apartment. The maid glared at them with fury when she opened the door. She would probably have slammed it in their faces if Maigret had not thought of putting his foot inside first.

'Madame is . . .'

'Never mind Madame. If you know how to read, take a look at this. It's a search warrant, drawn up by an examining magistrate. Unless you wish to be arrested for obstructing the law.'

'What do you want to see?'

'I don't need your help. I know the flat.'

Maigret started to walk towards the solicitor's rooms, followed by Lapointe. He was particularly interested in the mahogany desk and the contents of its four drawers. It was the only piece of furniture in the flat which was locked.

'Why don't you open the window? It's stuffy in here.'

He tried three of the keys before he found the right one. There was nothing in the first drawer except for some writing paper with Sabin-Levesque's name printed on it, some envelopes and two fountain pens, one of them in solid gold.

The contents of the second drawer were more interesting. It contained several snapshots, most of them taken in the garden of a huge villa. It was Sabin-Levesque's house on the Riviera and looked as though it had been built at the turn of the century. The photographs were of Nathalie, who seemed about twenty years younger, and of the solicitor in his shirt-sleeves, looking like a student.

The words 'La Florentine' were written on the back; this was obviously the name of the villa.

In one of the pictures, there was a huge Alsatian standing close to Sabin-Levesque.

It occurred to Maigret, seeing the picture of the dog, that he had seen no pets anywhere in the apartment.

He was about to close the drawer when he noticed, right at the back, a small passport photograph taken in a Photomat. It was of Nathalie, looking even younger than in the Cannes pictures and also very different. In this photo, she had a mysterious expression and her smile was deliberately provocative.

One word was written on the back: Trika.

It was obviously an invented name and equally obvious that she had not adopted it just to go and work as a lawyer's secretary in the Rue de Rivoli.

When she had told Maigret about her past life, he had begun to get suspicious, especially after he discovered that her so-called employer had been dead for ten years.

When she had spoken to him, she had known the lawyer was dead, so that no one could contradict her story, She had probably never been a secretary, or a typist for that matter.

'Lapointe, look at this. . . . What does it remind you of?'

'Of a high-class call-girl. . . .'

'And we know where the solicitor looked for his lady friends.'

Maigret carefully slipped the photograph into his wallet. He now opened the two left-hand drawers. The top one contained some cheque-books, all unused, except for one in which every cheque stub had been made out to 'The Bearer'.

There were a few odds and ends in the last drawer: a platinum wrist-watch, some gold-embossed cuff-links, rubber bands, stamps.

'Having fun?'

Nathalie had just come into the room. Claire must have woken her up. She had already drunk a good deal of brandy, for they could smell it on her breath three feet away.

'Hello, Trika . . .'

She had enough self-control not to seem too taken aback. 'I don't understand.'

'Never mind. Read this. . . .'

He showed her the search warrant. She drew away.

'I know. My maid told me. Make yourselves at home. Do you want to search the pockets of my dressing-gown?'

Her expression was no longer the same as on the previous day. There had been a look of anxiety in her eyes before; now there was a look of barely disguised terror. Her lips were trembling even more than usual, as were her hands.

'I haven't finished searching this suite yet.'

'Am I disturbing you? . . . It's been such a long while since I came to this part of the house. . . .'

Ignoring her, Maigret began to open and close other drawers and cupboards. There were at least thirty suits in the wardrobe, most of them light-coloured and all bearing the label of one of the best tailors in Paris.

'I see your husband didn't wear a hat?'

'How should I know? I never went out with him. . . .'

'Congratulations for that act you put on with the reporters yesterday.'

She smiled, flattered in spite of her circumstances.

The bed was huge and very low; there was something very masculine about the whole bedroom, with its leather-covered walls.

The bathroom looked as though the solicitor had only just left it. The toothbrush was in its mug, the razor on a shelf with some shaving-soap and a pumice stone. The bath-tub, the basin, the floor and the walls were all made of white marble. The window overlooked a large garden which Maigret noticed for the first time.

'Is that your garden?' he asked.

'Why shouldn't it be?'

It was unusual to see such fine trees in a private garden right in the centre of Paris.

'Tell me, Trika, you were a hostess in which night-club?'

'I know my rights. I don't have to answer you.'

'You'll have to answer the examining magistrate.'

'I'll have my lawyer with me then.'

'Have you got a lawyer?'

'I've had one for a long time.'

'The one in the Rue de Rivoli?' he asked ironically.

He did not know why he was so hard on her, but there was something about her manner which constantly irritated him.

'That's my business.'

'We'll go to your rooms now. . . .'

On the way, he glanced at the titles of some of the books in the study. There were quite a few good modern authors, including some in English; Maigret assumed the solicitor had spoken the language fluently.

They went through the smaller drawing-room, then into the main one, finally reaching Nathalie's boudoir. She stood watching them while Maigret opened a few drawers, which contained only trinkets.

He went into her bedroom. Her bed was as large as her husband's, but it was white, like the rest of the furniture. In the drawers, Maigret found nothing but some very fine made-to-measure underwear.

The grey-blue marble bathroom was untidy, as though it had just been used in a hurry. There was a bottle of brandy and a glass on a small table.

In the wardrobe, Maigret found only dresses, coats, suits and at least thirty pairs of shoes on special racks.

'Do you know how your husband died?'

She looked at him, tight-lipped, without answering.

'Someone hit him on the head with a blunt instrument, probably a car-jack. He was hit not once, but at least a dozen times, so that his skull is in little pieces . . .'

She remained quite still and went on staring at the chief superintendent. There was a glazed look in her eyes and anyone seeing her at that moment would have taken her for a madwoman.

CHAPTER FIVE

MAIGRET PAID ANOTHER VISIT to the concierge in his lodge.

'Tell me, didn't the solicitor have a dog when he got married?'

'Yes, a beautiful Alsatian; he was very fond of it and the dog was devoted to him.'

'Did it die?'

'No. They gave it away a few days after they came back from Cannes, where they had spent their honeymoon.'

'Didn't you think it odd?'

'I hear the dog would snarl at Madame Sabin-Levesque every time she came near. It almost bit her once and tore the hem of her dress. She was terrified of it and so she made her husband give it away. . . .'

When he got back to his office, Maigret sent for the photographer who worked for the Criminal Identity Department. He produced the snapshot of the couple with the dog in Cannes.

'Can you enlarge this for me?'

'The result won't be perfect, but you'll be able to recognize the people in it.'

'What about this one?'

He took out the passport photograph.

'I'll do my best. When do you want them for?'

'Tomorrow morning.'

The photographer sighed. The superintendent always wanted things done in a hurry. He was used to it by now.

Madame Maigret looked at her husband somewhat anxiously, the way she always did when he was conducting a difficult investigation. She was used to his silences and his grumpy manner. He would wander about the flat, not knowing what to do with himself.

Sometimes, when he was eating in an absent-minded way, his wife would ask him, smiling:

'Are you there?'

In fact, his thoughts had wandered far away. His wife recalled a conversation between Pardon and her husband one evening, when they were having dinner at the doctor's home.

Pardon had said:

'There's one thing I just can't understand. You're the exact opposite of most policemen; why, you seem to hate having to arrest a criminal.'

'Yes, that's sometimes true. . . .'

'Yet you carry out your investigations as though the outcome affected you personally.'

Maigret had answered:

'That's because each case is a personal experience in which I become involved. When you go to visit an unknown patient, don't you get emotionally involved too? Don't you struggle with death as though the patient were someone dear to you?'

He was weary and in a bad mood. The sight of the corpse on the Quai de Grenelle had been enough to upset even a forensic doctor like Grenier.

Maigret was fond of Sabin-Levesque, even though he had never met him personally. At school, he had known a boy who was rather like the solicitor, light-hearted and unconcerned. This boy had been the most undisciplined pupil in the class, interrupting the teacher or drawing in his exercise books during lessons.

When the teacher sent him out of the room for an hour, he would look in through the window and make faces at the class.

In spite of this, the teachers did not bear him a grudge and they even ended up by laughing at his antics. But then of course, he was also one of the three top boys in his class at every exam.

After leading the life of a playboy, Sabin-Levesque had suddenly got married. Why? Had he fallen madly in love with Nathalie, alias Trika? Or had she cleverly manipulated his feelings for her?

What did she expect? A brilliant social life, a luxurious home, exotic holidays and fashionable resorts?

Then, about three months after the wedding, Sabin-Levesque had begun to go off on his own again.

Why?

Maigret kept on asking himself this question and could not find a satisfactory answer to it. Had she gradually revealed herself to be the way she was now? They were not getting along well together and then, at some point, they simply stopped being on speaking terms.

Yet neither of them had asked for a divorce.

Maigret finally fell asleep, still turning things over in his mind. When he woke up the next morning, he first drank the cup of coffee his wife had brought him in bed and then got up. It was raining a little outside.

'Are you going to have a busy day?'

'I don't know. I never know what's waiting for me.'

He took a taxi, which was significant, for he nearly always went by bus or métro.

He found the photographs lying on his desk; they were surprisingly clear. He took one copy of each and went to Peretti's office at the other end of the corridor. Peretti was head of the Vice Squad and he was the only police inspector to wear a diamond ring, as though something of the underworld had rubbed off on him.

A good-looking man with jet-black hair, he was still young and dressed in a rather flashy way.

'Hello there! Haven't seen you for a long time.'

It was true. The two men had their offices in the same corridor yet they hardly ever met and when they did it was usually at the Brasserie Dauphine.

'I don't suppose you know this lady?'

Peretti studied the enlargement of Nathalie's passport photograph, going over to the window to examine it more closely.

'Isn't it an old picture of that solicitor's wife, the one who was in the papers yesterday?'

'Yes, it's her, about fifteen years ago. . . . Here's another one of her with her husband, taken a few weeks or maybe months later.'

Peretti studied the Cannes photograph as intently as he had done the other one.

'I can't place either one of them.'

'I didn't expect you to. But there's something else I'd like to know. My men have drawn up a list of all the nightclubs in Paris. Here's a copy of it. Do you see any clubs there which are still run by the same people as fifteen years ago? I'm particularly interested in clubs round the VIIIth *arrondissement.*'

Peretti looked at the list.

'Most of these clubs didn't exist fifteen years ago. Fashions change. At one time, the smart place for night-life used to be Montmartre. Then it was Saint-Germain-des-Prés. . . .

'Wait a moment . . . *Le Ciel de Lit*, Rue de Ponthieu. That used to be run by a nice old crook whom I've never been able to pin anything on; he still owns it. . . .'

'Any others?'

'*Chez Mademoiselle*, Avenue de la Grande Armée. A very classy place run by a woman called Blanche Bonnard. She must be well over fifty by now, but she still looks pretty good. She has another club called *Le Doux Frisson* in Montmartre, Rue Fontaine; it's less genteel than the other one. . . .'

'Do you know where she lives?'

'She's got a flat in the Avenue de Wagram; I gather she spent a small fortune doing it up.'

'I'll leave you the list. I've more copies of it. If you happen to think of any others. . . .

'I forgot to ask you where the owner of *Le Ciel de Lit* lives. . . .'

'Marcel Lenoir? In the same building as his club, on the third or fourth floor. I raided his place once, hoping to find some drugs. . . .'

'Thanks, old chap.'

'How's your case getting on?'

'So-so. . . .'

Maigret went back to his office. Then, as usual, he went to the office of the director for a briefing. During the briefing, he could not help recalling that he might have been sitting in his boss's place only a month hence.

'How are you getting on with your solicitor's case, Maigret?'

The superintendents of the other departments were all present, each carrying various files.

'I'm not getting anywhere. I'm just accumulating bits and pieces of information which may or may not come in useful later.'

He sent off the enlargement of Nathalie's photograph to the newspapers, with the caption: *Madame Sabin-Levesque, aged twenty*.

He then went upstairs to the police archives and looked up the names Trika and Nathalie Frassier. He found nothing.

Nathalie did not have a police record and had never had any encounters with the law.

'Will you take me to the Rue de Ponthieu?'

Lapointe or Janvier drove Maigret everywhere; he had never sat behind the wheel of a car in his life. He had bought a car recently to go to his little house in Meung-sur-Loire on a Saturday evening or Sunday morning, but it was Madame Maigret who did all the driving.

'Anything new, chief?'

'We're going to see the proprietor of a nightclub. He's been running the same place for twenty years. . . .'

The gates of the nightclub were shut, but they could see, through the grating, some large framed photographs of nearly-nude women.

They went in by the main doorway. The concierge sent them up to the third floor on the left. A rather grubby little maid opened the door for them.

'Monsieur Lenoir? . . . I don't know if he can see you. He's only just got up and he's eating his breakfast. . . .'

'Tell him Superintendent Maigret wishes to see him.'

A moment later, Lenoir came out into the hall to greet his visitors. He was huge, very fat and not very clean-looking. He wore an old, wine-coloured dressing gown over faded pyjamas.

'To what do I owe the pleasure . . . ?'

'Pleasure has nothing to do with it. Please carry on with your breakfast.'

'I apologize for receiving you in this fashion.'

Lenoir was an old rogue who had run a brothel twenty-five years earlier. He was probably about sixty but he looked older; he was unshaven and his eyes were still heavy with sleep.

'Will you please come this way. . . .'

The apartment was as untidy as its occupant, whose belongings lay strewn everywhere. They went into a small dining-room which had a window overlooking the street.

Lenoir had finished one boiled egg and was just opening a second.

'I need a good start in the morning.'

He was drinking black coffee. The ash-tray was full of cigarette ends.

'Well, what can I do for you?'

'I want to show you a photograph and you must tell me if it reminds you of anyone. . . .'

Maigret showed him the enlargement of Nathalie's passport photograph.

'She looks vaguely familiar. What's her name?'

'In those days, about fifteen years ago, she used to call herself Trika. . . .'

'They all love to choose the most idiotic names. . . . Trika . . .'

'Do you recognize her?'

'No, I don't to tell you the truth.'

'Can you look up her name in your files?'

Lenoir was a messy eater; there was egg yolk on his chin and on the lapel of his dressing-gown.

'Do you imagine I keep a file on every girl who works in my nightclub? . . . Those women come and go. . . . A lot of them get married and you'd be surprised how many of them make really good marriages. . . . One of my girls became an English duchess. . . .'

'Don't you even keep their photographs?'

'They nearly all take their photographs with them when they go. . . . And if they leave them, I just tear them up and throw them away.'

'Thank you, Lenoir.'

'It's been a pleasure. . . .'

He got up, his mouth still full, and accompanied them back to the door.

'31, Avenue de Wagram.'

Number 31 was the luxury apartment block where Blanche Bonnard lived, as well as a dentist, two doctors and a barrister.

'Whom shall I say is calling?' the maid asked. She was dressed like the classic housemaid in a French comedy.

'Maigret.'

'The inspector?'

'Yes.'

Blanche Bonnard was not eating her breakfast but she was talking on the phone. They could hear her from another room.

'Yes. . . . Yes. . . . My dear boy. I can't just commit myself like that . . . I need more information, my architect will have to make a survey. . . . Yes. . . . No, I don't know how long it'll take. . . . I'll see you this evening at the club, all right? . . . If you like. . . . Bye. . . .'

When she walked into the room, the sound of her footsteps was muffled by the brightly-coloured rugs which lay strewn everywhere on the carpet.

She stared at Maigret for a long time, glancing only briefly at Lapointe.

'You're lucky not to find me in bed. I usually get up late but today I've got an appointment with my business manager. . . . Do come in.'

The living-room was sumptuous, much too sumptuous for Maigret's liking. Blanche must have been in her late fifties but she was still a good-looking woman, even at this time in the morning. She was plump, but pleasantly so, and she had beautiful eyes.

'I suppose you've come because of the Sabin-Levesque affair? I was expecting you one of these days, but I had no idea you'd be so quick.'

She lit a gold-tipped cigarette.

'Please smoke your pipe. It won't disturb me, or my parrot for that matter. . . . When I saw that picture in the papers yesterday, I immediately thought I recognized her from somewhere. So I checked and of course I was right. . . .'

'Did you know Madame Sabin-Levesque in the days when she called herself Trika?'

'And how!'

She got up, went into another room and reappeared, carrying an enormous album.

'My memory isn't very good so I keep everything. I've got five albums like this one, all stuffed with photographs. Look. . . .'

She opened the album and showed it to Maigret. There was a photograph on the right-hand page, of the kind taken by photographers in nightclubs.

It was of Nathalie, looking very young and demure. She was wearing a low-cut dress which showed her cleavage.

Sabin-Levesque was sitting by her side, bending slightly towards her. . . . There was a bottle of champagne in an ice-bucket on the table. . . .

'He met her here. . . . She'd been a hostess for about two months. . . .'

'Do you know where she had come from?'

'Yes. She had been working in a rather sleazy nightclub in Nice. . . .'

'Did she speak about her past to you?'

'Oh, they all do. Most of them live on their own and have no one to talk to . . . so they come and tell Mama Blanche everything. . . . Can I offer you a drink? . . . I don't drink much myself, but I have a glass of port about now.'

The port was exceptional; Maigret had never drunk a finer one.

'Her family name was Frassier. Her father died when she was about fifteen. He was an accountant or something of that sort. . . . Her mother was the daughter of a Russian count and she liked people to know it. . . . You see, I haven't got such a bad memory after all. . . .

'She always sat at the same table in my club. At first, the customers were a bit shy with her because she looked so young and innocent. They would hesitate before going up to her table; she would always smile and act friendly, but she was rather withdrawn. . . .

'She hardly ever went off with anyone. I don't think she did more than three times.'

'Did she have a steady boyfriend?'

'No. She lived alone in a little hotel room not far from here, in the Rue Brey. I liked her, but I never could quite figure her out. . . .'

'One evening, Gérard Sabin-Levesque came in . . . I mean Monsieur Charles, because that was the name we knew him by. . . . He had been coming to the club for a long time. . . . He liked gentle and quiet women and he noticed Trika the moment he came in. . . . He went over to sit at her table. . . . He asked her to go off with him but she refused. . . .

'He came back every evening for a week before she finally agreed to leave with him. . . . She left me some of her belongings, a couple of dresses, some underwear and a few odds and ends. . . .

'She came back a few days later to fetch her things.

'"Madly in love?" I asked her.

'She looked at me without answering.

'"Is he setting you up?"

'"It's not definite yet."

'Then she kissed me and thanked me and I never saw her again.

'Two months later, though, I saw a wedding picture of them in the *Figaro*. Trika was wearing a wedding-dress and her husband a tail-coat.

'"Monsieur Gérard Sabin-Levesque, well-known society solicitor, was married this morning to . . ."'

Maigret and Lapointe exchanged looks, wondering

what to make of the story. The little girl from Quimper, the hostess who had worked in a sleazy Nice nightclub and after that in Blanche Bonnard's establishment, had become the wife of one of the richest and best-known solicitors in Paris.

Gérard's father was still alive in those days. He was a man of principles. What had been his reaction to his son's marriage? And how did the three of them get along when they were all living together in the same flat?

Was Nathalie already drinking in those days? And did she spend most of the time in her rooms, the way she did now?

The years had passed and she drank more than ever. The solicitor had given up hope of a real married life. Husband and wife had grown estranged, almost becoming enemies.

'She's free now . . . free and rich. . . . Is that what's bothering you, Superintendent?'

'What the newspapers haven't said yet is that Sabin-Levesque was hit a dozen times over the head with a blunt instrument, which broke his skull into small fragments. . . .'

'Would a woman be capable of doing that?'

'In certain circumstances, women can show as much strength as men, if not more. . . . Let us suppose she did it. . . . Where would she have committed the murder? . . . In their flat? . . . He lost a great deal of blood. It would have left stains and she's too clever not to realize that. . . .

'Besides, how would she have got the body to the Seine? How would she have got it out of a car and into the river?'

'Of course. Perhaps he was murdered by some ruffian he met in a deserted street?'

'Nothing was removed from his wallet and there was over two thousand francs in it.'

'A revenge killing?'

'Why would anyone want to revenge themselves on him?'

'A lover . . . the lover of one of those women he picked up in the nightclubs. . . .'

'That sort of lover isn't jealous of a paying customer. Unless perhaps one of them was trying to blackmail him. . . .'

Maigret took another look at the photograph of the young couple drinking their champagne. He finished his port.

'Will you have another?'

'No thank you, though it's delicious.'

He had learned a few more details about Nathalie's past, but had it got him any further in his investigations?

Madame Maigret was surprised when her husband came home for lunch, but it obviously did not mean very much, for he was sullen and withdrawn as before.

He usually loved the *pot-au-feu* with *pauvre-homme* sauce which she had made for him, but today he hardly noticed what he was eating.

'Can I have a really large cup of coffee?'

She knew this meant one like his morning cup, which held a good third of a litre. He glanced at the papers: there were interviews with the concierge and with one of the employees from the practice. The reporters had also tried to interview Vito, but he had not been very forthcoming.

When Maigret got back to his office, he found a transcript of all the telephone calls made to and from the Sabin-Levesque flat.

Nathalie had not telephoned once since the police had started to tap her phone, but she had received an incoming call that morning. It had been very brief.

'Is that you?'

'Yes.'

'I must see you. . . .'

Without waiting or saying anything, she had hung up. On the same line, but probably on another extension, the cook had ordered some veal from the butcher, which the chauffeur would collect later on.

The practice, however, had been flooded with incoming calls from clients. Many of them sounded worried. Lecureur had tried to reassure them and to answer their questions as best he could.

Maigret went up to see the examining magistrate, although he had nothing much to tell him. But Coindet was in no hurry. He sat at his desk, slowly sucking on an old pipe and looking through some files.

'Sit down, Maigret.'

'I've got practically nothing to tell you. You must have received the report of the autopsy.'

'Yes, I did, this morning. . . . The murderer won't be able to claim that he didn't mean to kill his victim. . . . Have you any idea where the crime was committed?'

'No, I haven't, not so far. The experts at the Criminal Identity Laboratory are examining his clothes and shoes down to the last little seam. . . . But the body's been in the water for such a long time that it may well yield no results.'

Maigret filled his pipe, lit it and offered Coindet some tobacco from his pouch.

'I've had some successes in one area. Madame Sabin-Levesque claims she was working as a secretary for a lawyer in the Rue de Rivoli when she met her future husband. This lawyer turns out to have been dead for ten years, so he can't refute her story.

'I found some photographs in one of the solicitor's drawers. One of them was of Nathalie when she was much younger; there was a name written on the back of it: Trika.

'That's a false name, of course. I knew what sort of women the solicitor liked, so I did some investigating around the nightclubs. I learned that his wife used to be a hostess, not a secretary. I even know in what nightclub she met Sabin-Levesque. . . .'

Coindet gazed thoughtfully at the smoke coming out of his pipe.

'Do you think she ever went back to her old haunts?' he asked in his mild voice.

'I shouldn't think so. . . . After her marriage, she must have thoroughly despised that world; she had always felt it was unworthy of her. . . .

'This morning, someone telephoned her. It was a man's voice but we didn't have time to find out where he was ringing from. He just said:

' "I must see you. . . ."

'She hung up without answering. I still have the feeling that she knows far more than she's telling us; that's why I'm hounding her rather. I'll go back and see her, not for any reason in particular.'

The two men smoked their pipes in silence for a moment; then they shook hands and Maigret returned to his office.

He went into the adjoining room and asked Janvier:

'Who's on duty out there at the Boulevard Saint-Germain?'

'Inspector Baron.'

Lapointe was looking at him expectantly. Maigret turned to him and said:

'I'm going there alone. . . . It's an experiment. . . . She might be less wary and perhaps . . .'

He finished his sentence with a gesture, implying that he did not really believe there was much hope of it.

He took a taxi and when he got there he could see Inspector Baron across the street walking up and down; he went over to speak to him.

'Has she gone out?'

'No. I've nothing to report. The chauffeur went out in the Fiat this morning; I assume he only went to do the shopping because he came back soon afterwards . . .'

The concierge was such a nice fellow and so proud to shake hands with a police superintendent that Maigret went to pay him a brief visit.

'I gather she hasn't gone out?'

'No. All the people who've come in were for the doctor up on the third floor.'

'How many years have you been working here?'

'Sixteen years. My feet get sore easily, so it didn't suit me to be in the City Police force.'

'Did you know Sabin-Levesque when he was still a bachelor?'

'He was married six months after I came here.'

'Did he disappear for several days at a time even then?'

'Yes, except during the last two or three weeks before he got married.'

'And was his father still alive in those days?'

'Yes. He was a fine-looking man, the picture of a solicitor, with a youthful face and snow-white hair.'

'How did he get on with his son?'

'I don't think he was especially proud of him, but he had resigned himself . . .'

Maigret went up to the first floor and rang the bell.

The maid, Claire, opened the door and said with a sneer:

'Madame Sabin-Levesque has gone out.'

'Are you quite certain of that?'

'Yes.'

'What time did she leave the house?'

'About two o'clock. . . .'

It was ten past three.

'Did she take one of the cars?'

'I don't think so.'

Maigret knew that Baron could not have missed Nathalie; and besides, the concierge would have seen her going out too.

He walked into the flat, closing the door behind him.

'What are you going to do?'

'Nothing. Pay no attention to me. If you're frightened I'll steal something, you can follow me around. . . .'

He started searching the left-hand side of the apartment, which was Nathalie's section.

He even peered into the wardrobes, which made Claire smile.

'Why do you think she would hide in a closet?'

'It's as good a hiding-place as any.'

'She has no reason to hide.'

'She has no reason not to go out by the main door, either. . . .'

He walked around the drawing-room, studying the austere looking portraits of Sabin Levesque's ancestors; he thought of the life their descendant had led and wondered if they had carried on in the same fashion when they were not sitting for their portraits.

'Where's the other way out of the house?'

'I suppose I can tell you, since everyone else knows about it.'

'By the courtyard?'

'No. There's a little glass door next to the lift. You open it and walk down a few steps into the garden. You cross the garden and you come to a door in the wall. If you go out by there, you find yourself in the Rue Saint-Simon.'

'Isn't the door locked?'

'Yes, it is. But Monsieur and Madame Sabin-Levesque happen to be the owners, so they've got a key.'

'Where do they keep the key?'

'I don't know. . . .'

It was an interesting point. Did Gérard or his wife keep the key? And if it was Gérard, when had she taken it from him?

He went into the solicitor's small study and sat down in a comfortable leather armchair.

'Are you planning to stay here for long?'

'Until your mistress comes back.'

'She won't be pleased.'

'Why not?'

'Because you're not supposed to be here while she's out.'

'You're very loyal to her, aren't you?'

'Why shouldn't I be?'

'Is she nice to you?'

'She can be extremely disagreeable sometimes, rude and unfair, but I don't hold it against her.'

'Do you feel she's not responsible for her actions?'

'Not at those moments. . . .'

'Do you think of her as a sick woman?'

'It's not her fault if she only has drink to fall back on.'

'If she asked you to lie for her, to perjure yourself, would you do it?'

'Certainly.'

'It can't be very nice for you when she vomits in her bed at night. . . .'

'Nurses have to cope with far worse things than that.'

Maigret thought he heard a sound in the hall, coming from the door. He did not stir and the maid did not seem to have heard.

'What would you do if I began to scream and then accused you of having tried to rape me?'

Maigret could not help laughing.

'Why don't you try? . . . It might be amusing. . . .'

She shrugged and walked off through the main drawing-room in the direction of Nathalie's rooms. She did not return, but Nathalie soon came into the study from the drawing-room, very unsteady on her feet.

She was white as a sheet and there were dark circles around her eyes. The lipstick on her mouth looked like a gash. She almost fell as she came in and Maigret rose to help her.

'Please don't worry about me. I can still stand up by myself. . . .'

She sank down into the armchair opposite the chief superintendent and stared at him with a dazed look in her eyes.

'Who told you . . .'

She shook her head as though to erase the words she had just spoken.

'Could you please ring that bell over by the door?'

Maigret rang the bell, which would summon one of the servants.

'It's hot. . . .' Without getting up, she took off her brown tweed jacket. 'Aren't you warm?'

'Not right now. You must have walked too fast.'

'What makes you think I've been walking?'

'Because you knew I would find your driver if you took a taxi and that I'd learn where you've just been that way. . . .'

She stared at him, a look of shock in her eyes. She seemed incapable of pulling herself together.

'You're clever. . . . But you're cruel. . . .'

He had hardly ever seen anyone as acutely distressed and crushed as Nathalie was at that moment. Claire must have known why she had been called, for she came in carrying a tray with a bottle of brandy, a glass and a packet of cigarettes on it. She filled the glass herself and handed it to Nathalie, who almost dropped it.

'You won't have one, will you? You're not an alcoholic yet. . . .'

She had trouble pronouncing the word alcoholic and had to repeat it.

'Hasn't your doctor ever suggested you should go to a hospital for treatment?'

'Oh yes! If he had his way I'd have been locked up in an asylum long ago. . . . Which would have suited my husband perfectly. . . . You see how odd life is . . .'

She stopped abruptly, as though she had lost her train of thought.

'Odd . . . odd . . .' she kept on repeating to herself, with a far-away look in her eyes. . . . 'Ah yes. . . . Life. . . . Now my husband's dead and I'm still alive. . . .'

She looked around the study, then glanced towards the drawing-room, and a rather satisfied expression came into her face. She took another gulp of brandy and said in a joyless tone:

'Everything's mine.'

He expected to see her collapse on the floor any minute and yet, in spite of her drunkenness, she retained some sense of reality.

'I never used to come in here. . . .'

She was now gazing at the walls of the study.

'He only came in here to read.'

'Do you remember the *Chez Mademoiselle* nightclub?'

She gave a start and her eyes grew hard again.

'What did you say?'

'Madame Blanche, the owner of *Chez Mademoiselle*. . . .'

'Who told you about it?'

'Never mind. I've got a very nice photograph of you and Gérard drinking a bottle of champagne together. This was before your marriage. . . .'

She did not stir; her manner had grown defensive again.

'You never were a secretary. You worked in a third-rate club in Nice where you were forced to go upstairs with the customers. . . .'

'You're a bastard, Superintendent.'

She swallowed the rest of her brandy in one gulp.

'I'm the wife of Monsieur Sabin-Levesque now. . . .'

She corrected herself.

'I mean the widow of Monsieur Sabin-Levesque.'

She was panting slightly.

'I don't believe you killed your husband. . . . You're a very energetic woman but you wouldn't be physically capable of such a murder. . . . Unless an accomplice . . .'

'I never even went out that evening.'

'On the 18th of February?'

'Yes.'

'You remember the date?'

'You told me that was the date. . . .'

'Who rang you up this morning?'

'I don't know.'

'Someone was determined to see you and said it was absolutely necessary. . . .'

'It must have been a wrong number.'

'You hung up, guessing that the phone was tapped, but by a strange coincidence you went out this afternoon. . . . You did not leave by the main door but by the little door in the garden. By the way, was it your husband or you who kept that key?'

'It was me.'

'Why?'

'Because he never went into the garden and I did from time to time. I used to go and sit there in the summer. I hid the key in a crevice in the wall.'

'Did you ever use it?'

'Yes, to go and buy cigarettes across the way. Or maybe to go and have a drink. . . . They'll tell you . . . I'm the local drunk, aren't I?'

'Where did you go this afternoon?'

'I went for a walk.'

'And where did you stop?'

'I don't know. In a bar, perhaps.'

She was swaying and he began to feel sorry for her. He got up.

'I'll ring for your maid and she'll put you to bed.'

'I don't want to go to bed. . . .'

The idea seemed to frighten her; she was living in a nightmare.

'I'll ring for her, anyway.'

'No. Stay here. . . . I'd rather even you were here. . . . Do you know anything about medicine?'

'No.'

'Give me your hand.'

She put his hand on her chest; her heart was throbbing violently.

'Do you think I'm going to die?'

'No, I don't. What's your doctor's name?'

'I don't want to see him either. . . . He'll have me locked up. . . . He's a beastly man. . . . One of Gérard's friends. . . .'

Maigret looked up the doctor in the directory. He lived just around the corner, in the Rue de Lille.

'Hello . . . Doctor Bloy? . . . It's Superintendent Maigret speaking. I'm at Madame Sabin-Levesque's house. She isn't feeling at all well and I think she needs your help. . . .'

'Are you sure she isn't putting on an act?'

'Does she do that sometimes?'

'Yes. Unless she's dead drunk. . . .'

'I'd say that was the case today.'

'I'll come over right away.'

'He's going to give me an injection,' she was moaning. 'He always gives me an injection every time he comes. He's a fool and he thinks he's smarter than anyone else. Don't go. . . . Don't leave me alone with him. . . . He's a wicked man. . . . The world is full of wicked people and I'm all alone. . . . Do you realize that? . . . All alone.'

She began to weep; the tears rolled down her cheeks and her nose was running.

'Haven't you got a handkerchief?'

She shook her head and Maigret gave her his, as he would have done to a child.

'Whatever happens, don't let him send me to a hospital. . . . I can't bear the idea of going there. . . .'

There was no way of stopping her from drinking still more. She would suddenly grab her glass and empty it in a flash.

They heard the door-bell ring. A moment later, Claire ushered in a very tall, athletic-looking man. Maigret found out later that the doctor had once been a rugby player.

'Glad to meet you,' he said, shaking hands with Maigret.

He glanced at Nathalie with indifference; she did not stir but stared at him, terrorized.

'Well? Like on the previous occasions? Come into your room.'

She tried to protest but he caught her by the hand, holding his medical bag in his other hand.

'Monsieur Maigret. . . . Don't let them send me . . .'

Claire followed them out of the room. Maigret wondered what to do next and finally sat down in an armchair in the main drawing-room; he knew the doctor would have to cross the room on his way out.

The doctor reappeared much sooner than Maigret had

expected. His expression remained as indifferent as before.

'It must be the hundredth time,' he said. 'She ought to be sent to a clinic and kept there for quite a while.'

'Was she like that already when Sabin-Levesque married her?'

'Yes, but not quite as bad. She was already a heavy drinker and she couldn't do without it even in those days. Then there was some story about her being scared out of her wits by a dog. . . . Though I must admit the dog really did snarl at her every time she went near it or her husband. . . . She made Gérard fire the chauffeur and get another at least two or three times in succession, just as she got rid of one maid after another.'

'Would you say she was mad?'

'Not in the clinical sense of the word. Let's just call her neurotic. Because of all her drinking.'

For some reason, the doctor changed the subject abruptly.

'Have you discovered who killed poor Gérard? . . . I've lived around the corner ever since I was a child and we used to play in the Luxembourg Gardens together. We went to the same school, then we were students at the same time. . . . He was the nicest chap you can imagine.'

They went downstairs together and continued talking outside on the pavement for a while before they parted.

CHAPTER SIX

MAIGRET WALKED along the *quais*, vaguely looking at the waters of the Seine. He kept his pipe clasped between his teeth and his hands in his pockets, and he seemed to be in a bad mood.

He could not help feeling rather guilty. He had been hard, almost ruthless, with Nathalie, yet he felt no animosity towards her.

He had been particularly tough today. She was helpless, incapable of acting her part, and then, suddenly, she had collapsed. He felt quite sure that her collapse had not been part of an act, that she really was at the end of her tether. But he had been doing his work and was only being conscientious in carrying out his duty; if he had been cruel, it was only because he felt it was necessary.

Besides, the doctor who had known her for a long time had been just as hard on her.

She must be fast asleep by now, thanks to the injection the doctor had given her; but what would happen when she woke up?

There was only one person in that huge apartment who cared about her and that was the maid, Claire Marelle. It had been like that for fifteen years.

Marie Jalon, the cook, who had been almost like a mother to Gérard Sabin-Levesque, always looked upon his wife as an intruder. The butler, Honoré, watched all those bottles of cognac vanish with disgust. There was also a cleaning-lady called Madame Ringuet, who came to the flat every morning. Maigret had only met her briefly, but he suspected that she too belonged to the husband's camp.

There had been something rather childlike about the

solicitor, and this made people forgive him everything. He was basically selfish, like a child, and at the same time honest about it.

Shortly after his marriage he returned to the kind of life he had been leading as a bachelor. He was brilliant at his legal work and success came easily to him. And, whenever he wished, he would turn into Monsieur Charles again for the evening.

He was known in most of the nightclubs around the Champs-Elysées; that in itself was odd. He never went to clubs in Montmartre or Saint-Germain-des-Prés. He hunted his quarry, so to speak, only within a defined territory, in the most elegant and chic places.

When those doormen with their gold braid saw him arrive, they called out with a mixture of respect and familiarity:

'Good evening, Monsieur Charles . . .'

And he would remain Monsieur Charles for the whole of that evening, a young man who would never grow old, who smiled at everyone and gave generous tips.

The hostesses would eye him, wondering if it would be their turn tonight. Sometimes he only drank a bottle of champagne with one of them. Or else he took the girl away with him and the manager did not dare complain.

He had been a happy man with no problems. He did not mix with people from his own world; you never saw him at their parties. He liked the convenience of going out with professionals, and if he spent a few days with one of them, it amused him to help her with little household tasks.

He had certainly not intended to get married. He did not feel the least inclination towards matrimony.

Yet he had married Nathalie. Had she won him over by playing the gentle, docile and helpless little woman? It was likely. There was something touching about her in

the passport photograph; in it, she looked like a vulner
able little girl.

She was asking for his protection, making him feel big
and strong . . .

She was married in white, like a chaste young maiden.
She had been dazzled by the house in the Boulevard
Saint-Germain. And the big old-fashioned villa in Cannes
must have seemed like paradise to her at first; she had
put up with everything, even the presence of the strange
dog which snarled at her.

What had gone wrong?

She was alone in the huge apartment for days on end.
Her husband and her father-in-law were working in their
offices downstairs. Mealtimes were rather formal affairs.
She did not have Claire with her yet but another maid,
for whom she was merely the boss's wife.

She had gradually grown harder. She started by insisting that her husband got rid of the dog, which he did
very reluctantly. They had nothing to say to each other
in the evenings. She did not read books and did nothing
except watch television.

They still slept together in the same bed, but they never
really became intimate.

Then, one day, Gérard left without warning anyone,
to go and play the part of Monsieur Charles again in the
Etoile district.

This was his real nature, his childlike side. He was
happy-go-lucky and cheerful; everyone welcomed him
and was pleased to see him.

Nathalie had thought that she would be the centre of
attraction; instead, she discovered that she was super-
fluous. Her husband tolerated her. He did not ask for a
divorce, but they began to sleep in separate rooms and
she would lie in bed, brooding over all her grievances.

It was a mild day. The sun was slowly sinking in the

west and Maigret strolled along, without hurrying. Twice he bumped into a passer-by coming in the opposite direction.

Nathalie was already drinking in her hostess days. She started to take to the bottle in earnest when she found herself all alone in the flat; she was trying to knock herself out.

Maigret wondered if it had all really happened the way he imagined. The more Nathalie drank, the more her husband grew away from her.

Then her father-in-law died. Gérard had to shoulder new responsibilities and as a result he needed to relax more than ever before.

They had both held out for fifteen years. This was what really astonished Maigret. For fifteen years they had met without exchanging a word in those rooms where no one seemed to live. In the end, she could no longer even bear to sit and eat her meals with him.

She had become a stranger and her only good fortune was to have found someone like Claire, who was her ally.

Why didn't she leave? How could she bear to continue leading that stifling existence?

She went to the cinema in the afternoons. At least she claimed she did. She would ask the chauffeur to drive her to a bar in the Champs-Elysées district from time to time. There she would sit perched on a high stool at the bar and drink by herself.

The barmen would fill her glass the moment it was empty, without waiting for her to ask. She spoke to no one. No one spoke to her. She was known as 'the woman who drinks'.

Had she finally met a man who was prepared to look after her and to restore her shattered ego?

So far, Maigret had found nothing in his investigations to make him suppose such a thing had occurred. Vito claimed that she always left the various bars alone, staggering a little.

She was a widow now. The house, the practice and the money belonged to her, but wasn't it too late? She was drinking more than ever. She was frightened of something. She seemed to be fleeing from reality, from life itself.

Where did she go when she slipped out by the garden door?

Who had telephoned her that morning?

It was hard to know when she was lying or when she was speaking the truth. She was a clever actress; within minutes, she had been able to transform herself into a high society lady for the benefit of those photographers and reporters.

Maigret went half way across the Pont-Neuf and stopped at the Brasserie Dauphine.

'A *pastis* like the other day?'

'No, a brandy.'

It was a challenge. He would do the same as her. He would have a brandy. The first sip burned his throat. Yet he had a second brandy before he went back to the Police Judiciaire.

The file which he had shown to his colleague in the Vice Squad lay on his desk.

He picked it up and took it to the inspectors' duty room, which contained at that moment about twenty inspectors.

'I need ten of you, those who don't look too much like policemen. . . .'

The men smiled, some of them a trifle sourly.

'Here's a list of all the nightclubs in Paris. . . . Forget about the ones in Saint-Germain-des-Prés and Montmartre. Concentrate on the ones in the VIIIth *arrondissement* and thereabouts.'

He gave Lucas the list, with a dozen copies of the Cannes photograph.

'You don't have to hide your profession, but don't be too obvious about it either. . . . Each one of you will be given a photograph and some addresses. . . . You must go there at about midnight and question the barmen, the *patron* and the hostesses. . . . Keep the date of the 18th of February in mind. . . . Also the name Monsieur Charles. . . . I forgot, also talk to the flower-sellers who go from one club to another. I know it'll be a miracle, but I want to find someone who saw Monsieur Charles on February 18th. . . .'

He gave Lucas the whole file and returned to his office, still looking preoccupied.

It was probably a stab in the dark, but people did sometimes remember a date because of a birthday or because of some particular incident which happened that day.

Lapointe had followed him.

'May I come in, chief? I wanted to tell you about a phone call which came through for you while you were out. I took the liberty of answering in your place.

'The municipal police rang. . . . A police officer in Puteaux reported a black Citroën abandoned apparently quite a while ago on some waste ground.

'Apparently there are some bloodstains on the front passenger seat, especially on the back of the seat. . . .'

'Who does the car belong to?'

'To a man called Dennery; he's a municipal engineer who lives in the Rue La-Boétie.'

'When was the car stolen?'

'On the 18th of February, which is the interesting part. He reported the theft to his local police station. . . . No one thought of looking for the car in that god-forsaken corner of Puteaux. . . .'

'Were the number plates removed?'

'No, they weren't. That's what allowed them to trace the owner immediately.'

'Where's the car?'

'I asked the police commissioner of Puteaux to leave it where it was and to send a police officer to keep a watch on it.'

So they had one positive clue at last!

It was not definite yet, but it might eventually lead them somewhere.

'Put me through to Doctor Grenier. . . .'

Maigret hoped that the doctor was not busy with some other autopsy.

'Grenier? Maigret speaking. I need you. . . .'

'Right away?'

'The sooner the better.'

'Another corpse?'

'No. But maybe the car which transported the corpse.'

'Where do I have to go?'

'Come over here. I don't know the exact location; we'll drop in at the Puteaux police station and they'll tell us.'

'All right. I'll be with you in fifteen minutes.'

He then rang up Moers at the Criminal Identity Department.

'I need those specialists who worked on the solicitor's case.'

'They're right here. Where do you want me to send them?'

'To the police station in Puteaux; they'll be told where to go from there.'

Maigret had almost forgotten how difficult the afternoon had been. They picked up Doctor Grenier and Lapointe drove them off to Puteaux, no easy job at that time of day.

'We don't often see you in these parts, Superintendent Maigret.'

'I'd like one of your men to take us to the car you've just found.'

'That's easily done.'

He gave instructions to a policeman, who just managed to squeeze into the small car with them.

'It's very near. . . . Next to a demolition site. . . . They're pulling down an old house to build a block of flats.'

The car was very dusty. The headlamps and the tyres had been stolen. A policeman was standing guard over it and a man of about fifty came rushing over to Maigret.

'Look at the state my car is in!'

'Are you the owner?'

'My name is Georges Dennery. I'm an engineer. . . .'

'Where was your car stolen?'

'Right in front of my house. My wife and I had just finished dinner and we were going to drive to a cinema in the Latin Quarter. . . . The car had disappeared. . . . I dashed over to the police station. . . . Who is going to pay for the repairs, the tyres and the headlamps?'

'You'll have to inquire at the appropriate department.'

'Which is the appropriate department?'

'I don't know,' Maigret had to admit, a little testily.

The grey material of the upholstery had absorbed the blood. Doctor Grenier took a small glass phial out of his medical kit and began his intricate task.

The men from the Criminal Identity Department were searching for fingerprints on the doors, the steering-wheel, the hand-brake and the gear-lever.

'Can you find any?'

'There are some beautiful ones on the steering-wheel. The other prints aren't so clear. . . . Somebody was smoking Gitanes . . . the ashtray's full of them.'

'What's on the dead man's side?'

'Nothing except for the blood on the upholstery.'

'And bits of brain,' the doctor added. 'The traces here correspond exactly to those which would have been left by the corpse I examined. . . .'

They went on working meticulously for another hour. A small crowd of curious people had gathered to watch them and two Puteaux policemen were keeping them at bay.

The car was parked in the middle of the building site, which seemed abandoned for the moment.

Monsieur Dennery nervously went from one police officer to the other, obsessed by the question of who would pay for the damage done to his car.

'Aren't you insured against theft?'

'Yes, but the insurance companies never pay the whole amount. And I don't want to have to fork out for the rest. This sort of thing wouldn't happen if the streets of Paris were better patrolled.'

'Had you left the keys in the car?'

'I never dreamt that someone might steal it. The seats will have to be replaced. I don't even know if my wife will want to ride in a car which has carried a corpse. . . .'

The men from the Criminal Identity Department had found a few woollen threads which probably belonged to a tweed jacket.

'Boys, I'll let you get on with your work. Try to establish a preliminary report for me by tomorrow morning, even if it's incomplete.'

'We'll do our best, chief.'

'My job won't take long at all,' Doctor Grenier said. 'I only have to do a blood test. I'll ring you at your flat this evening.'

Lapointe dropped Maigret off at the Boulevard Richard-Lenoir.

Madame Maigret came to the door to greet her husband. She took one look at him and frowned.

'Not too tired?'

'Very tired.'

'Are you getting somewhere?'

'Could be . . .'

He was still quite grumpy and did not seem to notice what she gave him for dinner. After the meal, he sank into an armchair, filled a pipe and watched television.

He was thinking of Nathalie.

Maigret was dozing in his armchair when the phone rang, rudely jolting him out of his little oasis of silence. Only one lamp was lit. They had turned the television off. Madame Maigret sat on a chair a few feet away, sewing.

She never sat down in an armchair, claiming that it made her feel imprisoned.

With heavy footsteps, he walked over to the phone.

'Superintendent Maigret?'

'Yes. Speaking.'

His voice must have been slurred, for his caller asked:

'Have I woken you up?'

'No. Who is it calling?'

He did not recognize the voice.

'Doctor Bloy. I'm at the Boulevard Saint-Germain. Madame Sabin-Levesque has just tried to commit suicide.'

'Is her condition serious?'

'No. I thought you might like to see her before I give her another stronger injection.'

'I'll come over right away. . . . Thank you for calling.'

His wife was already helping him on with his jacket; she went to fetch his overcoat.

'I suppose you'll be away a long time?'

'Will you call a taxi . . . ?'

While she rang for the taxi, he filled his pipe and poured

himself a small glass of *prunelle*. Madame Maigret noticed how upset he was. Of course, he did not know any of the details, yet he felt partially to blame for what had happened.

'The taxi will be here in a minute. . . .'

He gave his wife a kiss. She followed him to the door and opened it for him. Leaning over the balustrade, she watched him going down the stairs, giving him a little wave of her hand.

The taxi arrived a couple of minutes later. Maigret was about to give the address when the taxi-driver asked him in a sly tone:

'To the Quai des Orfèvres?'

'No. Not this time. Boulevard Saint-Germain. Number 207 *bis* . . . at the far end of the boulevard.'

He noticed a street clock which said that it was twenty past ten. This meant that he must have been asleep for nearly two hours, without realizing it.

He paid the taxi-driver and rang at the main door.

The ex-policeman turned concierge came to open it for him.

'I don't know what's happened, but the doctor's up there.'

'He rang me a moment ago.'

Maigret raced up the stairs and Claire Marelle opened the door for him. Doctor Bloy was waiting for him in Gérard Sabin-Levesque's little study.

'Is her condition serious?'

'No. The maid happens to have worked for a doctor once and she immediately tied a tourniquet above her wrist, even before she phoned me.'

'I thought the injection was supposed to knock her out until tomorrow morning, if not later. . . .'

'It ought to have done. I don't understand how she woke up or how she was able to get up and walk around.

The maid was sleeping in a camp bed in the boudoir so as not to leave her alone. . . . She woke up suddenly and saw her mistress walking through the room like a ghost, as she put it, or a sleepwalker. . . .

'She went across the main drawing-room and into the dining-room. . . . Then she went into her husband's rooms . . .

'"Madame, what are you doing? You must go back to bed. You know what the doctor said. . . ."

'She was smiling in a peculiar, twisted sort of way.

'"You're a good girl, Claire. . . ." '

Here the doctor added:

'And don't forget that all the lights were out at that moment, except for the one in the boudoir. It must have been quite an awesome sight, but the maid kept her nerve.

'"Give me something to drink."

'"I don't think I ought to."

'"Then I'll go and fetch the bottle myself. . . ."

'Claire preferred to get it for her. She put her mistress to bed, then she telephoned me. I was playing bridge with some friends. I dashed over. It's a deep wound; I had to make three stitches. . . .

'She didn't speak to me. She just stared at me without any expression on her face, except perhaps indifference.'

'Does she know you telephoned me?' Maigret asked.

'No. I called you from the study. I thought you might like to speak to her before I really knocked her out with another injection. That woman is incredibly tough.'

'I'll go and see her.'

Once again, Maigret crossed the apartment and went into the boudoir; he could still see the imprint of Claire's body on the camp bed.

'You see what you've done?' Claire said to him; her voice was not angry but sorrowful.

'How is she?'

'She's lying without moving, and staring at the ceiling; she won't answer when I speak to her. All I ask is that you treat her humanely.'

Maigret felt awkward as he went into the bedroom. Nathalie lay with the sheet pulled up to her chin; only her bandaged arm was resting on top of the bedclothes.

'I had a feeling they'd get in touch with you.'

Her voice sounded weary.

'I really wanted to die. . . . It's the only solution, isn't it? . . .'

'Why do you say that?'

'Because I've nothing left to live for.'

Maigret was startled to hear her say this, as it did not fit in with what he knew. She had not loved her husband. She had not even pretended to like him.

She could never have felt that Gérard was her reason for living.

'I know you were only doing your job, but you were cruel. . . .'

'Have you anything to tell me?'

She did not answer him immediately.

'Pass me the bottle. . . . It'll be too late once the doctor gives me another injection. . . .'

He hesitated, then took down the bottle from the chest of drawers.

'Don't bother about a glass. My hand is shaking too much; I'd spill it. . . .'

She drank straight from the bottle, a sorry sight to see in those luxurious surroundings.

She almost dropped the bottle on the bedspread and Maigret caught it just in time.

'What are you going to do with me?'

Was she in her right mind? Her words, spoken in a muffled voice, could be interpreted in several ways.

'What do you expect?'

'Nothing. I don't expect anything any more. I don't want to be alone in this big house. . . .'

'It's yours now.'

Her mouth grew twisted once again.

'Yes . . . it's mine. . . . It's all mine. . . .'

Her voice was full of a melancholy irony.

'If they had told me such a thing in the days when I was just a little nightclub hostess. . . .'

Maigret did not reply and for once did not even feel his usual urge to take his pipe out of his pocket.

'I'm Madame Sabin-Levesque. . . .' She tried to laugh, but only succeeded in producing a sob.

'You can leave me now. I promise you I won't try to kill myself again. . . . Go back to your wife. . . . Because at least you're not alone. . . .'

She turned her head slightly to one side and looked at him. 'You've chosen a dirty sort of job, but I suppose it's not your fault. . . .'

'I hope you sleep well.'

'Don't worry. This time, Doctor Bloy will increase the dose and heaven knows when I'll wake up. . . .'

'Good night.'

Maigret left the room on tiptoe, rather as he would have left a deathbed. Claire was waiting for him in the boudoir.

'Did she talk to you?'

'Yes.'

'Did she reveal anything to you?'

'No. Is the doctor still in the study?'

'I think so.'

Maigret went to find him.

'Your turn now. . . . I'll wait for you here.'

He filled his pipe and sank down into an armchair. Claire came into the room a few seconds later. She seemed much less hostile to him now.

'Why are you so hard on her?'

'Because I'm convinced that she knows who killed her husband.'

'What proof have you got?'

'I haven't any proof. If I had, I would already have arrested her.'

Oddly enough, the young woman did not protest.

'She's an unhappy woman.'

'I know that.'

'Everyone in the house hates her except me.'

'I know that, too.'

'It's as though she usurped someone else's place by marrying Monsieur Gérard.'

'Did you ever go out anywhere with her?'

'No.'

'Do you know where she went?'

'To the cinema.'

'Did you ever find any old cinema tickets in her handbag or in her pockets?'

'No,' Claire answered, after thinking over his question carefully.

'Did she spend a great deal of money?'

'Monsieur Gérard gave her all she wanted. She would ask me to prepare a handbag for her and to put a specific sum of money in it. . . .'

'How much, for example?'

'Sometimes a few hundred francs, sometimes two or three thousand. . . .'

She bit her lip. 'I shouldn't have told you that.'

'Why not?'

'You know as well as I do. . . . She hardly ever went shopping. All the tradesmen came here to the flat. She never went anywhere personally except to the hairdresser. . . .'

The doctor came into the study and said to the maid:

'This time I think you'll get a good night's rest. I've given her the dose used for sleeping cures. . . . Don't worry if she doesn't wake up tomorrow morning. . . . I'll drop in shortly before noon.'

'Thank you, Doctor.'

She left the room and the doctor sat down and crossed his legs.

'Did she say anything interesting? Sometimes, when they're in that kind of state, people are more outspoken than they mean to be. . . .'

'One of the things she asked me was what I was planning to do with her.'

'She's just been asking me the same question.'

'I think she knows quite a lot about her husband's death.'

'In any case, she's certainly trying hard to hide something. That's what has reduced her to this condition. I'm surprised she hasn't had an actual breakdown yet.'

'She asked me for something to drink and she was so insistent that I gave her the bottle. . . .'

'You were right. . . . Practically nothing could make her worse at this stage.'

'What's going to happen to her medically speaking?'

'Her condition will continue to deteriorate.'

'Do you mean that she'll go mad?'

'I'm not a psychiatrist. . . . And indeed, I'd like a psychiatrist to examine her in a day or two. . . . Anyway, if she goes on drinking at this rate, she'll be finished soon. She can't stay here; I haven't got the sort of equipment I'd need to look after her. She'll have to go to a clinic. Not necessarily a psychiatric clinic. . . . They'll dry her out and make her take the rest she needs.'

He sighed.

'I don't like dealing with this kind of patient. . . . By the way, do you know when the funeral will take place?'

'I didn't dare bring up the subject with her.'

'Do you think she'll want a lying-in?'

'The head clerk will probably deal with it. She's in no condition to do so herself.'

'It'll be much better for her if there isn't too much upset in the flat itself. I can't imagine a catafalque lying in the hallway or in the drawing-room.'

The two men got up and said good-bye to each other in the street. Maigret went home to bed. He slept badly and had nightmares. When his wife woke him up by bringing him his morning coffee, he discovered that he was aching all over, as though he had performed strenuous physical feats.

'Lapointe?' he asked over the phone. 'Is he there yet?'

'He's just coming in.'

'Let me speak to him, Lucas.'

'I'm listening, chief,' he heard Lapointe say.

'Come and get me at my place. First make sure that nothing new has happened.'

He had a bath, shaved and got dressed; then he swallowed a couple of aspirins, since he had a bad headache. He hardly touched his breakfast.

'I'll be glad when this inquiry is over,' Madame Maigret said in a low voice. 'You're taking it so much to heart you'll end up by falling ill.'

He looked at her gloomily and forced himself to smile.

'How come the papers hardly mention it any more?'

'Because there's nothing to say for the time being.'

He found Lapointe sitting behind the wheel of the car and got in next to him.

'Anything on my desk?'

'A report by the experts. . . . The woollen threads found in the car are of the same type as the material of the dead man's jacket. . . .'

'What about the men I sent out to the nightclubs?'

'Almost all the clubs saw Monsieur Charles and they all thought highly of him. . . .'

'What about the 18th?'

'Not a single barman, *maître d'hôtel* or hostess remembered that particular date. Jamin may be on to something, though. An old flower-seller who goes round the clubs in that district remembers the 18th of February because it's her daughter's birthday. She claims that Monsieur Charles, who always used to buy flowers from her, was at the *Cric-Crac* that evening, in the Rue Clément Marot.'

'Did she say anything else?'

'He was with Zoé and he gave her some red carnations. . . .'

'Have we got her address?'

'Jamin wrote it down. She's longing to come and see you in person because she knew you long ago, when you used to be walking the beat. . . .'

They were standing in front of the large oak door which Maigret knew so well by now.

'Shall I wait for you?'

'No. Come inside with me.'

He said hello to the concierge as he walked past the lodge, then went into the office. The receptionist let him go through and, crossing the solicitor's office, he went into Lecureur's room. The head clerk was dictating a letter to his secretary. He stopped, sent her away and got up to shake hands with Maigret.

'I gather she tried to commit suicide during the night and that the doctor had to come?'

'It was nothing serious. She's asleep now.'

'Why did she do it, do you think?'

'If I knew, the inquiry would soon be over. What have you arranged, professionally speaking?'

'The will is to be read out this afternoon at three o'clock. I know what's in it, more or less, because I was one of the witnesses who signed it. Madame Sabin-Levesque inherits the money, the Cannes villa and the profits of the practice. . . . The Institute of Solicitors will decide my position, since my employer expressed the wish that I should succeed him. . . .'

'There's another urgent matter to be looked after: the funeral.'

'I know the family has a vault in the Montparnasse cemetery.'

'That's one point settled. I suppose it wouldn't do for the coffin to be fetched directly from the Forensic Institute to be taken to the cemetery. Madame Sabin-Levesque is in no condition to deal with the question. I don't imagine it will be possible to arrange a lying-in in the apartment.'

'Why not here in the office?'

'That's what I had in mind. Will you deal with it?'

'I'll ring up an undertakers right away. Should we send out announcements to all the clients?'

'Yes, I think so. And don't forget to put an announcement in the papers. Incidentally, aren't you besieged by reporters?'

'We've had at least ten who came along and asked me all sorts of indiscreet questions; I threw them out. Two of them even wanted to know how much Monsieur Sabin-Levesque had left. . . .'

'Keep in touch with me concerning the funeral arrangements, but Madame Sabin-Levesque is not to be disturbed.'

'Won't she be going to the church?'

'I don't think so. It'll depend on the doctor.'

Maigret then went upstairs with Lapointe. Claire opened the door.

'I had business to do downstairs so I came up to find out how everything was going.'

'She's asleep.'

'Have there been any phone calls?'

'No. Only one from a journalist who wanted to see her and who got very angry when I told him it wasn't possible.'

She was obviously tired and had probably not slept much.

'Drive me to the Rue Clément Marot.'

He felt like taking a look. At night, the street must be almost deserted. The multi-coloured door of the nightclub stood ajar.

Two cleaning-ladies were sweeping the floor, which was covered with confetti and paper streamers. The walls were hung with gaudy-coloured cloth.

'What do you want? If you're looking for Monsieur Felix, he isn't here.'

'Who is Monsieur Felix?'

'The barman.'

A man came in, looking very self-possessed.

'Well, well! The chief superintendent in person. . . . One of your inspectors came to see us yesterday evening . . .'

'Tell me what you think of Louisa.'

'She used to be a street-walker and she's never left the district. But she had to change jobs in the end, so now she sells flowers in nightclubs and restaurants.'

'Is she reliable?'

'In what way?'

'She won't let her imagination run away with her? Can I believe what she tells me?'

'Certainly. She also knows how to keep a secret. Most of our young ladies have secrets and she knows every single one.'

'Thanks.'

'Why are you interested in her?'

'Because she claims to have seen Monsieur Charles here with a hostess on the evening of February 18th.'

'How can she remember the date?'

'Because it's her daughter's birthday.'

'Then she's telling you the truth.'

The club was not far away from the banks of the Seine; there was a ramp which led to the water's edge.

CHAPTER SEVEN

ONCE AGAIN, Maigret had lunch at the Brasserie Dauphine with Lapointe. He hardly said a word during the entire meal. Not that he was particularly depressed, but he was in a mood which Lapointe knew well: a solemn and introspective mood, in which he kept his thoughts very much to himself.

When they returned to the Quai des Orfèvres, they saw an old woman through the glass partition of the waiting-room. Maigret did not know who she was at first, but she instantly recognized him and smiled.

It was old Louisa, as they called her now. Maigret had known her when she was young and sexy, one of the best-looking prostitutes along the Champs-Elysées.

He asked her into his office and took off his hat and coat.

'Just think, Inspector, what a long time it's been since we last met! You were a young fellow in those days and once you arrested me I really thought for a moment that you were about to make a pass at me!'

'Please sit down, Louisa.'

'You've come a long way since then, haven't you? Mind you, I haven't done too badly myself. I had my daughter raised by some decent folk in the country and now she's the wife of a cashier at the Crédit Lyonnais bank. . . . She has three kids, which makes me a granny three times over. . . . Her birthday's on the 18th of February, that is why I remembered the date.'

'What exactly did you see?'

'To start with, I saw a black car with a fellow in it, about a hundred yards from the *Cric-Crac*. Then, inside

the club, I saw Monsieur Charles sitting at a table with
Zoé, a nice little girl. When I left, the car was still there
and the man was sitting in the driver's seat, smoking . . .
I could see the little red glow of his cigarette end in the
dark. . . .'

'Can you describe the man to me?'

'It was too dark . . . I did my rounds . . . I have my
routine and I know my customers. . . . Then I came back
at about three. . . . The car had gone and so had Monsieur
Charles. . . . Zoé was now sitting with a strapping
American fellow. . . .'

'Is that all you can tell me?'

'Yes. I really came here because I wanted to see you
again. . . . Men are lucky. . . . They don't age as fast as
we do.'

The phone rang and Maigret picked it up.

'Yes . . . speaking. . . . What? . . . A dead man in the
Rue Jean-Goujon? . . . Five bullets through the chest?
. . . I'll come over right away. . . . Warn the Magistrates'
Court and Coindet, the examining magistrate.'

He turned to the old flower-seller.

'Thanks for coming. I have to go now.'

'That's all right. . . . I've seen you and that's what
matters. . . .'

She shyly held out her hand to Maigret before leaving
the room.

'Lapointe! We're off again. . . .'

The Rue Jean-Goujon was only two hundred yards
from the Seine. The two policemen who were guarding
the building saluted respectfully when they saw Maigret.

'It's on the top floor.'

They took the lift. The door was ajar and Maigret
shook hands with the police commissioner, who was
probably new as Maigret had not met him before.

'The concierge alerted us. She came up here to do the

housework as usual. . . . The tenant didn't answer so she used her pass-key and found the body. . . .'

The doctor was leaning over the corpse of a tall young man in his early thirties lying stretched out on the carpet.

It was not really an apartment but an artist's studio, for one entire wall, as well as part of the ceiling, was made of glass.

'Have you discovered who he is?'

'Joe Fazio. . . . Came from Marseilles four or five years ago. . . . Was a pimp before he got a job as barman in a rather sleazy little bar called the Paréo. He left about two years ago and we don't know how he's made a living since.'

The doctor stood up and shook hands with Maigret.

'It's odd. . . . Someone shot him point blank, almost touching him, with a small-calibre gun. As far as I can tell, two bullets perforated the left lung and another one is lodged in the heart.'

There was a startled look on the dead man's face. As far as Maigret could tell, he had been handsome. He was wearing a very smart gaberdine suit of a shiny, almost luminous brown.

'Has the weapon been found?'

'No.'

The men from the Criminal Identity Department had arrived with their various bulky instruments. Next came a rather elderly deputy who disliked the police commissioner but who shook hands with him all the same.

Coindet, the examining magistrate, was puzzled.

'Why did you ask to have me put in charge of this case? Do you think it has any connection with the solicitor's death?'

'It may well have. I was expecting something like this to happen. When Nathalie slipped out via the garden yesterday, she must have had a reason. . . .'

He turned to Lapointe.

'Are you coming?'

There were too many people in the flat. He would come back when the experts and the magistrates were gone.

He went into the concierge's lodge with Lapointe. The concierge was a small, dark, energetic-looking woman.

'How long had this Fazio been living here?'

'For two years. He was a good tenant; he was quiet and he paid his rent regularly. . . . He lived by himself and he had asked me to do his housework for him. I went up there every day around noon.'

'Was he at home when you went up there?'

'No, usually not, because he ate his meals at a restaurant. I didn't always see him going out. I'm very busy. The tenants come and go and I don't notice. . . .'

'Did he have many visitors?'

'No. Just one lady.'

Her tone was full of respect as she mentioned the 'lady'.

'Every day?'

'Nearly every day.'

'At what time?'

'Around three in the afternoon.'

'Would he come back with her?'

'No. He'd be upstairs already.'

'Describe her to me.'

'She was a real lady, you could see that right away. She wore a fur coat in winter and she must have owned at least three different ones. She usually wore suits in summer. Those suits of hers came from top couturiers. I've got an eye for those things. . . .'

'What about her face?'

'It's hard to say.'

An orange cat was rubbing its head against Maigret's legs.

'Was she young?'

'Not young, but not old either. . . . She could have been attractive. . . . She certainly must have been once. . . . I'd say about forty, but her face was rather battered. . . .'

'What do you mean, battered?'

'She nearly always had dark circles under her eyes and her features were very drawn. Her lips twitched in a funny way. . . .'

'Did she speak to you?'

'No. She went straight upstairs.'

'How long would she stay?'

'She would leave at about five or five-thirty.'

'By car?'

'No. I noticed that she arrived by taxi, but she would get out at the street corner so that the driver wouldn't know where she was going.'

Maigret took the Cannes photograph out of his pocket and showed it to the concierge, who went to fetch her glasses from the other room.

'Do you recognize her?'

'I'm not sure. The one here is so young and she's got a different mouth. . . . Yet the face is pretty much the same. . . .'

The chief superintendent then showed her the passport photograph. 'What about this one?'

'Now that's more like it. . . . At a distance of twenty years. . . .'

'Would you say it was the same person?'

'I think so.'

The police commissioner was walking past the lodge. Maigret ran after him.

'Did the doctor extract the bullets?'

'That's the forensic doctor's job and he hasn't arrived yet. But I think they've found one which hit a rib and ricocheted.'

144

'Will you go and fetch it, Lapointe?'

He thanked the police commissioner and went back to see the concierge.

'Did your tenant work?'

'I don't think so. He didn't keep regular hours except for mealtimes.'

'Did he come home late at night?'

'Do I have to tell you everything?'

'You might as well, since you'll be summoned as a witness anyway.'

'Apart from the three o'clock lady, as I used to call her, he had another girl-friend who was much younger and prettier. . . . She usually came here at about two or three in the morning, either with him or alone, and spent the rest of the night up there. . . . I once overheard him calling her Géraldine. . . .'

Maigret remained expressionless, as though he were not thinking at all.

'Do you know where she lives?'

'No, I don't. She probably works locally, since they always came back on foot. . . .'

Lapointe had come down again with the bullet. Maigret thanked the concierge and walked out of the lodge.

'Where are we going now?'

'To Gastinne-Renette.'

Gastinne-Renette was the gunsmith who usually gave ballistic advice to the Police Judiciaire. When they got there, the shop assistant went to fetch his employer.

'Well, well! Maigret.'

The two men had known each other for twenty years.

The chief superintendent showed him the bullet.

'Can you tell me at a glance what sort of gun this bullet comes from?'

Like the concierge, Gastinne-Renette put on a pair of spectacles.

'This won't be a strictly accurate assessment; I'd need more time for that. It obviously comes from a small-calibre gun, like a Browning 65, for example. They make those models in Belgium; some of them have mother-of-pearl handles. I sold a gold-encrusted one to a client.'

'How lethal is it?'

'Not very, from a distance. The aim isn't accurate further than three yards away.'

'The doctor thinks the shots were fired point-blank.'

'In that case, of course. . . . How many shots?'

'Three or four. One in the heart, two in the lungs.'

'The murderer must have meant business. Who was the victim?'

'A man by the name of Joe Fazio . . . barman turned gigolo. . . .'

'Nice to have seen you. Shall I keep the bullet?'

'I'll tell our forensic expert to send you the others.'

'Thanks. Happy hunting. . . .'

Maigret did not laugh at the joke but mustered a strained smile.

CHAPTER EIGHT

ON THE GROUND FLOOR, the undertakers were busy
turning the solicitor's office into a mortuary chapel. They
were draping the walls with black cloth; the coffin had
been left in a corner, as though no one knew what to do
with it.

'Is the body inside?'

'Of course.'

Jean Lecureur came out of his office.

'The funeral is tomorrow at eleven,' he said. 'The
church is just across the way. We've sent off the announcements. Do you think Madame Sabin-Levesque will attend
the funeral service?'

'I'm certain she won't.'

'That might be best. How is she? I don't know what's
going on up there.'

'Doctor Bloy probably went to see her late this morning.
I'll go up now.'

As they walked up the stairs, he said to Lapointe:

'You're to take down everything which is said.'

'All right, *patron.*'

The footman opened the door.

'Where's Claire?'

'In the boudoir, I think. . . .'

But Claire was just coming forward to meet them.

'Is she asleep?' Maigret asked her.

'No. She's been sitting on the bed in her nightgown
ever since the doctor left. She won't speak to me or take
her bath or allow me to do her hair. . . .'

'What did the doctor say to you?'

'Nothing much. Just to watch her.'

'Has she eaten anything?'

'No. She just shakes her head or nods at me instead of answering.'

'What about you? Have you been eating?'

'I just can't. I feel as though I were at someone's death-bed. . . . What's going to happen, Superintendent? I gather the coffin is downstairs. . . .'

'Yes, it is. Before I go in and see her, I'd like you to put a dressing-gown on her if you can. . . .'

'I don't mind trying.'

Claire was no longer hostile towards him. He could see that she was at a loss as to what to do. The two men waited in the drawing-room for a long time. Finally, after a quarter of an hour, the maid returned.

'She's in the boudoir. I had to give her the bottle.'

Maigret went in first. Nathalie was sitting in her usual easy-chair. She was holding the brandy bottle in one hand. Yet her eyes remained steady and her expression was almost calm.

'May we come in?'

She did not seem to have heard him. Maigret sat down opposite her. She was stroking the bottle as though it were her most precious possession.

'I've just come from the Rue Jean-Goujon,' he told her, his tone gentle, as though he did not want to frighten her.

When she finally opened her mouth, it was only to say a single word in an indifferent voice:

'Already!'

Having said this, she drank straight from the bottle as Maigret had seen her do once before. Her pale cheeks grew slightly flushed and her lips began to twitch again.

'I don't suppose it matters much any more, does it?'

'Were you afraid that he would denounce you as his accomplice if he was arrested?'

She shook her head.

'No. It was worse than that. . . . He only wanted to see me yesterday to demand a very large sum of money, assuring me that he would leave me alone after that and go back to Marseilles. . . .'

'Did you love him?'

She did not answer; there was a despairing look on her face.

'Why did you go there with the gun if you loved him?'

This question seemed to make her become even more desperate.

'I've never had any illusions about him. . . . He was my last chance. . . . Don't you understand? . . .'

She tried to light a cigarette but her hands were trembling too much. Maigret bent forward with a lighted match. She did not thank him.

'You've always been a proud person, haven't you?'

She corrected him in a dull voice.

'I am proud. I mean I was proud once. . . . Now . . .'

She did not finish her sentence.

'You found it humiliating to work in a cabaret and you would have found it even more humiliating to work as a sales-girl in a department store.'

She was listening to him, showing interest, as she always did whenever anyone spoke about her.

'Sabin-Levesque fell in love with you. . . . You soon found out Monsieur Charles's real identity. . . .'

She said nothing and listened tensely.

'You hoped to lead a dazzling, luxurious existence with cocktail parties, receptions, dinners. . . .'

'I soon found out that he was the most selfish man I had ever met.'

'Why? Because he refused to let you come before him?'

She seemed startled and Maigret went on:

'He was the king of this household and you counted for nothing.'

Her eyes grew hard.

'Everyone loathed me except Claire.'

'Why didn't you get a divorce?'

She looked around as though taking in the whole apartment, the house and the entire fortune of Sabin-Levesque.

'Because you were greedy. . . . You didn't care if he went off from time to time to go and look for a pretty girl. . . . You were Madame Sabin-Levesque . . . and you intended to remain that, whatever happened. . . .'

She drank. The gesture had become automatic.

'You turned to drink. I suppose you must have had lovers too? . . .'

'One-night stands. . . . Men I met in bars. . . .'

Now that the truth was out, she no longer cared to defend herself. It was almost as though she got pleasure from baring her soul.

'Hotel rooms. . . . Some of the men got the wrong idea and tried to give me money. . . .'

Her lips were quivering.

'You met Joe Fazio two years ago . . .'

'That was different. I loved him.'

'He was a barman . . .'

'I rented a studio flat for him and kept him. . . .'

She admitted this cynically, once again showing defiance.

'I couldn't expect him to love me for my sake alone. I'm too much of a wreck now. . . . He pretended to love me and I pretended to believe him. . . .'

'Whose idea was it to kill your husband?'

'I think we both thought about it.'

'Fazio found out which clubs Monsieur Charles went to. . . . He followed him several times and waited for the right occasion. . . .'

She shrugged. It was all so obvious!

'Your husband came out of the *Cric-Crac* one night and

Joe Fazio took advantage of the fact that the street was deserted to kill him. He dragged him into a stolen car and carried him to the Seine. He then abandoned the car on a building-site at Puteaux. . . .'

'I didn't go into any of the details. . . .'

'Did he ring you up afterwards to tell you what he'd done?'

'Yes.'

'What sort of life would you have led with your ex-barman?'

'I never thought about it.'

'Admit it wasn't out of love for Joe Fazio that you let him kill your husband. . . .'

'I don't know any more.'

'You just wanted to remain Madame Sabin-Levesque. You would then be undisputed mistress of the house-hold. . . .'

'You don't think much of me, do you?'

'No. But I also can't help feeling sorry for you because, although you're hard, you're vulnerable too. . . .'

'Vulnerable?' She gave a harsh laugh.

'Yes, vulnerable,' Maigret repeated.

'I suppose you're taking me away with you?'

'Yes. It's my duty. Go and get dressed. Keep an eye on her, Lapointe. I don't want her to slip out again by another little door.'

Maigret slowly filled his pipe and began to pace up and down in the room. He waited for nearly half an hour. She came back with Claire, who was carrying a pigskin suit-case.

Nathalie took one last, seemingly endless swig from the bottle of brandy before she started walking towards the staircase.

'I don't suppose they'll let me have any there, will they?'

She would certainly be found guilty. But given the

appalling state she was in, she would probably go straight into the prison hospital.

The door of the solicitor's office was open. The undertakers had finished hanging up their black drapery. She took a couple of steps forward and looked at the coffin.

Her face remained expressionless.

'Is he in there?'

'Yes. He's being buried tomorrow.'

'And I'm being buried today. . . .'

They put her suitcase in the boot and Maigret sat down next to his prisoner. She gazed at the Quais, the bridges, the people in the streets, the buses, the cars, as though they were all part of an already distant past.

When they got to the Palais, Lapointe carried the suitcase, which was too heavy for her. Maigret knocked on the examining magistrate's door.

'She's all yours . . .' he said in a faltering voice.

He looked at her but she paid no attention to him. Before anyone asked her to, she sat down opposite Coindet; she seemed very much at her ease.

Epalinges
February 11, 1972

MAIGRET
AND THE DOSSER

★

*Translated from
the French by*
JEAN STEWART

CHAPTER ONE

FOR A MOMENT, somewhere between the Quai des Orfèvres and the Pont Maric, Maigret halted, so briefly that Lapointe, who was walking beside him, did not notice. And yet, during the space of a few seconds, perhaps for less than a second, the Superintendent had become a young man again, no older than his companion.

It was probably due to the quality of the air, the brightness, the smell, the taste of it. There had been a morning just like this, other mornings like it, when, as a young detective newly appointed to the Police Judiciaire, which Parisians still called the Sûreté, Maigret had belonged to the Public Highways Squad and had walked the streets of Paris from morning till night.

Although this was the 25th of March, today was the first real spring day, specially clear after a last heavy shower that had fallen during the night, accompanied by the distant rumble of thunder. For the first time that year, too, Maigret had left his overcoat hanging in the cupboard of his office, and from time to time the breeze blew open his unbuttoned jacket.

Because of that breath from the past, he had unconsciously begun to walk at his old pace, neither fast nor slow, not exactly the pace of an idler pausing to watch trivial incidents in the street, nor yet that of a man making for a definite goal.

His hands clasped behind his back, he looked about him, to right and left and into the air, mentally recording visual images to which he had long ceased to pay attention.

For so short a journey, there had been no point in

taking one of the black cars lined up in the courtyard of Police Headquarters, and the two men walked along the embankment. As they crossed the square in front of Notre-Dame, a flight of pigeons took off; a big yellow coach, come from Cologne, had already brought the first party of tourists.

Crossing the iron footbridge, they had reached the Ile Saint-Louis, and at one of the windows Maigret had noticed a young housemaid in uniform and muslin cap, looking like a character out of a Boulevard comedy. A butcher's boy, also in uniform, was delivering meat a little farther on; a postman was leaving a block of flats.

Buds had burst open that very morning, and the trees were speckled with pale green.

'The Seine's still high,' observed Lapointe, who had not spoken until now.

It was true. For the past month the rain had barely stopped for more than a few hours at a time and almost every evening the television showed rivers in spate, towns and villages with water pouring through their streets. The Seine was a yellowish flood, carrying along refuse, broken boxes, branches of trees.

The two men walked along the Quai de Bourbon as far as the Pont Marie, and as they crossed the bridge at the same leisurely pace, they could see downstream a greyish-coloured barge with the red and white triangle of the Compagnie Générale painted on her bow. Her name was *Le Poitou*, and a crane, whose grunting and creaking mingled with the confused noises of the city, was unloading the sand with which her holds were full.

Another barge was moored above the bridge, some fifty yards upstream from the first. She was cleaner-looking, as if she had been polished that very morning, and a Belgian flag was fluttering lazily over her stern, while, close to the white cabin, a baby lay asleep cradled in a canvas ham-

156

mock, and a very tall man with pale blond hair was looking out expectantly towards the river bank.

The boat's name, in gilt letters, was *De Zwarte Zwaan*, a Flemish name which meant nothing to either Maigret or Lapointe.

It was two or three minutes to ten. The policemen reached the Quai des Célestins, and as they were about to go down the ramp towards the port a car stopped and three men got out, slamming the door behind them.

'Hullo! That's well timed . . .'

They had come from the Palais de Justice too, but from the more imposing part of it reserved for magistrates. There was Parrain, the Deputy Public Prosecutor, Dantziger the examining magistrate, and an old clerk of the court whose name Maigret could never remember, although he had met him hundreds of times.

Passers-by on their way to work, children playing on the pavement opposite did not suspect that a police investigation was under way. In the clear morning light, there was nothing impressive about it. The Deputy Public Prosecutor pulled a gold cigarette case from his pocket and automatically offered it to Maigret, who had his pipe in his mouth.

'Of course . . . I was forgetting. . . .'

He was tall and slender, fair-haired and distinguished-looking, and the Superintendent reflected, not for the first time, that this was typical of the Public Prosecutor's department. Dantziger, the examining magistrate, was short and tubby and casually dressed. There are all sorts of examining magistrates. Why were the Parquet people always as elegant, as polite and often as haughty, as the private secretaries of Cabinet Ministers?

'Shall we go, messieurs?'

They went down the unevenly paved ramp as far as the water's edge, not far from the barge.

'Is that the one?'

Maigret knew no more about it than his companions. He had read the brief newspaper reports of what had happened during the night, and a telephone call half an hour previously had asked him to be present at the Parquet's investigation.

He was quite glad to do so. He was back among people and in an atmosphere with which he was not unfamiliar. The five men walked together towards the motor-barge, while the tall blond bargee set out to meet them along the plank that connected it with the bank.

'Take my hand,' he said to the Deputy Public Prosecutor, who was walking in front. 'It'll be safer, *n'est-ce pas?*'

He had a pronounced Flemish accent. His strongly marked features, his pale eyes, his long arms and his way of moving recalled those Belgian racing cyclists whom one sees being interviewed after an event.

The noise of the crane unloading sand could be heard even more loudly here.

'Your name is Josef Van Houtte?' Maigret asked, after glancing at a piece of paper.

'Jef Van Houtte, yes, monsieur.'

'Are you the owner of this boat?'

'Of course I'm the owner of it, monsieur, who else could be?'

A good smell of cooking rose from the cabin, and at the foot of the stairs, which were covered with floral-patterned linoleum, a very young woman could be seen coming and going.

Maigret pointed to the baby lying in its cradle.

'Is that your son?'

'That's not a son, monsieur, that's a daughter. Yolande, her name is. My sister's called Yolande too, and she's its godmother. . . .'

Parrain, the Deputy Public Prosecutor, felt impelled to intervene, after motioning to the clerk to take notes.

'Tell us what happened.'

'Well! I fished him out and the chap on the other boat helped me. . . .'

He pointed to the *Poitou*, at the stern of which a man, leaning against the tiller, was looking at them as if waiting for his turn.

A tug hooted repeatedly and sailed slowly past, going upstream with four barges behind it. Each time one of them drew level with the *Zwarte Zwaan*, Jef Van Houtte raised his right arm in greeting.

'Did you know the drowned man?'

'I'd never set eyes on him before. . . .'

'How long have you been berthed at this quay?'

'Since last night. I've come from Jeumont with a cargo of slates for Rouen. . . . I meant to pass through Paris and stop for the night at the Suresnes lock. . . . I suddenly noticed that something was wrong with the engine. . . . Us lot aren't keen on sleeping in the middle of Paris, you understand?'

From a distance, Maigret caught sight of two or three down-and-outs sitting about under the bridge, including a very stout woman whom he fancied he had seen before.

'How did it happen? Did the man jump into the water?'

'I don't think so, you know, monsieur. If he'd jumped into the water what would the other two have been doing here?'

'What time was it? Where were you? Tell us everything that happened during the evening. You had moored by the quay shortly before nightfall?'

'That's right.'

'Did you notice a vagrant under the bridge?'

'That's not the sort of thing one notices. There's nearly always some of them.'

'What did you do next?'

'We had our supper, Hubert and Anneke and me.'

'Who's Hubert?'

'He's my brother. He works with me. Anneke's my wife. Her name's Anna but we call her Anneke. . . .'

'And then?'

'My brother put on his good suit and went to a dance. He's the age for that, isn't he?'

'How old is he?'

'Twenty-two.'

'Is he here?'

'He's gone shopping. He'll be back.'

'What did you do after supper?'

'I went to work on the engine. I saw straight away that there was an oil leak, and as I wanted to set off this morning I began to mend it.'

He was casting watchful glances at them each in turn, with the mistrustful air of people who are unused to dealing with the Law.

'When did you finish the job?'

'I didn't finish it, not until this morning.'

'Where were you when you heard cries?'

He scratched his head, staring at the great gleaming spotless deck.

'First I went up once to smoke a cigarette and see if Anneke was asleep.'

'What time was that?'

'About ten o'clock . . . I don't know exactly. . . .'

'Was she asleep?'

'Yes, monsieur. And the baby was asleep too. Some nights she cries, because she's beginning to cut her first teeth. . . .'

'Did you go back to your engine?'

'Of course.'

'Was it dark in the cabin?'

'Yes, monsieur, because my wife was asleep.'

'And on deck too?'

'Sure.'

'And then?'

'Then, a long time after, I heard the noise of an engine, as if a car was stopping not far from the boat.'

'Didn't you go and find out?'

'No, monsieur. Why should I have?'

'Go on.'

'A little later, there was a splash. . . .'

'As if someone was falling into the Seine?'

'Yes, monsieur.'

'And then?'

'I went up the ladder and stuck my head through the hatchway.'

'What did you see?'

'Two men running towards the car. . . .'

'So there really was a car?'

'Yes, monsieur. A red car. A Peugeot 403.'

'Was it light enough for you to make it out?'

'There's a street lamp just above the wall.'

'What were the two men like?'

'One was a short man in a light-coloured raincoat, and he had broad shoulders.'

'And the other?'

'I didn't see him so clearly because he got into the car first. He started up the engine immediately. . . .'

'You didn't notice the registration number?'

'The what?'

'The number on the plate?'

'I only know there were two 9's and it ended in 75.'

'When did you hear the shouts?'

'When the car started off. . . .'

'In other words, there was an interval between the time when the man was thrown into the water and the moment when he called out? Otherwise you'd have heard the shouts earlier?'

'I guess so, monsieur. At night it's much quieter than now.'

'What time was it?'

'After midnight.'

'Were there any people on the bridge?'

'I didn't look up. . . .'

On the embankment, beyond the wall, some passers-by had stopped, their curiosity aroused by the sight of these men arguing on the deck of a barge. It struck Maigret that the vagrants had moved several yards nearer. Meanwhile the crane kept on scooping up sand from the hold of the *Poitou* and emptying it into lorries which stood waiting for their turn.

'Did he call out loudly?'

'Yes, monsieur.'

'What sort of a shout was it? Was he calling for help?'

'He shouted. . . . Then there was nothing more to be heard. . . . Then . . .'

'What did you do?'

'I jumped into the punt and unfastened it. . . .'

'Could you see the drowning man?'

'No, monsieur. Not right away. . . . The skipper of the *Poitou* must have heard too, for he was running the whole length of his craft trying to catch hold of something with his boathook. . . .'

'Carry on. . . .'

The Fleming seemed to be doing his best, but he found it hard and beads of sweat appeared on his forehead.

'He was saying: There! . . . there! . . .'

'Who was?'

'The skipper of the *Poitou*.'

'And could you see?'

'Sometimes I could see, other times I couldn't.'

162

'Because the body was sinking?'

'Yes, monsieur. And it was being carried away by the current. . . .'

'Your punt was, too, I suppose?'

'Yes, monsieur. The other chap jumped into it. . . .'

'The chap from the *Poitou*?'

Jef gave a sigh, probably reflecting that his interlocutors were not very bright. The whole thing was quite straightforward to him, and he must have been through similar scenes more than once in his life.

'Between you, you fished him out?'

'Yes.'

'What state was he in?'

'His eyes were still open and when he was in the boat he was sick. . . .'

'He didn't say anything?'

'No, monsieur.'

'Did he seem frightened?'

'No, monsieur.'

'What did he seem like?'

'Nothing in particular. He stopped moving at last and the water went on running out of his mouth.'

'Were his eyes still open?'

'Yes, monsieur. I thought he was dead.'

'Did you go for help?'

'No, monsieur. It wasn't me.'

'Was it your mate from the *Poitou*?'

'No. Somebody shouted to us from off the bridge.'

'So there was someone on the Pont Marie?'

'By then there was. He asked us if somebody had been drowned. I said yes. He shouted that he would go and tell the police.'

'Did he do so?'

'He must have done, for not long after a couple of cops came up on bikes.'

'Was it raining already?'

'It started raining and thundering when we'd hoisted the chap on to the deck.'

'Of your barge?'

'Yes. . . .'

'Did your wife wake up?'

'The light was on in the cabin and Anneke had put on her coat and was watching us.'

'When did you see the blood?'

'When we'd laid the man down beside the tiller. It was pouring out of a crack he'd got in his head.'

'A crack?'

'A hole. . . . I don't know what you'd call it. . . .'

'Did the policemen arrive immediately?'

'Almost immediately.'

'And the passer-by who'd informed them?'

'I didn't see him again.'

'You don't know who it was?'

'No, monsieur.'

In the morning light, it required some effort to imagine that midnight scene, which Jef Van Houtte was describing as best he could, groping for his words as if he had to translate them one by one from Flemish.

'I suppose you know that the dosser had been knocked on the head before being thrown into the water?'

'That's what the doctor said. Because one of the cops went to fetch a doctor. Then an ambulance came. Once they'd taken away the man's body I had to swab the deck, where there was a great pool of blood . . .'

'What happened, in your opinion?'

'I couldn't say, monsieur.'

'You told the policemen . . .'

'I told them what I believed, didn't I?'

'Tell me again.'

'I suppose he'd been sleeping under the bridge. . . .'

'But you hadn't seen him before?'

'I hadn't taken any notice. There's always people sleeping under the bridges. . . .'

'All right. Then a car drove down the ramp. . . .'

'A red car. . . . That I'm sure of. . . .'

'It stopped not far from your barge?'

He nodded, and flung out his arm towards a certain point on the river bank.

'Did the engine keep on running?'

This time he shook his head.

'But you heard footsteps?'

'Yes, monsieur.'

'Two people's footsteps?'

'I saw two chaps coming back towards the car. . . .'

'You didn't see them go towards the bridge?'

'I was working down below, on the engine.'

'Might these two men, one of whom was wearing a light-coloured raincoat, have knocked out the vagrant as he lay asleep and then thrown him into the Seine?'

'When I went up he was in the water already. . . .'

'The doctor's report states that he could not have received that injury to his head while falling into the water. Not even if he had accidentally fallen on the edge of the quay. . . .'

Van Houtte stared at them as though to say that it was none of his business.

'Can we question your wife?'

'I don't mind your talking to Anneke. Only she won't understand you, for she only speaks Flemish.'

The Deputy Public Prosecutor glanced at Maigret as if to ask him whether he had any questions to put, and the Superintendent shook his head. If he had any, they would come later, when the gentlemen from the Parquet had gone away.

'When shall we be able to leave?' the bargee asked.

'As soon as you've signed your statement. On condition you let us know where you are going.'

'To Rouen.'

'You'll have to keep us informed of your subsequent movements. My clerk will bring you the documents to sign.'

'When?'

'Probably in the early afternoon.'

This clearly annoyed the bargee.

'By the way, what time did your brother come back on board?'

'Soon after the ambulance had left.'

'Thank you.'

Once again Jef Van Houtte helped him across the narrow gangway, and the little party made its way towards the bridge, while the down-and-outs withdrew a few yards.

'What d'you think about it, Maigret?'

'I think it's odd. It's pretty uncommon for a down-and-out to be attacked.'

Under the arch of the Pont Marie, up against the stone wall, a kind of nook had been contrived. It was shapeless and nameless, and yet it had apparently provided for some time past a resting-place for a human being.

The stupefaction of the Deputy Public Prosecutor was comical to behold, and Maigret could not help telling him:

'There are places like that under all the bridges. In fact you can see a shelter of this sort just opposite Police Headquarters.'

'And the police do nothing about it?'

'If we demolish them they spring up again a little further off. . . .'

It was made of old boxes and pieces of tarpaulin. There was just enough room there for a man to lie curled up.

The ground was covered with straw, torn blankets and newspapers, which exuded a strong smell in spite of the draught under the bridge.

The Deputy Public Prosecutor carefully avoided touching anything and it was Maigret who bent down to make a rapid inventory.

An iron cylinder with holes and a grill had served as a stove and was still covered with whitish ash. Beside it lay pieces of charcoal, picked up heaven knows where. Turning over the blankets, the Superintendent uncovered a secret hoard: two hunks of stale bread, a few inches of garlic sausage and, in another corner, some books whose titles he read out in an undertone.

'Verlaine's *Sagesse*. . . . Bossuet's *Oraisons Funèbres* . . .'

He picked up a journal which must have been lying about in the rain for a long time and which had probably been extracted from someone's dustbin. It was an old number of *La Presse Médicale*.

Finally, part of a book, the second half of Las Cases's *Mémorial de Sainte-Hélène*.

Dantziger, the magistrate, seemed just as stupefied as the man from the Parquet.

'Funny sort of things he read,' he commented.

'I don't suppose he had much choice.'

Still looking under the tattered blankets, Maigret discovered some garments: a much patched grey sweater, with paint stains on it, which had presumably belonged to a painter, a pair of yellowish twill trousers, some felt slippers with worn-out soles, and five odd socks. Finally a pair of scissors with one of the points broken.

'Is the man dead?' inquired Deputy Public Prosecutor Parrain, keeping at a safe distance for fear of catching fleas.

'He was alive an hour ago, when I rang up the Hôtel-Dieu.'

'Are they hoping to save him?'

'They're trying to. . . . He's got a fractured skull, and furthermore they're afraid of pneumonia developing. . . .'

Maigret was fingering a dilapidated pram which the man must have used when he went rummaging in dustbins. Turning towards the little group of watchful onlookers, he scanned their faces each in turn. Some of them looked away. Others expressed nothing but bewilderment.

'Come here, you!' he told the woman, beckoning to her.

If it had happened thirty years earlier, when he was working on the Public Highways Squad, he could have put a name to each face, for at that period he had known most of the down-and-outs in Paris.

They had not altered much, in fact, but they had become far fewer. 'Where d'you sleep?'

The woman smiled at him ingratiatingly.

'Over there,' she said, pointing to the Pont Louis-Philippe.

'Did you know the chap they fished out last night?'

She had a puffy face and her breath smelt of sour wine. She stood with her hands on her stomach, nodding her head.

'We used to call him Doc.'

'Why?'

'Because he was an educated sort of chap . . . they say he really used to be a doctor once. . . .'

'Had he been living under the bridges a long time?'

'Years. . . .'

'How many?'

'I don't know . . . I've stopped counting them. . . .'

This made her laugh and she tossed back a lock of grey hair that hung over her face. When her mouth was shut she looked about sixty. But when she spoke she disclosed an almost toothless jaw and she seemed much older. There was still a twinkle in her eyes, however. From time to time she turned towards the others as though calling them to witness.

'It's true, isn't it?' she asked them.

They nodded, although ill at ease in the presence of the Law and these over-dressed gentlemen.

'Did he live alone?'

That made her laugh afresh.

'Who'd he have lived with?'

'Has he always lived under this bridge?'

'Not always . . . I used to know him under the Pont-Neuf . . . and before that in the Quai de Bercy. . . .'

'Did he do the Halles?'

For that was where most down-and-outs forgathered at night.

'No,' she replied.

'Did he forage in dustbins?'

'Sometimes.'

In spite of the child's pram, therefore, he could not have been a collector of old papers and rags, and this would account for his already being abed at nightfall.

'He was mostly a sandwich-man. . . .'

'What else do you know?'

'Nothing.'

'Did he never talk to you?'

'Of course he did. . . . In fact it was me that used to cut his hair now and then. . . . Folks must help one another. . . .'

'Did he drink much?'

Maigret knew that the question was meaningless, since practically all of them drank.

'Red wine?'

'Like we all do.'

'A lot?'

'I've never seen him sozzled. Not like me. . . .'

And she began laughing again.

169

'I know you, you know, and I know you're not a bad chap. You had me up for questioning once in your office, a long time ago, twenty years ago maybe, when I was still on the job at the Porte Saint-Denis. . . .'

'Did you hear nothing last night?'

She flung out her arm to point at the Pont Louis-Philippe, as though to show what a distance it was from the Pont Marie.

'It's too far off. . . .'

'You saw nothing?'

'Only the headlights of the ambulance. . . . I came a little closer, not too close for fear of being picked up, and I recognized it was an ambulance. . . .'

'And the rest of you?' Maigret asked the three down-and-outs.

They shook their heads, still ill at ease.

'Suppose we went to see the skipper of the *Poitou*?' suggested the Deputy Public Prosecutor, who felt uncomfortable in these surroundings.

The man was expecting them. He was very unlike the Fleming. He, too, had his wife and children on board, but the barge did not belong to him and it almost always did the same journey, between the sandpits of the upper Seine and Paris. His name was Justin Goulet; he was forty-five. He was short and squat, with shrewd eyes, and an unlit cigarette clung to the corner of his lips.

Here, they had to speak loud because of the noise from the nearby crane which went on unloading sand.

'It's queer, isn't it?'

'What's queer?'

'That people should bother to do in a bum and chuck him in the water.'

'Did you see them?'

'I didn't see anything at all.'

'Where were you?'

'When they beat up the fellow? In my bunk.'

'What did you hear?'

'I heard somebody yelling. . . .'

'No car?'

'I may have heard a car, but there are cars going by all the time up there on the embankment and I didn't pay attention.'

'Did you go up on deck?'

'In pyjamas . . . I didn't waste time putting on my trousers. . . .'

'And your wife?'

'She said in her sleep: Where are you going? . . .'

'Once you were on deck what did you see?'

'Nothing. The Seine flowing by as usual, with eddies. I shouted "Ahoy!" so that the chap might answer and so's I could find out whereabouts he was. . . .'

'Where was Jef Van Houtte at this point?'

'The Fleming? I finally caught sight of him on the deck of his barge. . . . He started to unfasten his punt. . . . When the stream brought him level with me, I jumped in. . . . The chap in the water kept surfacing and then disappearing again. . . . The Fleming tried to catch him with my boathook. . . .'

'A boathook with a big iron hook at the end?'

'They're all like that. . . .'

'Couldn't he have incurred that injury to his head when you were trying to catch hold of him?'

'Surely not . . . in the end we got him by the seat of his trousers. I leaned over at once and caught him by one leg. . . .'

'Had he fainted?'

'His eyes were open.'

'Did he say nothing?'

'He sicked up some water. . . . Afterwards, on the Fleming's boat, we saw that he was bleeding. . . .'

'I think that's all?' muttered the Deputy Public Prosecutor, who seemed to find the story rather tedious.

'I'll look after the rest,' Maigret replied.

'Are you going to the hospital?'

'I'll go there presently. The doctors say it'll be several hours before he's in a fit state to speak. . . .'

'Keep me informed.'

'I certainly will.'

As they went back under the Pont Marie, Maigret said to Lapointe: 'Go and ring up the district police station and ask them to send me an officer.'

'Where shall I find you, Chief?'

'Here.'

And he solemnly shook hands with the people from the Department of Public Prosecution.

CHAPTER TWO

'ARE THOSE JUDGES?' queried the fat woman as she watched the three men walking away.

'They're magistrates,' Maigret corrected her.

'It's the same thing, isn't it?'

And, after giving a faint whistle: 'They're taking as much trouble as if he'd been one of the nobs, aren't they? Was he a real doctor, then?'

Maigret did not know. He seemed in no hurry to find out. He was living in the present, with a persistent sense of having experienced these things before, a long time ago. Lapointe had disappeared at the top of the ramp. The Deputy Public Prosecutor, flanked by the little magistrate and the clerk, was picking his steps carefully for fear of soiling his shoes.

Black and white in the sunshine, the *Zwarte Zwaan* was as spotless outside as its kitchen must have been. The tall Fleming, standing beside the steering wheel, was looking in his direction, and a small, slender woman, a real child-wife with hair so fair as to be almost white, was bending over the cradle, changing the child's napkin.

Despite the unceasing noise of the cars along the Quai des Célestins, and of the crane unloading sand from the *Poitou*, Maigret could hear birds singing and the lapping of the water.

The three down-and-outs still kept out of the way, and only the stout woman followed the Superintendent under the bridge. Her blouse, which must once have been red, was now a faded pink.

'What's your name?'

'Léa. Big Léa, they call me. . . .'

This set her laughing and her enormous breasts shook.

'Where were you last night?'

'I told you.'

'Was there nobody with you?'

'Only Dédé, the smallest of them, over there with his back to you.'

'Is he your friend?'

'They're all my friends.'

'Do you always sleep under the same bridge?'

'I sometimes move around. . . . What are you looking for?'

For Maigret was once again bending over the queer collection of objects which constituted the worldly goods of the Doc. He felt more at ease now that the magistrates had left. He took his time, and brought out from under the rags a frying pan, a billy-can, a spoon and fork.

Then he tried on a pair of spectacles with steel rims, one glass of which was cracked, and everything became a blur.

'He only uses them for reading,' explained the fat woman.

'What surprises me,' he began, looking at her intently, 'is not to find . . .'

She did not let him finish, but moved a couple of yards away and from behind a big stone pulled out a litre bottle still half full of purplish wine.

'Have you drunk some of it?'

'Yes. I was going to finish it up. It won't be any good, after all, when the Doc comes back.'

'When did you take it?'

'Last night, after the ambulance had taken him off. . . .'

'You've touched nothing else?'

She spat on the ground, with a solemn face. 'I swear I haven't!'

He believed her. He knew from experience that the

down-and-out do not rob one another. Indeed it is unusual for them to rob anybody at all, not only because they would be spotted immediately but through a kind of indifference.

Across the river, on the Ile Saint-Louis, open windows revealed cosy flats, and a woman could be seen brushing her hair at her dressing table.

'Do you know where he bought his wine?'

'I've seen him more than once coming out of a *bistrot* in the Rue Ave-Maria. It's quite close by . . . at the corner of the Rue des Jardins. . . .'

'How did the Doc get on with the others?'

She thought hard, trying to please him.

'I couldn't really say. . . . He wasn't all that different.'

'Did he never speak about his life?'

'None of us do. Not without being really boozed up. . . .'

'Was he never boozed up?'

'Not really. . . .'

Out of the pile of old newspapers that served to keep the dosser warm, Maigret had just pulled out a small painted toy horse with one leg broken. He was not surprised to see it, neither was Big Léa.

Someone had just come down the ramp with silent, springy steps, wearing rope-soled sandals, and was making for the Belgian barge. In each hand he carried a string bag full of provisions, from which protruded two long loaves and some fishes' tails.

This was undoubtedly the brother, for he was like a younger version of Jef Van Houtte, with less pronounced features. He was wearing blue jeans and a white-striped jersey.

Once on board the boat, he spoke to the other man, then glanced in Maigret's direction.

'Don't touch anything. I may need you again. . . . If you should hear anything . . .'

'Can you see me turn up at your office, looking like this?'

That set her laughing again. Pointing to the bottle, she asked:

'May I finish it off?'

He nodded, and went to meet Lapointe, who was now returning accompanied by a uniformed policeman. He gave the latter instructions: to watch over the heap of rubbish that constituted the Doc's fortune until the arrival of a specialist from the Police Records Office.

After which, with Lapointe by his side, he made his way towards the *Zwarte Zwaan*.

'You are Hubert Van Houtte?'

The youth, more taciturn or more suspicious than his brother, merely nodded.

'Did you go dancing last night?'

'Is there anything wrong about that?'

His accent was less pronounced. Maigret and Lapointe, standing on the bank, had to raise their heads to speak to him.

'What dance hall were you at?'

'Near the Place de la Bastille. . . . A narrow street where there are half-a-dozen of them. . . . This one was called *Chez Léon*.'

'Did you know it already?'

'I'd been there a number of times. . . .'

'So you know nothing about what has happened?'

'Only what my brother told me. . . .'

Smoke was rising from a brass funnel on the deck. The woman had gone down into the cabin with her child, and from where they stood the Superintendent and the inspector could smell cooking.

'When shall we be able to leave?'

'Probably this afternoon. . . . As soon as the magistrate has got your brother to sign the statement. . . .'

Hubert Van Houtte, clean-looking and well-groomed, had the same pink skin and pale blond hair as his brother.

A little later, Maigret and Lapointe crossed the Quai des Célestins, and at the corner of the Rue de L'Ave-Maria they found a *bistrot* bearing the sign *Au Petit Turin*. The proprietor, in his shirt-sleeves, was standing in the doorway. There was nobody inside.

'May we come in?'

He drew aside, astonished to see people like themselves entering his establishment. The place was minute, and apart from the counter there were only three tables for customers. The walls were painted apple green. From the ceiling there hung sausages, salami, and queer yellow cheeses shaped like bulging goatskin-bottles.

'What can I bring you?'

'Some wine. . . .'

'Chianti?'

Flasks in straw covers lined a whole shelf, but the proprietor filled their glasses from a bottle standing under the counter, meanwhile watching the two men with curiosity.

'Do you know a vagrant who's known as the Doc?'

'How is he? I hope he hasn't died?'

The Italian accent and the gesticulations of the proprietor contrasted with the Flemish accent and calm bearing of Jef Van Houtte and his brother.

'You know what has happened?' Maigret asked.

'I know something happened to him last night.'

'Who told you?'

'Another of the dossers, this morning. . . .'

'What were you told, exactly?'

'That there had been a to-do near the Pont Marie and that an ambulance had come to fetch away the Doc.'

'Anything else?'

'Seems that the bargees fished him out of the water. . . .'

'Did the Doc buy his wine from you?'

'Often.'

'Did he drink a lot?'

'About two litres a day . . . when he had the money. . . .'

'How did he earn it?'

'Like they all do. . . . Odd jobs in the market or else-where. . . . Or else walking the streets with advertisement boards. . . . I was always glad to let him have it on credit.'

'Why?'

'Because he wasn't a no-good like the rest. . . . He saved my wife. . . .'

The woman was there in the kitchen, almost as stout as Léa but very alert.

'You're talking about me?'

'I was telling how the Doc . . .'

Then she came into the bar, wiping her hands on her apron. 'Is it true that someone tried to kill him? Are you from the police? D'you think he's going to get over it?'

'We don't know yet,' the Superintendent replied evasively. 'What did he do for you?'

'Well, if you'd seen me a couple of years ago you'd not have recognized me. I was covered with eczema and my face was as red as a piece of meat on a butcher's slab. It had been going on for months and months. . . . At the outpatients' they tried out all sorts of treatments on me, they gave me ointments that smelt so horrible that I was disgusted with myself. . . . Nothing did any good. I was hardly allowed to eat anything and in any case I'd lost my appetite. . . . And they gave me injections. . . .'

The landlord listened, nodding.

'One day when the Doc was sitting there, in that corner by the door, and I was complaining to the green-grocery woman, I felt he was looking at me in an odd sort of way. . . . A little later he said to me in the same tone of voice as though he'd been ordering a glass of wine:

' "I think I can cure you."

'I asked him if he was really a doctor and he smiled.

' "I've not been disqualified from practising," he said quietly.'

'Did he give you a prescription?'

'No. He asked me for a little money, two hundred francs if I remember rightly, and he went off himself to get some little packets of powder from the chemist.

' "Take one in warm water before each meal. And wash yourself, morning and night, in very salt water. . . ."

'Believe it or not, two months after that my skin was all right again.'

'Did he attend anyone else besides you?'

'I don't know. He didn't talk much.'

'Did he come here every day?'

'Practically every day, to buy his couple of litres.'

'Was he always by himself? Did you never see him with anyone you didn't know?'

'No.'

'Did he never tell you his real name, nor where he lived formerly?'

'I only know he had a daughter. . . . We've got one, who's at school now. Once when she was staring at him curiously he said to her:

' "Don't be afraid of me . . . I've got a little girl, too. . . ." '

Lapointe was probably somewhat surprised to see Maigret attach so much importance to the story of this down-and-out. In the press it would have provided merely a few lines among the news items.

What Lapointe did not know, because he was too young, was that this was the first time in Maigret's career that a crime had been committed against one of the down-and-out.

'How much do I owe you?'

179

'Won't you have one more? To drink the health of poor old Doc?'

They drank the second glass, for which the Italian refused to let them pay. Then they crossed over the Pont Marie.

A few minutes later they went in underneath the grey archway of the Hôtel-Dieu. Here they had a lengthy argument with a cantankerous woman keeping guard behind a window.

'You don't know his name?'

'Only that he's known on the embankment as the Doc and that he was brought here last night. . . .'

'Last night I wasn't here. . . . Which department have they taken him to?'

'I don't know. Just now I spoke on the telephone to an intern who said nothing about an operation.'

'Do you know the name of the intern?'

'No.'

She flicked over the pages of a register and made two or three telephone calls.

'What did you say your name was?'

'Superintendent Maigret.'

The name meant nothing to the woman, who repeated into the receiver:

'Superintendent Maigret. . . .'

Finally, after about ten minutes, she sighed, as though granting them a favour:

'Take staircase C. . . . Go up to the third floor. . . . Ask for the Sister in charge of that floor. . . .'

They met nurses, young doctors, patients in hospital uniform, and through open doors caught sight of rows of beds.

On the third floor they had to wait yet again, for the Sister in charge was having an animated discussion with two men, whose request she appeared to be refusing.

'I can't do anything about it,' she finally flung at them. 'Speak to the head office. I don't make the rules.'

They went off, muttering uncomplimentary remarks between their teeth, and she turned to Maigret.

'Is it you who've come about the vagrant?'

'Superintendent Maigret,' he repeated.

She was searching her memory. The name meant nothing to her either. This was another world, a world of numbered wards, of separate departments, of beds lined up in huge rooms, each bed having at its foot a card inscribed with mysterious signs.

'How is he?'

'I believe Professor Magnin is with him at this moment.'

'Has he been operated on?'

'Who said anything to you about an operation?'

'I don't know . . . I thought . . .'

Maigret did not feel at home here and it made him diffident.

'Under what name have you registered him?'

'The name on his identity card.'

'Have you got the card?'

'I can show it to you.'

She went into a small glass-panelled office at the end of the passage and promptly found a filthy identity card still damp from the water of the Seine.

Surname: Keller.

First names: François Marie Florentin.

Occupation: rag-and-bone man.

Birthplace: Mulhouse, Bas-Rhin.

According to this document, the man was sixty-three years old and his address in Paris was a doss-house in the Place Maubert, which the Superintendent knew quite well and which served as official residence for a number of vagrants.

'Has he recovered consciousness?'

She tried to take back the identity card, which the Superintendent was putting into his pocket, and she grumbled:

'It's not in order. . . . The regulations. . . .'

'Is Keller in a private ward?'

'Whatever next?'

'Take me to him.'

She hesitated, but eventually gave way.

'Well, you'll have to settle things with the Professor.'

Leading the way, she opened the third door, disclosing two rows of beds, all occupied. Most of the patients were lying down, and their eyes were open; two or three were standing about at the far end of the room, wearing hospital clothes, and chatting in low voices.

Beside one of the beds, in the middle of the room, a dozen young men and women in white coats and caps stood round a short, broad-shouldered man with crew-cut hair, also clad in white, who appeared to be giving them a lecture.

'You can't disturb him just now. . . . You see he's busy.'

However, she went up and whispered a few words in the ear of the professor, who cast a glance in Maigret's direction and went on with his explanations.

'He'll have finished in a few minutes. He asks you to wait in his office.'

She took them there. It was a small room with only a couple of chairs in it. On the desk stood the silver-framed photograph of a woman and three children with their heads close together.

Maigret hesitated, then emptied his pipe into the ashtray, which was crammed with cigarette-ends, and filled himself another.

'Sorry to have kept you waiting, Superintendent. When Sister told me you were there I was a bit surprised. . . . After all . . .'

Was he, too, going to say that after all, the patient was merely a down-and-out? No.

'. . . It's a straightforward business, I suppose?'

'I scarcely know anything about it yet and I'm counting on you to enlighten me.'

'It's a fracture of the skull, a nice clean one, luckily, as my assistant must have told you over the phone this morning. . . .'

'They hadn't X-rayed him yet. . . .'

'That's been done now. . . . He's got a good chance of pulling through, for the brain doesn't appear to be damaged.'

'Could the fracture have been caused by a fall on the embankment?'

'Certainly not. The man had been struck a violent blow with some heavy instrument such as a hammer, a spanner or a tyre-lever. . . .'

'Did it make him lose consciousness?'

'He lost consciousness to such an extent that he's still in a coma and may remain in it for several days. Or on the other hand he might come round at any moment. . . .'

Maigret kept visualizing the river bank, the Doc's shelter, the muddy water flowing a few yards away, and he recalled the remarks of the Flemish bargee.

'Forgive me for persisting. . . . You say he'd had a blow on the head. . . . Only one?'

'Why do you ask that?'

'It might be important.'

'At first glance I thought he might have received several blows. . . .'

'Why?'

'Because one ear is torn and there are a number of superficial wounds on the face. . . . Now that he's been shaved I've had a closer look. . . .'

'And your conclusion?'

'Where did it happen?'

'Under the Pont Marie.'

'During a fight?'

'Apparently not. The man seems to have been lying asleep when he was attacked. . . . According to your observations, is that plausible?'

'Quite plausible.'

'And do you think he lost consciousness immediately?'

'I'm practically sure of that. . . . And after what you've just told me, I can account for the torn ear and the scratches on the face. He was picked up out of the Seine, wasn't he? . . . These minor injuries suggest that instead of being carried there he was dragged over the stones along the embankment. . . . Is there any sand on that part of the embankment?'

'They're unloading sand from a barge a few yards away.'

'I found traces of sand in the wounds.'

'In your opinion, then, the Doc . . .'

'What did you say?' the professor asked in some surprise.

'That's what they call him, on the embankment. . . . It's possible he may really have been a doctor.'

And this was the first time, in thirty years, that Maigret had come across a doctor living under the bridges. He could remember finding there a former chemistry master from a provincial *lycée*, and a few years later a woman who had been a famous circus rider in her time.

'I'm convinced that he was lying down and probably asleep when his attacker, or attackers, struck him.'

'Only one person must have struck him, since there was only a single blow.'

'Quite true. . . . He then lost consciousness, so that he must have appeared dead. . . .'

'That's very plausible.'

'He was then dragged rather than carried to the edge of the Seine and tipped into the water. . . .'

The doctor was listening gravely, with a thoughtful look.

'Does that hold together?' Maigret persisted.

'Perfectly well.'

'Is it medically possible that when he was in the river, being swept away by the current, he should have begun to scream?'

The professor scratched his head.

'You're asking a good deal of me and I shouldn't like to give you a categorical answer. Let's say that I don't consider the thing impossible. On coming into contact with the cold water . . .'

'Would he have recovered consciousness, then?'

'Not necessarily. . . . Patients in a coma sometimes speak and move about. . . . Let's assume . . .'

'Did he say nothing at all while you were examining him?'

'He gave an occasional moan.'

'I was told that when he was picked out of the water his eyes were open.'

'That proves nothing. . . . I suppose you'd like to see him? . . . Come with me.'

He took them along to the third floor, and the Ward Sister watched them pass in with some surprise and also no doubt with some disapproval.

The patients lying in their beds stared at the little party as it moved forward and came to a halt at one of the bedsides.

'There's not much to be seen. . . .'

Indeed, there was nothing to be seen but the bandages that surrounded the dosser's face and head, revealing only his eyes, nose and mouth.

'What are his chances of recovery?'

'Seventy per cent. . . . Say eighty, for his heart's still strong.'

'Thank you very much.'

'You'll be informed as soon as he recovers consciousness. Leave your phone number with the Ward Sister.'

It felt good to be outside again and to see the sun, the people in the street, a red and yellow coach unloading its tourists on the parvis of Notre-Dame.

Once again, Maigret walked along in silence, his hands behind his back, and Lapointe, realizing that he was preoccupied, avoided speaking.

They went under the archway of Police Headquarters, and climbed up the big staircase which looked even dustier than usual in the sunlight, finally reaching the Superintendent's office.

The first thing Maigret did was to fling the window wide open and look down at a string of barges drifting downstream.

'We'll have to send somebody from up there to look at his things. . . .'

Up there meant the Police Records Office, with its technicians and specialists.

'The best thing would be to take the van and remove the whole lot.'

He had no fear of other vagrants seizing the Doc's few belongings, but he was afraid, rather, of thieving urchins.

'Will you go to the Highways Department, meanwhile. . . . There can't be all that many red 403's in Paris. . . . Make a note of all the numbers that include two nines. . . . Get help from as many men as you need to check up on the owners. . . .'

'Right, Chief.'

Once he was alone, Maigret set out his pipes and looked through the official correspondence piled up on his desk.

Because of the fine weather, he wondered whether to lunch at the Brasserie Dauphine and finally decided to go home.

At this time of day the dining-room was flooded with sunlight. Madame Maigret was wearing a dress with pink flowers and it reminded him of Big Léa's blouse, which was almost the same pink.

He was deep in thought as he ate his *foie de veau en papillotes*, and his wife asked him:

'What are you thinking about?'

'About my tramp.'

'What tramp?'

'A fellow who may once have been a doctor. . . .'

'What has he done?'

'Nothing, as far as I know. But he nearly got his head split open while he was asleep under the Pont Marie . . . and then he was thrown into the water. . . .'

'Did he die?'

'Some bargees fished him out in time.'

'Why had somebody got it in for him?'

'That's what I'm wondering. . . . As it happens, he comes from the same part of the world as your brother-in-law. . . .'

Madame Maigret's sister lived at Mulhouse with her husband, a civil engineer. The Maigrets had quite often been to visit her.

'What's his name?'

'Keller . . . François Keller.'

'It's funny, but the name seems to ring a bell. . . .'

'It's a fairly common name in those parts.'

'Suppose I rang up my sister?'

He shrugged his shoulders. Why not? He did not put much faith in it, but it would give his wife pleasure.

As soon as she had served coffee, she rang up Mulhouse; she had only a few minutes to wait for the connection, and during that time she kept saying to herself, as though trying to recollect:

'Keller . . . François Keller. . . .'

The telephone bell rang.

'Hullo! . . . Hullo, yes! . . . Yes, mademoiselle, I asked for Mulhouse. . . . Is that you, Florence? . . . What d'you say? . . . Yes, it's me . . . why no, nothing's the matter. . . . From Paris . . . I'm at home. . . . He's just beside me, drinking his coffee. . . . He's fine. . . . Everything's fine. . . . Yes, so it is here. . . . Spring at last. . . .

'How are the children? . . . Flu? I had it last week . . . not badly. . . . Listen. That's not what I'm ringing up about. . . . Do you by any chance remember somebody called Keller? . . . François Keller? . . . What's that? . . . I'll ask him? . . .'

Turning to Maigret, she inquired: 'How old is he?'

'Sixty-four.'

'Sixty-four. . . . Yes. . . . You didn't know him personally? . . . What's that you said? . . . Don't disconnect us, mademoiselle. . . . Hullo! . . . Yes, he was a doctor. . . . For the past hour I've been trying to remember who had told me about him. . . . D'you think it was your husband? . . .

'Yes. . . . Wait . . . I'm going to repeat what you've said to *my* husband, who seems to be getting impatient. . . . He married the Mervilles' daughter. . . . Who are these Mervilles? . . . An Appeal Court Judge? . . . He married the daughter of an Appeal Court Judge? . . . Right. . . . The father died a long time ago. . . . Right. . . . Don't be surprised if I repeat everything, but otherwise I'd be afraid of forgetting something. . . . An old Mulhouse family. . . . The grandfather had been Mayor and . . . I can't hear you very well. . . . His statue . . . I don't think that's very important. . . . It doesn't matter if you're not sure. . . .

'Hullo! . . . So Keller married her. . . . Their only daughter. . . . Rue du Sauvage? . . . The couple lived in the Rue du Sauvage? . . . An eccentric? . . . why? . . . You don't exactly know. . . . Oh yes, I get your point . . . a bit of a savage himself. . . .'

She glanced at Maigret as though to say she was doing her utmost.

'Yes. Yes. . . . It doesn't matter if it's not interesting. . . . . Where he's concerned, you never know. . . . Sometimes a detail that may seem quite unimportant. . . . Yes. . . . In which year? . . . About twenty years ago, then . . . she was left some money by an aunt. . . . And he went away. . . . Not immediately. . . . He still lived with her for a year or so. . . .

'Had they any children? . . . One daughter? . . . Who? . . . Rousselet, pharmaceutical products? . . . Does she live in Paris? . . .'

She repeated, for her husband's benefit:

'They had a daughter who married young Rousselet of the pharmaceutical products firm, living in Paris.'

She returned to the telephone:

'I understand. . . . Listen. . . . Try to find out some more. . . . Yes. . . . Many thanks. . . . Love to your husband and the children. Call me back any time . . . I'm not going out. . . .'

There followed the sound of kisses. Now she spoke to Maigret.

'I was sure I knew the name. Did you understand? It seems as if it really was the same François Keller, who was a doctor and who married the daughter of a magistrate. . . . Her father died shortly before the marriage. . . .'

'And the mother?' he enquired.

She looked at him sharply, wondering whether he was speaking ironically.

'I don't know. Florence said nothing about her. . . .

About twenty years ago Madame Keller inherited some money from one of her aunts. . . . She's a very rich woman now. . . . The doctor was an eccentric. . . . You heard what I said? . . . A bit of a savage, as my sister put it. . . . They left their home and settled in a big house near the cathedral. . . . He stayed with her for one year more and then all of a sudden he disappeared. . . .

'Florence is going to ring up her friends, particularly the older ones, to get more information. . . . She's promised to call me back. . . . Does it interest you?'

'Everything interests me,' he sighed, getting up from his armchair to fetch a fresh pipe from the rack.

'Do you think it'll involve a journey to Mulhouse?'

'I don't know yet.'

'Would you take me along?'

They smiled at one another. The window was open. The sun streamed in on them and made them think of holidays.

'See you this evening. . . . I'll make a note of everything she tells me . . . even if it makes you laugh at us both. . . .'

CHAPTER THREE

YOUNG LAPOINTE was presumably scouring Paris for red 403's. Janvier was not at his desk in the inspectors' room, either, for he had been summoned to the nursing-home where he was now pacing the corridors, waiting for his wife to present him with a fourth child.

'Are you doing anything urgent, Lucas?'

'Nothing that can't wait, Chief.'

'Come into my room for a minute.'

It was to send him to the Hôtel-Dieu to collect the Doc's belongings. Maigret had forgotten about this in the morning.

'They'll probably send you from one office to another and rebuff you with lord knows what rules and regulations. . . . You'd do well to provide yourself with a letter that'll impress them, with as many official stamps as possible.'

'Who shall I get to sign it?'

'Sign it yourself. . . . With them, it's only the stamps that count. . . . I'd also like to have this François Keller's fingerprints. . . . Actually, it'll be simpler to ring up the head of the hospital.'

A sparrow, on the window-sill, was watching them both bestirring themselves in what must have appeared to it as a human nest.

With the utmost politeness, Maigret gave notice of Sergeant Lucas's forthcoming visit, and everything went off quite smoothly.

'You won't need a letter,' he declared, hanging up the receiver. 'They'll take you straight to the Director, and he'll show you round himself.'

Left alone, a little later, he was looking through the pages of the Paris telephone directory.

'Rousselet . . . Rousselet . . . Amédée . . . Arthur . . . Aline . . .'

There were scores of Rousselets, but he found one entry in heavy type:

Laboratoires René Rousselet.

The labs were in the fourteenth *arrondissement*, near the Porte d'Orléans. This particular Rousselet's private address was given immediately below: Boulevard Suchet, XVIe.

It was half past two. The weather was still just as radiant, after a flurry of wind which had raised the dust of the pavements and seemed to threaten a storm.

'Hullo! . . . May I speak to Madame Rousselet, please?'

A woman's voice, low-pitched and pleasant, asked:

'Who is speaking?'

'Superintendent Maigret, of the Police Judiciaire.'

There was a pause, then:

'Can you tell me what it's about?'

'It's a personal matter.'

'I am Madame Rousselet.'

'Were you born at Mulhouse and was your maiden name Keller?'

'Yes.'

'I should like to talk to you as soon as possible. . . . May I call on you?'

'Have you bad news for me?'

'I only want some information.'

'When would you like to come?'

'As soon as I can get to you.'

He heard her say to somebody, presumably a child:

'Let me talk, Jeannot.'

She was evidently surprised, intrigued and uneasy.

'I'll expect you, Superintendent. Our flat is on the third floor. . . .'

That morning he had enjoyed the atmosphere of the *quais* which brought back to his mind so many memories, particularly of the walks he had often taken with Madame Maigret, when they used to stroll alongside the Seine from one end of Paris to the other. He was equally appreciative of the peaceful tree-lined avenues and elegant houses of the wealthy districts to which he was now driven by Inspector Torrence in a small police car.

'Shall I come up with you, Chief?'

'I think better not.'

The block of flats had a wrought iron doorway lined with glass and the entrance hall was of white marble; the roomy lift rose silently, without a jar or a creak. He had barely time to press the bell when the door opened and a manservant in a white jacket relieved him of his hat.

'This way, please. . . .'

There was a red ball lying in the entrance hall, and a doll on the carpet, and he caught sight of a nurse taking a little girl in white along the passage. Another door opened, leading into a small sitting-room adjoining the large drawing-room.

'Come in, Superintendent.'

Maigret had reckoned that she must be about thirty-five. She looked younger. She was dark-haired, and wore a lightweight suit. Her eyes, which had the same mellow softness as her voice, looked at him questioningly, while the manservant closed the door.

'Do sit down. . . . Ever since you rang up I've been wondering . . .'

Instead of going straight to the heart of the matter he asked automatically:

'You have several children?'

'I've got four . . . eleven, nine, seven and three.'

It was probably the first time a policeman had entered her home and she kept her eyes fixed on him.

'I wondered at first whether anything had happened to my husband. . . .'

'Is he in Paris?'

'Not at the moment. He's at a conference in Brussels, and I rang him up immediately.'

'Do you remember your father well, Mme Rousselet?'

She seemed to relax slightly. There were flowers everywhere, and the trees of the Bois de Boulogne could be seen through the large windows.

'I remember him, yes. Although . . .'

She seemed reluctant to go on.

'When was the last time you saw him?'

'It was a very long time ago . . . I was thirteen. . . .'

'Were you still living in Mulhouse?'

'Yes . . . I only came to Paris after my marriage.'

'Was it at Mulhouse that you met your husband?'

'At La Baule, where we used to go every year, mother and I . . .' Children could be heard shouting and sliding about in the passage.

'Excuse me a moment.'

She closed the door behind her and said something in a low but forceful tone.

'I'm sorry about that. . . . They're not at school today and I had promised to take them out. . . .'

'Would you recognize your father?'

'I suppose so. . . . Yes. . . .'

He produced the Doc's identity card from his pocket. According to the date of issue, the photograph was some five years old. It had been taken by one of those automatic cameras that are to be found in big stores and stations, and even at Police Headquarters.

François Keller had not shaved for the occasion and had made no attempt to spruce himself up. His cheeks were covered with a two- or three-inch growth of beard, which he must have cut from time to time with scissors. His hair had begun to recede on his temples and the expression in his eyes was blank and indifferent.

'Is that him?'

She held the document in an unsteady hand and bent down to see it better. She was evidently short-sighted.

'This is not how I remembered him, but I'm practically sure it's my father. . . .'

She bent down closer.

'With a magnifying glass, I might be able to—— Wait, I'll fetch one. . . .'

She left the identity card on a small table, disappeared and came back a few minutes later with a lens.

'He had a scar above his left eye, quite small but deep, . . . See . . . you can't make it out very well on this photograph, but I think it's there. . . . Look for yourself. . . .'

Maigret peered through the magnifying glass.

'I remember it so clearly because it was on account of me that he hurt himself. . . . We were having a walk in the countryside one Sunday. . . . It was very hot and there were masses of poppies growing alongside a field of corn. . . .

'I wanted to go and pick some. There was a barbed wire fence round the field . . . I was about eight years old. . . . My father held the barbed wire apart to let me get through. . . . He held the lower wire down with his foot and he was bending forward. . . . It's funny that I can picture the scene so clearly, when I've forgotten so many other things. . . . His foot must have slipped and the barbed wire sprang up suddenly and hit him in the face. . . .

'My mother was afraid his eye might have been hurt. He was bleeding a lot . . . we went to a farm to get water and something to dress the wound with. . . . He was left with the scar. . . .'

All the time she spoke, she was watching Maigret

anxiously and she seemed to be trying to put off the moment when he would tell her exactly why he had come.

'Has anything happened to him?'

'He was injured last night, on the head again, but the doctors don't think his life is in danger.'

'Did it happen in Paris?'

'Yes. . . . On the bank of the Seine. . . . Whoever attacked him then threw him into the water. . . .'

He kept his eyes fixed on her, watching her reactions, and she made no attempt to avoid his scrutiny.

'Do you know how your father was living?'

'Not exactly. . . .'

'What do you mean?'

'When he left us . . .'

'You were thirteen, you told me. Do you remember his leaving?'

'No. . . . One morning I didn't see him about the house, and as I expressed surprise my mother told me he had gone for a long journey.'

'When did you learn where he was?'

'A few months later, mother informed me that he was in Africa, in the wilds, looking after natives.'

'Was it true?'

'I assume it was. Later, in fact, people who had met him out there told us about him. . . . He was living in Gabon, at a station some hundreds of kilometres from Libreville.'

'Did he stay there long?'

'For several years, at any rate. . . . In Mulhouse, some people considered him a kind of saint. . . . Others . . .'

He waited. She seemed hesitant.

'Others called him reckless and crazy.'

'And your mother?'

'I think mother had resigned herself once and for all.'

'How old is she now?'

'Fifty-four. . . . No, fifty-five. . . . I know now that he had left her a letter which she never showed me, in which he said that he would probably never come back and that he was ready to let her divorce him.'

'And did she?'

'No. Mother's a very devout Catholic. . . .'

'Does your husband know about it?'

'Of course. We hid nothing from him.'

'Were you unaware that your father had come back to Paris?'

Her eyelids fluttered briefly, and she was on the point of telling a lie; Maigret was convinced of it.

'Yes and no . . . I never saw him again myself . . . we knew nothing for certain, mother and I . . . but somebody from Mulhouse told her about a sandwich man he had met on the Boulevard Saint-Michel, who looked strangely like my father. . . . An old friend of mother's, it was. . . . Apparently when he spoke the name François the man gave a start, but afterwards pretended not to have recognized him. . . .'

'Did it never occur to you or to your mother to approach the police?'

'What would have been the good? . . . He had chosen his own way of life. . . . He was probably not fitted to share ours. . . .'

'Did you never wonder about him?'

'We talked about him several times, my husband and I. . . .'

'And what about your mother?'

'I asked her various questions, of course, before and after I got married. . . .'

'What is her point of view?'

'It's hard to say, right away, in a few sentences. . . . She's sorry for him. . . . So am I. Although I sometimes wonder if he isn't happier this way. . . .'

She added in a lower tone, with some embarrassment:

'There are some people who can't fit in with the kind of life we lead. . . . And besides, Mother . . .'

She rose, restlessly, went to the window and looked out for a moment before turning to face him again.

'I don't mean to blame her. . . . She has her own attitude to life . . . I suppose everyone has. One can't exactly call her authoritarian, but she does like to have everything happen according to her wishes. . . .'

'After your father left, did you get on well with her?'

'More or less well. All the same I was glad to get married and . . .'

'And escape from her authority?'

'Something of that sort. . . .'

She smiled. 'It's not at all special, and a great many girls are in the same position. . . . My mother loves going out, entertaining, meeting important people. . . . In Mulhouse everyone of any consequence in the town used to come to her parties. . . .'

'Even in your father's time?'

'During the last two years, yes.'

'Why the last two?'

He remembered Madame Maigret's lengthy telephone conversation with her sister, and felt a bit sorry that he was learning more here than his wife would be able to find out.

'Because Mother had inherited some money from her aunt. Before that, we lived quite humbly, in a small house . . . we weren't even in one of the better-class districts, and my father's practice was chiefly working-class. . . . None of us had expected this inheritance. . . . We moved. . . . Mother bought a large house near the cathedral and she wasn't sorry that there was a coat of arms carved over the doorway. . . .'

'Did you know your father's family?'

'No . . . I'd only seen his brother a certain number of times before he was killed in the war, in Syria I believe, at any rate not in France. . . .'

'His father? His mother?'

Children's voices could be heard again, but this time she took no notice.

'His mother died of cancer when my father was about fifteen. . . . His father had a carpenters' and joiners' business. One fine day, while my father was still at university, he was found hanging in the workshop and it turned out that he was on the verge of bankruptcy. . . .'

'But your father managed none the less to finish his studies?'

'By working in a chemist's shop. . . .'

'What was he like?'

'Very gentle. . . . I know this hardly answers your question, but that's the chief impression he left on me . . . very gentle and rather sad. . . .'

'Did he quarrel with your mother?'

'I never heard him raise his voice. . . . It's true that when he was not in his surgery he spent most of his time visiting patients. I remember Mother scolding him for taking no care about his appearance, for always wearing the same crumpled suit and sometimes going without shaving for three days. . . . I used to tell him his beard was prickly when he kissed me. . . .'

'I suppose you know nothing about your father's relations with his colleagues?'

'All that I know comes through Mother . . . only with her it's difficult to distinguish what's true from what's more or less true. She doesn't tell lies. She arranges the truth so that it bears some resemblance to what she'd like it to be. . . . Since she had married my father, he had to be somebody quite remarkable. . . .

' "Your father's the best doctor in the town", she used

to tell me, "probably one of the best in France. . . . Unfortunately . . ." '

She smiled once more.

'You can guess the rest. He couldn't adapt himself. He refused to behave like other people. . . . She let it be understood that if my grandfather had hanged himself it was not because of his imminent bankruptcy but because of mental depression. . . . He had a daughter, who spent some time in a mental home. . . .'

'What became of her?'

'I don't know. . . . I don't think my mother knows, either. . . . In any case she left Mulhouse.'

'Does your mother still live there?'

'She's been living in Paris for a long time now.'

'Can you give me her address?'

'It's 29b Quai d'Orléans.'

Maigret gave a start, but she did not notice.

'It's in the Ile Saint-Louis. Since the island became one of the most fashionable parts of Paris . . .'

'Do you know where your father was attacked last night?'

'Of course not.'

'Under the Pont Marie . . . three hundred yards from your mother's home.'

She knitted her brows anxiously.

'It's on the other branch of the Seine, isn't it? Mother's windows look out on to the Quai des Tournelles . . .'

'Has she a dog?'

'Why do you ask that?'

During the few months that Maigret had spent in the Place des Vosges, while the house in the Boulevard Richard-Lenoir was being done up, he and his wife used to take a walk in the evenings round the Ile Saint-Louis. That was when dog-owners or their servants used to walk their animals along the embankment.

'Mother only has birds. She detests dogs and cats.'

And changing the subject: 'Where has my father been taken to?'

'To the Hôtel-Dieu, the nearest hospital.'

'I suppose you'd like me to . . .'

'Not just yet . . . I may perhaps ask you to come and identify him, so that we may be absolutely certain, but for the moment his head and face are covered with bandages.'

'Is he in much pain?'

'He's in a coma and not conscious of anything.'

'Why did they do such a thing?'

'That's what I'm trying to find out.'

'Was there a fight?'

'No. In all probability he was attacked while he was sleeping. . . .'

'Underneath the bridge?'

Maigret now rose.

'I suppose you're going to see Mother?'

'I'm afraid I shall have to.'

'May I ring her up and tell her the news?'

He hesitated. He would have preferred to watch Madame Keller's reactions. However, he did not insist.

'Thank you, Superintendent. Will it be in the papers?'

'There'll have been a brief report of the assault by now, but your father's name will certainly not appear in it, for I only learnt it myself in the middle of the morning.'

'Mother won't want it talked about. . . .'

'I'll do my best.'

She went with him to the front door, while a small girl clung to her skirt.

'We're going out right away now, darling. Go and ask Nanny to dress you.'

Torrence was pacing up and down the pavement in front of the house and the little black police car cut a poor figure amongst the gleaming cars belonging to the local residents.

'Quai des Orfèvres?'

'No . . . Ile Saint-Louis . . . Quai d'Orléans.'

The house was an old one, with a huge carriage gateway, but it was as well cared for as a piece of valuable furniture. The brasswork, the handrail of the stairs, the steps and walls were clean and polished, without a speck of dust; the concierge herself, in a black dress and white apron, looked like a maid from some upper-class household.

'Have you an appointment?'

'No. Madame Keller is expecting me.'

'One moment, please . . .'

The lodge was a little parlour which smelt of polish rather than of cooking. The concierge picked up the telephone.

'What is your name?'

'Superintendent Maigret.'

'Hullo . . . Berthe. . . . Would you tell Madame that a certain Superintendent Maigret is asking to see her? . . . Yes, he's right here. Can he go up? . . . Thanks. . . . You can go up. . . . Second floor on the right.'

Maigret wondered, as he climbed the stairs, whether the Flemings' boat was still moored at the Quai des Célestins or whether, the statement having been duly signed, they were already travelling downstream towards Rouen. The door opened without his having to ring. The maid, young and pretty, examined the Superintendent from head to foot as if it were the first time in her life that she had seen a real live detective.

'This way. . . . Let me take your hat.'

The flat was high-ceilinged and decorated in baroque style, with a great deal of gilt and richly carved furniture. From the entrance hall he could hear the chirping of budgerigars, and when the drawing-room door was opened he beheld a huge cage with almost a dozen pairs of birds in it.

He waited for about ten minutes, and finally by way of protest lit his pipe. However, he removed it from his mouth when Madame Keller made her entry. It came as a surprise to him to find her so tiny, so fragile-looking and yet so young. She seemed barely ten years older than her daughter; she was dressed in black and white, she had a fresh complexion and forget-me-not blue eyes.

'Jacqueline rang me,' she said immediately, waving Maigret towards an armchair with a high upright back, as uncomfortable as possible. She herself sat on a stool covered in antique tapestry, holding herself as she must have been taught to at her convent school.

'So you've found my husband . . .'

'We weren't looking for him,' he retorted.

'I'm sure. . . . There's no reason why you should have been looking for him. Everyone's free to live as he chooses. . . . Is it true that his life is not in danger, or did you tell my daughter that to spare her feelings?'

'Professor Magnin thinks he has an eighty per cent chance of recovering.'

'Magnin? . . . I know him quite well. He's often been here. . . .'

'Did you know your husband was in Paris?'

'I knew it without really knowing it. Since he left for Gabon nearly twenty years ago I have had two postcards from him, and that's all. . . . And that was right at the beginning of his stay in Africa . . .'

She made no pretence of grief, but looked him squarely in the face, like a woman familiar with every kind of situation.

'Are you sure, at least, that it's really him?'

'Your daughter recognized him. . . .'

He showed her, too, the identity card with its photograph. She fetched her spectacles from the top of a chest of drawers and examined the portrait attentively, her face betraying not the least trace of emotion.

'Jacqueline was quite right. . . . Of course he's changed, but I'd swear, too, that it's François. . . .'

She looked up.

'Is it true that he lived a few steps away from here?'

'Under the Pont Marie. . . .'

'And to think that I cross that bridge several times a week, for I have a friend who lives just the other side of the Seine . . . Madame Lambois. You must know her name. Her husband . . .'

Maigret did not wait to be told of the important position held by Madame Lambois's husband.

'You've never seen your husband again since the day he left Mulhouse?'

'Never.'

'Did he never write to you or telephone you?'

'Apart from the two postcards, I never had any news of him. . . . At any rate, not directly. . . .'

'And indirectly?'

'I did happen to meet, at a friend's house, a former governor of Gabon, Pérignon by name, who asked me whether I was related to a certain Dr. Keller.'

'What did you reply?'

'I told him the truth. He looked embarrassed. . . . I had to worm it out of him. At last he admitted that François had failed to find what he was searching for out there. . . .'

'What was he searching for?'

'He was an idealist, do you see. He was not fitted for modern life. . . . After his disappointment at Mulhouse . . .'

Maigret showed some surprise.

'Did my daughter not tell you about it? . . . It's true that she was very young and saw so little of her father. . . .

Instead of acquiring the practice he deserved. . . . Will you take a cup of tea? . . . No? . . . Excuse me for having some in front of you, but it's my tea-time.'

She rang the bell.

'My tea, Berthe. . . .'

'For one?'

'Yes. . . . What can I offer you, Superintendent? . . . Some whisky? . . . Nothing? . . . Just as you please. What was I saying? . . . Oh yes. Didn't someone write a novel called *The Poor Man's Doctor*? Or am I thinking of *The Country Doctor*? . . . Well, my husband was a kind of poor man's doctor, and if I hadn't inherited money from my aunt we should have become as poor as his patients. . . . Note that I'm not blaming him for it. It was in his nature. His father . . . well, no matter. Every family has its problems. . . .'

The telephone rang.

'Excuse me. . . . Hullo. . . . Yes, speaking. . . . Alice? . . . Yes, darling . . . I may be a little late. . . . Oh no! . . . Very well, on the contrary. . . . Have you seen Laure? . . . She'll be there? . . . I won't go on now, because I have a visitor . . . I'll tell you all about it . . . I'll see you presently. . . .'

She came back to her place smiling.

'That was the wife of the Minister of the Interior. Do you know her?'

Maigret merely shook his head, and instinctively put his pipe back into his pocket. The budgerigars irritated him. So did the interruptions. The next thing was the maid bringing in tea.

'He'd got it into his head to become a hospital doctor and for two years he worked hard for the competitive examination. Everyone in Mulhouse would tell you it was flagrantly unfair . . . François was certainly the best and cleverest doctor there. And I think he would have felt in the right place. . . . As usual, they appointed the protégé of one of the departmental heads. But that was no reason for giving everything up.'

'And it was as a result of this disappointment . . .'

'I suppose so . . . I saw so little of him! When he was at home he would shut himself up in his consulting room. . . . He had always been rather unsociable but from that time on he seemed to go off the rails completely. I don't want to say anything unkind about him. . . . It never even occurred to me to divorce him when he wrote to suggest this. . . .'

'Did he drink?'

'Did my daughter say so?'

'No.'

'He started drinking, yes. . . . Not that I ever saw him the worse for drink . . . but he always had a bottle in his consulting room and he was frequently seen coming out of little *bistrots* not usually frequented by a man in his position.'

'You had begun to tell me about Gabon.'

'I think he wanted to become a sort of Dr Schweitzer, if you see what I mean. To go and look after negroes in the wilds, to set up a hospital there and see as little as possible of white men, of people of his own class. . . .'

'And was he disappointed?'

'From what the Governor confided to me reluctantly, he succeeded in antagonizing the administration and the leading companies. . . . Perhaps on account of the climate, he took to drinking more and more. . . . Don't imagine I'm telling you this out of jealousy. I've never been jealous. Out there he lived in a native hut with a black woman and apparently he had children by her. . . .'

Maigret stared at the budgerigars in the sunlit cage.

'They gave him to understand that he was unsuited to the post. . . .'

'You mean he was turned out of Gabon?'

'More or less. . . . I don't know exactly how these things are done, and the Governor was rather vague about it. The fact remains that he left. . . .'

'How long ago was it that one of your friends met him in the Boulevard Saint-Michel?'

'Did my daughter tell you about that? Note that I can't be sure of it. . . . The man, who was carrying a board on his back advertising a local restaurant, looked like François, and apparently he gave a start when my friend addressed him by his name . . .'

'Did your friend not speak to him?'

'François stared at him as if he did not recognize him. That's all I know. . . .'

'As I told your daughter just now, I cannot ask you to come and identify him yet, because his face is covered with bandages. . . . As soon as there is some improvement . . .'

'Don't you think it may be painful?'

'For whom?'

'I'm thinking of him. . . .'

'We have to make sure of his identity.'

'I'm practically certain . . . if only because of the scar. It was one Sunday in August. . . .'

'I know.'

'In that case I don't see what else I have to tell you. . . .'

He rose, longing to get outside and away from the chattering budgerigars.

'I suppose the papers . . .'

'The papers will say as little as possible, that I can promise you.'

'It's not so much for my own sake as for my son-in-law's. For a business man it's always unpleasant to . . . Note that he knows all about it and has understood the situation very well. . . . Can I really not offer you anything?'

'No, thanks.'

And on the pavement he said to Torrence: 'Where can we find a quiet little *bistrot*? I've such a thirst!'

A glass of very cold beer with a creamy head to it!

They found the *bistrot*, as quiet and dark as they could have wished, but alas, the beer was lukewarm and flat.

CHAPTER FOUR

'YOU'LL FIND THE LIST on your desk,' said Lucas, who as usual had done a meticulous job.

There were, in fact, several typewritten lists. First, that of the various objects (classified under the heading 'unclaimed articles' by the specialist of the Police Records Department) found under the Pont Marie and constituting the entire worldly goods of François Keller. The whole lot, old boxes, child's pram, torn blankets, newspapers, frying pan, billy-can, the Funeral Orations of Bossuet and the rest, were now upstairs in a corner of the laboratory.

The second list was that of the clothes which Lucas had brought back from the Hôtel-Dieu, and a third, finally, inventoried the contents of the pockets.

Maigret preferred not to read it, and it was odd to see him, in the light of the setting sun, opening the brown paper bag in which the police sergeant had put the small articles.

His expression was rather like that of a child opening a surprise packet and expecting to find heaven knows what treasure.

The first thing he drew out was a dilapidated stethoscope, which he laid on his blotter.

'That was in the right-hand pocket of his jacket,' observed Lucas. 'I inquired at the hospital. It doesn't work.'

In that case why had François Keller carried it about with him? In the hope of getting it mended? Wasn't it rather as a last remaining symbol of his profession?

Next came a pocket knife with three blades and a corkscrew; its horn handle was cracked. Like the rest, it must have come out of some dustbin.

A briar pipe, the stem of which had been mended with wire.

'Left-hand pocket,' recited Lucas. 'It's still damp.'

Maigret sniffed at it instinctively.

'No tobacco?' he queried.

'You'll find a few cigarette ends at the bottom of the bag. They got so soaked that they're nothing but a mush.'

You could picture the man pausing on the pavement and bending down to pick up a fag-end, taking off the paper and poking the tobacco into his pipe. Secretly, Maigret was pleased to find that the Doc was a pipe-smoker. Neither the wife nor the daughter had mentioned this detail.

Nails and screws. What for? The tramp must have picked them up on his rounds and thrust them into his pocket without giving a thought to their use, considering them probably as talismans. The proof of which was that there were three objects of even less use to someone who lies under the bridges with newspaper wrapped round his chest to keep off the cold: three marbles, those glass marbles in which you see yellow, red, blue and green threads, the sort a child will swap for five or six ordinary marbles for the pleasure of seeing it shimmer in the sun. That was practically all, except for a few coins and, in a leather wallet, two fifty-franc notes stuck together by the water of the Seine.

Maigret kept one of the marbles in his hand and during the rest of the conversation rolled it about between his fingers.

'Have you taken the fingerprints?'

'The other patients watched me with great interest. I went up to check them in the files department.'

'What did you find out?'

'Nothing. Keller has never been involved with us or with the law.'

'Has he recovered consciousness?'

'No. When I was there, his eyes were half open, but he didn't appear to be seeing anything. His breathing is a bit wheezy. From time to time he gives a moan. . . .'

Before going home the Superintendent signed letters. In spite of his preoccupied air there was a certain light-heartedness about his mood, to match that of the air over Paris. Was it by accident that on leaving his office he slipped a marble into his pocket?

It was a Tuesday—macaroni *au gratin* for supper. Apart from Thursday's *pot-au-feu*, the menu varied from week to week, but for years now, for no apparent reason, Tuesday's evening meal had consisted of macaroni cheese with minced ham in it and occasionally a finely sliced truffle.

Madame Maigret, too, was in a lively mood, and from the sparkle in her eyes he gathered that she had some news for him. He did not tell her right away that he had seen Jacqueline Rousselet and Madame Keller.

'I'm hungry!'

She expected questions. He did not put any until they were both seated at table in front of the open window. The air was bluish, with a few lingering trails of red low down in the sky.

'Did your sister ring you back?'

'I think she's done a good job. She must have spent the whole afternoon calling up all her friends.'

She had a piece of paper with notes on it beside her plate.

'Shall I tell you what she said?'

The noises of the city made a resonant background to their conversation and they could hear the beginning of the television news talk from their neighbours' flat.

'Don't you want to turn on the news?'

'I'd rather listen to you.'

Two or three times while she was speaking he put his hand into his pocket to play with the marble.

'What are you smiling at?'

'At nothing . . . I'm listening.'

'To begin with, I know where the money came from that Madame Keller inherited from her aunt. . . . It's a longish story. Shall I tell it to you in detail?'

He nodded, while munching the crisp macaroni.

'She was a nurse, and still unmarried at forty-five. . . .'

'Did she live in Mulhouse?'

'No, Strasbourg. . . . She was Madame Keller's mother's sister. . . . D'you follow me?'

'Yes.'

'She worked at the hospital. The head men there each have a certain number of rooms at their disposal for their private patients. . . . One day, shortly before the war, she had to nurse a man about whom there's been a lot of talk in Alsace since, a certain Lemke, a dealer in scrap-iron who had already made a good deal of money and had rather a bad reputation. He was said to go in for usury. . . .'

'And he married her?'

'How did you know?'

He felt sorry for having spoilt her story.

'I guessed it from your expression.'

'Yes, he married her. Wait for the next bit. During the war he kept up his trade in non-ferrous metals. Inevitably he had to deal with the Germans, and he amassed a considerable fortune. . . . Am I being long-winded? Am I boring you?'

'Quite the contrary. What happened at the Liberation?'

'The F.F.I. hunted for Lemke to make him disgorge his wealth and then to shoot him. . . . He was never caught.

Nobody knows where he and his wife were hiding. . . .
Anyhow, they managed to reach Spain and from there
they took ship for the Argentine. A mill-owner from
Mulhouse met Lemke over there in the street. . . . A little
more macaroni?'

'Yes, please . . . some of the crispy top. . . .'

'I don't know whether he was still doing business or
whether the couple were travelling for pleasure. . . . One
day they took the plane for Brazil and the aircraft
crashed into the mountains. The crew and all the pas-
sengers were killed . . . and it was precisely because
Lemke and his wife died in a disaster that the money went
to Madame Keller, who never expected it. In the normal
way it should have gone to the husband's relatives. . . .
D'you know why the Lemkes got nothing and the wife's
niece inherited the whole estate?'

He shook his head; he was cheating, for in fact he had
understood.

'Apparently when a man and wife are victims of the
same accident, so that it can't be established which of the
two died first, the law assumes that the wife outlived her
husband, even if only by a few moments. . . . The doctors'
theory is that we are tougher than men; so the aunt
inherited the fortune first and then it went to her
niece. . . . Phew!'

She seemed pleased and rather proud of herself.

'So that, all things considered, it was partly because a
nurse married a scrap-iron merchant in a Strasbourg
hospital, and a plane crashed in the mountains of South
America, that Dr Keller became a down-and-out. If his
wife hadn't become rich overnight, if they'd gone on living
in the Rue du Sauvage, if . . . You see what I mean?
Don't you believe, yourself, that he'd have stayed in
Mulhouse?'

'Maybe.'

213

'I've got some information about her, too, but I warn you it's only gossip and my sister denies all responsibility for it.'

'Go on, tell me. . . .'

'She's a lively little person, always on the go, who adores social occasions and who's a regular lion-hunter. . . . Once her husband had left her, she went in for it to her heart's content, organizing big dinner parties several times a week. In this way she came to have a great influence on the Prefect, whose name is Badet and whose wife (she's since died) was an invalid. Scandal-mongers assert that she was his mistress and that she's had other lovers, including a general whose name I've forgotten. . . .'

'I've seen her.'

If Madame Maigret was disappointed, she showed no sign of it.

'What's she like?'

'Just as you've described her. . . . A lively, restless little lady, very well groomed, looking younger than her age and addicted to budgerigars. . . .'

'Why d'you bring in budgerigars?'

'Because her flat is full of them.'

'Does she live in Paris?'

'In the Ile Saint-Louis, three hundred yards from the Pont Marie, under which her husband used to sleep. . . . By the way, he smoked a pipe. . . .'

Between the macaroni and the salad, he had taken the marble out of his pocket and was rolling it about the table.

'What's that?'

'A marble. The Doc had three of them.'

She was watching her husband attentively.

'You're fond of him, aren't you?'

'I think I'm beginning to understand him.'

'You can understand how a man like that can become a tramp?'

'Perhaps. . . . He'd lived in Africa, the only white man in a station remote from towns and main roads. . . . And there, too, he was disappointed. . . .'

'Why?'

It was hard to explain this to Madame Maigret, who had always lived in clean and orderly surroundings.

'What I'm trying to guess,' he went on lightly, 'is what he could have been guilty of.'

She knit her brows.

'What do you mean? . . . Surely it was he who was knocked out and thrown into the Seine?'

'He was the victim, true.'

'Well then? Why do you say . . .'

'Criminologists, particularly American criminologists, have a theory on the subject, and it's maybe not as extravagant as it sounds.'

'What theory?'

'That in eight out of ten crimes the victim is to a large extent as responsible as the murderer. . . .'

'I don't understand.'

He was staring at the marble as though it fascinated him.

'Take the case of a quarrel between a woman and a jealous man. . . . The man accuses the woman, who taunts him . . .'

'That must sometimes happen.'

'Suppose he's holding a knife in his hand and says to her: "Take care. . . . Next time, I'll kill you." '

'That must sometimes happen, too.'

But not in the world she knew!

'Suppose, now, that she jeers at him: "You wouldn't dare! . . . You're not capable of it. . . ." '

'I see what you mean.'

'Well, in many crimes of passion, there's something of that sort. . . . You were talking about Lemke, who made his fortune partly by usury, driving his clients to desperation, and partly by trading with the Germans. Would you have been surprised to learn that he had been murdered?'

'The doctor . . .'

'He seemed to do no harm to anyone. He lived under the bridges, drank red wine straight out of the bottle and walked the streets with an advertisement board on his back. . . .'

'Well then!'

'And yet somebody went down on to the river bank by night and took advantage of his being asleep to deal him a blow on the head that might have been fatal, and then dragged him along and threw him into the Seine, from which he was only rescued by a miracle. . . . That person had a motive. . . . In other words, the Doc had consciously or unconsciously given him a motive for putting him out of the way. . . .'

'Is he still in a coma?'

'Yes.'

'Are you hoping that when he can speak you'll get something out of him?'

He shrugged his shoulders and began to fill his pipe. Soon afterwards they put out the light and remained there, sitting by the open window.

It was a pleasant, peaceful evening, with long pauses between remarks, which did not prevent them from feeling very close to one another.

When Maigret reached his office next morning the weather was as radiant as the previous day, and the tiny green specks on the trees had already given place to real little delicate leaves.

The Superintendent had barely sat down at his desk when Lapointe came in, in high spirits.

'I've got two customers for you, Chief.'

'Where are they?'

'In the waiting-room.'

'Who are they?'

'The owner of the red Peugeot and the friend who was with him on Monday night. I don't take much credit for it. . . . Contrary to what you might expect there aren't many red 403's in Paris and only three whose number-plates include two nines. One of those three has been under repair for the past week and the other is at the present moment in Cannes with its owner.'

'Have you questioned the men?'

'I only asked them one or two questions. I thought it best for you to see them yourself. . . . Shall I bring them in?'

There was something mysterious about Lapointe's attitude, as if he had another surprise in store for Maigret.

'Go along. . . .'

He waited, sitting at his desk, with the multi-coloured marble still in his pocket like a talisman.

'Monsieur Jean Guillot,' announced the inspector, ushering in the first customer.

He was a man of about forty, of average height, dressed with a certain studied smartness.

'Monsieur Hardoin, industrial draughtsman.'

The second man was taller and thinner and several years younger, and Maigret was soon to discover that he stammered.

'Sit down, messieurs. . . . I understand that one of you is the owner of a red Peugeot.'

Jean Guillot raised his hand, not without a certain pride.

'It's my car,' he said, 'I bought it at the beginning of the winter.'

'Where do you live, Monsieur Guillot?'

'Rue de Turenne, not far from the Boulevard du Temple.'

'Your profession?'

'Insurance agent.'

He was somewhat awestruck at finding himself in Police Headquarters, being interrogated by a Chief Superintendent, but he showed no signs of fear. He even stared about him with curiosity, as though planning to describe the scene in detail to his friends later.

'And you, Monsieur Hardoin?'

'I l . . . live in the same h . . . h . . . house.'

'The floor above ours,' Guillot helped him out.

'Are you married?'

'A b . . . b . . . bachelor.'

'*I'm* married with two children, a boy and a girl,' Guillot put in again without waiting for questions.

Lapointe, standing by the door, was smiling vaguely. The two men, each sitting on a chair with his hat on his knees, looked like performers in a double act.

'You are friends?'

They replied as simultaneously as Hardoin's stutter would allow:

'Very good friends.'

'Do you know François Keller?'

They looked at one another in surprise, as if hearing the name for the first time. It was the draughtsman who asked:

'Who . . . who . . . who's that?'

'He practised medicine in Mulhouse for a long time.'

'I've never set foot in Mulhouse,' declared Guillot. 'Does he claim to know me?'

'What were you doing on Monday night?'

'As I told your inspector, I had no idea it was against the law. . . .'

'Tell me in detail what you did.'

'When I got back from my round, about eight o'clock—I cover the western suburbs—my wife drew me into a corner so that the children shouldn't hear, and told me that Nestor . . .'

'Who is Nestor?'

'Our dog. . . . A Great Dane. . . . He was twelve years old and he was very gentle with the children, whom he'd known from birth, so to speak. When they were babies he used to lie at the foot of the cot and I hardly dared go near. . . .'

'So then, your wife told you . . .'

He went on, quite unruffled:

'I don't know if you've ever kept a Great Dane. . . . In general they don't live as long as other dogs, I can't think why. And when they grow old they suffer from nearly all the same weaknesses as men. . . . For the past few weeks Nestor had been almost paralysed and I'd suggested taking him to the vet to have an injection. My wife hadn't wanted that. . . . When I got home on Monday the dog was dying, and so that the children shouldn't witness such a sight my wife had fetched down our friend Lucien, who had helped her to carry the dog up to his flat. . . .'

Maigret glanced at Lapointe, who gave him a discreet wink.

'I went up to Hardoin's flat immediately to see what was happening to the dog. Poor Nestor was about done for. I rang up the vet and was told he was at the theatre and wouldn't be back before midnight. . . . For over two hours we stayed there watching the dog die. . . . I'd sat down on the ground and he'd laid his head on my knees. His body was shaking convulsively. . . .'

Hardoin was nodding in confirmation, and trying to put in a word.

'He . . . he . . .'

'He died at half past ten,' the insurance agent interrupted him. 'I went down to tell my wife. I stayed to look after the flat, where the children were asleep, while she went up to see Nestor for the last time. . . . I had a bite to eat, for I'd had no dinner. . . . I must confess I then drank a couple of glasses of brandy to set me up and when my wife came back I took the bottle upstairs to give some to Hardoin, who was as upset as I was. . . .'

In fact, it had been a little drama in the shadow of another drama.

'And that was when we wondered what we were going to do with the body. . . . I've heard tell that there's a cemetery for dogs, but I suppose it costs a lot, and besides, I can't afford to lose a day's work seeing to that. . . . As for my wife, she hasn't the time.'

'In short . . .' said Maigret.

'In short . . .'

And Guillot paused, having lost the thread of his ideas. 'We . . . we . . . we . . .'

'We didn't want to dump him on a piece of waste ground. . . . Have you any idea of the size of a Great Dane? Lying there in Hardoin's dining-room he looked even huger and more impressive. In short . . .'

He was relieved to have got back to that point.

'In short, we decided to put him into the Seine. I went back to our place to fetch a potato-sack. . . . It wasn't big enough and we couldn't get his paws in. It was quite a job carrying him downstairs and putting him into the boot of the car. . . .'

'What time was it?'

'Ten past eleven. . . .'

'How do you know it was ten past eleven?'

'Because the concierge hadn't gone to bed. She saw us go past and asked us what had happened. I explained to her. Her door was open and I instinctively looked at the clock, which said ten past eleven. . . .'

'You told her you were going to throw the dog into the Seine? You drove directly to the Pont des Célestins?'

'It was the nearest . . .'

'It only took you a few minutes to get there. I suppose you didn't stop on the way?'

'Not on the way there. We took the quickest route. It must have taken us five minutes. . . . I wasn't keen on driving down the ramp. . . . As I saw nobody there I took a chance. . . .'

'So it wasn't yet half past eleven?'

'Surely not. . . . You'll see. . . . We both took hold of the sack and we tipped it into the river. . . .'

'And you still saw nobody?'

'Nobody.'

'Was there a barge nearby?'

'That's true. We even noticed a light inside . . .'

'But you didn't see the bargee?'

'No.'

'You didn't go as far as the Pont Marie?'

'We had no reason to go any further. We threw Nestor into the water as close to the car as we could. . . .'

Hardoin kept on nodding assent, sometimes opening his mouth to put in a word and then closing it again, discouraged.

'What happened next?'

'We went away. . . . Once we were up there . . .'

'On the Quai des Célestins, you mean?'

'Yes. . . . I didn't feel too good and I remembered there was no more brandy in the bottle. . . . It had all been quite an ordeal. Nestor was almost one of the family. . . . In the Rue de Turenne, I suggested to Lucien that we should have a drink and we stopped at a café on the corner of the Rue des Francs-Bourgeois, close to the Place des Vosges. . . .'

'You had some more brandy?'

'Yes. . . . There was a clock there, too, and I looked at it. The landlord pointed out that it was five minutes fast. It was twenty to twelve. . . .'

He repeated, with a crestfallen air:

'I swear to you I didn't know it wasn't allowed. . . . Put yourself in my place. . . . It was chiefly for the children's sake, because I wanted to spare them the sight. They still don't know that the dog is dead. We've told them he's gone away, that he might turn up again perhaps. . . .'

Unconsciously Maigret had pulled the marble out of his pocket and was fingering it.

'I suppose you've told me the truth?'

'Why should I tell you a lie? If there's a fine to be paid, I'm ready to . . .'

'What time did you get home?'

The two men glanced at one another in some confusion.

Once again, Hardoin opened his mouth and once again it was Guillot who answered.

'Late. . . . About one in the morning. . . .'

'Did the café in the Rue de Turenne stay open until one in the morning?'

It was a district that Maigret knew well, where everything shuts at midnight or even a good deal earlier.

'No, we went for a last drink in the Place de la République.'

'Were you drunk?'

'You know how it is. You drink because you're upset. One glass, then another. . . .'

'You didn't go back along the Seine?'

Guillot looked surprised, and glanced at his companion as though asking him to confirm his evidence.

'Oh no! Why should we?'

Maigret turned to Lapointe.

'Take them next door and file their statements. . . .

Thank you, gentlemen. I need not tell you that we shall check up on everything you've just told us. . . .'

'I swear to you I've told the truth. . . .'

'So . . . so . . . so have I!'

There was something farcical about it. Maigret was left alone in his room, standing in front of the open window with a glass marble in his hand. In a brown study, he watched the Seine flowing beneath the trees, the boats passing, and the women's dresses making light patches on the Pont Saint-Michel.

At last he sat down again and rang up the Hôtel-Dieu.

'I'd like to speak to the Sister in charge of the Surgical Ward.'

Now that she had seen him with the Big Chief himself and had been given her instructions, she was all honey.

'I was just about to ring you, Superintendent. . . . Professor Magnin has just examined him. He finds him much better than last night and hopes that complications can be avoided. It's almost a miracle. . . .'

'Has he recovered consciousness?'

'Not quite, but he's beginning to look about him and to show some interest. It's hard to say if he's aware of his condition and of his surroundings. . . .'

'Has he still got his bandages on?'

'Not on the face. . . .'

'Do you think he'll recover consciousness today?'

'It may happen at any moment. . . . Would you like me to get in touch with you as soon as he speaks?'

'No. I'm coming over. . . .'

'Now?'

Now, yes. He was eager to make the acquaintance of the man whom he had only seen hitherto with his head bandaged. He went through the inspectors' room, where Lapointe was busy typing out the statements of the insurance agent and his stuttering friend.

'I'm off to the Hôtel-Dieu. I don't know when I'll be back. . . .'

It was almost next door. He walked there as though for a neighbourly call, taking his time, his pipe between his teeth and his hands behind his back, with vague thoughts floating through his mind.

When he reached the Hôtel-Dieu he saw Big Léa, still wearing her pink blouse, walking from the reception desk, a resentful look on her face. She hurried to meet him.

'You know, Superintendent, they not only stop me seeing him but they refuse to give me news of him. They nearly fetched a policeman to chuck me out. Have you got any news of him yourself?'

'I've just heard that he's a lot better.'

'Do they think he's going to pull through?'

'It's quite likely.'

'Is he in much pain?'

'I don't think he's conscious of it. I imagine they've given him an injection. . . .'

'Yesterday some plain-clothes men came to collect his things. Were they your people?'

He answered in the affirmative, and added with a smile:

'You needn't worry. He'll get everything back.'

'You've still got no idea who could have done such a thing?'

'And have you?'

'I've lived on the embankment fifteen years now and this is the first time anyone's attacked a dosser. For one thing we're harmless people, you must know that better than anyone.'

She was pleased with the word, and she repeated it:

'Harmless. . . . There aren't even any fights, ever. Each of us respects the others' liberty. . . . If we didn't respect each other's liberty, why should we sleep underneath the bridges?'

He scrutinized her more closely and noticed that her eyes were somewhat redder, her colour higher than on the previous day.

'Have you been drinking?'

'To get rid of the blues. . . .'

'What have your friends been saying?'

'They haven't said anything. . . . When you've seen all there is to see, you don't bother with gossip. . . .'

As Maigret was about to go in, she asked him: 'Can I wait till you come out to have some news of him?'

'I may be a long time.'

'It doesn't matter. . . . I may as well be here as anywhere else. . . .'

She had recovered her good humour, her childish smile.

'You wouldn't have a fag about you?'

He indicated his pipe.

'Well then, a pinch of tobacco . . . I chew it if I can't smoke.'

He went up in the lift at the same time as a patient on a stretcher and two nurses. On the third floor he met the Ward Sister coming out of one of the wards.

'You know the way. . . . I'll be with you in a moment. They've rung for me from Emergencies. . . .'

The patients lying in their beds turned to look at him, as on the previous day. Already, they seemed to recognize him. He made his way to Dr Keller's bed, hat in hand, and at last discovered a face on which only a few strips of plaster remained.

The man, who had been shaved the day before, bore little resemblance to his photograph. His face was sunken, his skin colourless, his lips thin and pale. What struck Maigret above all was to find a man's gaze suddenly confronting him.

For there was no doubt about it: the Doc was looking at him, and the gaze was not that of an unconscious man.

It embarrassed him to stand there silent. On the other hand he did not know what to say. There was a chair beside the bed and he sat down on it, murmuring uneasily: 'Are you feeling better?'

He was convinced that the words did not vanish into mist, that they had been noted and understood. But there was not a flicker in the eyes that remained fixed on him; they expressed nothing but complete indifference.

'Do you hear me, Dr Keller?'

It was the start of a long, frustrating struggle.

CHAPTER FIVE

MAIGRET SELDOM TALKED to his wife about an inquiry when it was under way. In fact he avoided discussing it with his closest collaborators, to whom he would merely give instructions. This was all part of his way of working, his attempts to understand, to immerse himself gradually in the way of life of people unknown to him the previous day.

'What do you think about it, Maigret?' an examining magistrate would often ask him during a visit from the Public Prosecutors' Department or the reconstitution of a crime.

His invariable reply was often quoted in the law-courts:

'I never think, *monsieur le juge.*'

And somebody had added one day: 'He's soaking it in . . .'

This was true, in a way; words were too precise for him, so that he preferred to keep silence.

This time it was different, at any rate with Madame Maigret, perhaps because thanks to her sister who lived in Mulhouse, she had lent him a helping hand. As they sat down to lunch he announced:

'This morning I made Keller's acquaintance. . . .'

She was surprised, not only because he had broached the subject first, but on account of the cheerfulness of his tone. That was not quite the right word, nor was it exactly sprightliness. None the less there was a certain light-hearted good humour in his voice and in his eyes.

For once, the papers were not harassing him, while the Deputy Public Prosecutor and the examining magistrate had left him in peace. A tramp had been attacked under the Pont Marie and thrown into the flooded Seine, but he had survived as though by a miracle and Professor Magnin was astonished at his powers of recovery.

In short, it was a crime without a victim, one might almost have said without a murderer, and nobody bothered much about the Doc except perhaps for Big Léa and two or three down-and-outs.

Maigret, however, devoted as much of his time to this affair as to some drama that aroused passionate interest throughout France. He seemed to have made it his personal concern, and from the way he had just announced his interview with Keller, he might have been speaking of somebody that he and his wife had been waiting to meet for a long time.

'Has he recovered consciousness?' asked Madame Maigret, trying not to display an excessive interest.

'Yes and no. . . . He did not utter a word. . . . He merely looked at me, but I'm convinced that he did not miss a word of what I said. The Sister in charge doesn't share my opinion. She maintains that he is still stupefied by the drugs he's been given, and that he's in the state of a punch-drunk boxer.'

As he ate, he looked out of the window and listened to the birds.

'Do you get the impression that he knows who attacked him?'

Maigret sighed, and finally gave a faint self-mocking smile that was uncharacteristic.

'I don't know . . . I'd find it hard to explain my impression.'

He had seldom, in all his life, felt as baffled as that morning in the Hôtel-Dieu, nor as passionately interested in any problem.

The conditions of the interview, for one thing, had

hardly been favourable. It had taken place in a ward where a dozen patients were lying and three or four more sitting or standing by the window. Some of them were seriously ill and in pain, and there was a ceaseless ringing of bells and a coming and going of nurses, bending over one bed or another.

Everyone was staring more or less intently at the Superintendent as he sat beside Keller, and all ears were on the alert.

Furthermore, the Ward Sister had appeared at the door from time to time, watching them uneasily and with obvious annoyance.

'You mustn't stay too long,' she had advised him. 'Don't tire him.'

Maigret, bending over the sick-bed, spoke gently in a low voice, so that a kind of murmur could be heard.

'Do you hear me, Monsieur Keller? . . . Do you remember what happened to you on Monday night when you were lying under the Pont Marie?'

Not a feature of the injured man's face stirred, but the Superintendent was concerned only with watching his eyes, which expressed neither distress nor anxiety. They were of a washed-out grey colour, which had seen a great deal and seemed almost worn out.

'Were you asleep when you were attacked?'

The Doc made no attempt to avert his gaze from Maigret, and a curious thing happened: it seemed as though Keller was scrutinizing his interlocutor, instead of the other way about.

This impression was so embarrassing that the Superintendent felt impelled to introduce himself.

'My name's Maigret . . . I'm in charge of the Criminal Squad of the Police Judiciaire. I'm trying to find out what happened to you. I've seen your wife and your daughter, and the bargees who pulled you out of the Seine. . . .'

The Doc gave no start at the mention of his wife and daughter, but Maigret could have sworn that a flicker of irony showed in his eyes.

'Are you unable to speak?'

The man made no effort to reply by even the slightest movement of the head or twitch of the eyelids.

'Are you conscious of being spoken to?'

Yes, yes! Maigret was convinced that he was right. Not only was Keller aware of his words, but he did not miss the least shade of their meaning.

'Does it bother you being questioned in the ward, with other patients listening to us?'

Then, almost coaxingly, he endeavoured to explain:

'I should have liked you to be in a private room. . . . Unfortunately that raises complicated administrative questions. . . . Our budget doesn't allow us to pay for one. . . .'

Paradoxically, things would have been simpler if, instead of being the victim, the doctor had been the aggressor or merely a suspect. There were no rules for dealing with victims.

'I'm going to have to bring your wife here, for it's necessary that she should make a formal identification. Shall you mind seeing her again?'

The lips moved slightly, without emitting a single sound, and there was neither a smile nor a grimace.

'Do you feel well enough for me to ask her to call in this morning?'

The man gave no sign of protest, and Maigret took advantage of this to allow himself a pause. He felt hot, almost stifled in the atmosphere of sickness and medicaments that pervaded the room.

He went to ask the Ward Sister if he could use the telephone.

'Are you going to keep on tormenting him?'

'His wife has got to identify him. . . . It'll only take a few minutes.'

He told the whole story, after a fashion, to Madame Maigret as they took their lunch in front of the window. 'She was at home,' he went on. 'She promised to come at once. I left instructions down below that she was to be allowed in. I walked about in the passage, where Professor Magnin eventually joined me.'

They had chatted together, standing in front of a window that overlooked the courtyard.

'Do you believe, as I do, that he's recovered his lucidity?' Maigret had asked.

'It's possible. . . . When I examined him just now he gave me the impression of knowing what was happening round about him. . . . But from a medical point of view I can't as yet give you a categorical answer. People imagine that we are infallible and can answer every question. But most of the time we're feeling our way. . . . I asked a neurologist to have a look at him this afternoon.'

'I suppose it would be difficult to put him in a private ward?'

'Not only difficult but impossible. Everything's full up. In some departments they've had to put beds in the corridors. . . . Or else he'd have to be taken to a private nursing home. . . .'

'Suppose his wife suggested it?'

'Do you think he'd like that himself?'

It was unlikely. If Keller had chosen to go off and live under the bridges it was not in order to find himself, as the result of an assault, living at his wife's expense.

She, meanwhile, emerged from the lift, looked round in some bewilderment, and Maigret went to receive her.

'How is he?'

She displayed little anxiety or emotion. She seemed, above all, to be out of her element here, and longing to get back as soon as possible to her flat on the Ile Saint-Louis and her budgerigars.

'He's quite calm. . . .'

'Has he recovered consciousness?'

'I think so, but I cannot prove it.'

'Am I to speak to him?'

He ushered her in ahead of him, and all the patients watched her walking across the polished floor of the ward. She, for her part, looked round for her husband, and of her own accord made her way towards the fifth bed, halting two or three yards from it as if she did not know what expression to assume.

Keller had seen her and was now watching her, with unchanged indifference.

She was extremely elegant in her beige shantung suit, with a hat to match, and her perfume mingled with the hospital smells.

'Do you recognize him?'

'Yes, it's him. . . . He's changed, but it's him. . . .'

There was a fresh silence, which was trying for everyone. At last she made up her mind to go forward, with a certain bravery. Her gloved fingers nervously fiddling with the clasp of her bag, she said:

'It's me, François. . . . I didn't expect to meet you again some day in such wretched circumstances. . . . They tell me you're going to recover very quickly. I'd like to help you. . . .'

What was he thinking, as he fixed that gaze on her? For seventeen or eighteen years he had been living in another world. It was as if he was surfacing to find himself confronted with a past from which he had fled.

His face betrayed no sign of bitterness. He merely gazed at the woman who had been his wife for so long, then turned his head a little to make sure that Maigret was still there.

And now the latter was explaining to Madame Maigret:

'I'd take my oath that he was asking me to bring this confrontation to an end.'

'You're talking about him as if you'd always known him.'

Was this not true, in a way? Maigret had never met Keller before, but during his career, how many confessions had he not listened to from men like Keller, in the privacy of his office? Perhaps not such extreme cases; but the human problem was the same, none the less.

'She did not insist on staying,' he went on. 'Before leaving him, she nearly opened her bag to take out some money. Fortunately she didn't do so. . . . In the corridor she asked me:

'"Do you think there's anything he needs?"

'And as I said no, she persisted:

'"I could perhaps hand over a certain sum for his benefit to the head of the hospital? . . . He'd be better in a private ward."

'"There's not one available . . ."

'She did not pursue the matter. "What ought I to do?"

'"Nothing for the moment. . . . I shall send an inspector to get your signature to a paper acknowledging that this is in fact your husband . . ."

'"What's the point, since it *is* François?"

'She went away at last. . . .'

They had finished eating and were sitting in front of their cups of coffee. Maigret had lit his pipe.

'Did you go back into the ward?'

'Yes. In spite of glares from the Ward Sister.'

He felt a kind of personal hostility towards her.

'Did he still not speak?'

'No. . . . I went on talking to him in a low voice while a houseman was attending the patient in the next bed.'

'What did you say to him?'

233

To Madame Maigret, this conversation over the coffee cups was almost a miracle. Usually she scarcely knew what cases her husband was dealing with. He would ring up to say he'd not be back for lunch or for dinner, sometimes that he was going to spend half the night in his office or elsewhere, and usually it was through the newspapers that she gathered any further information.

'I can't remember what I said to him,' he replied, somewhat uneasily. 'I wanted to gain his confidence. . . . I talked to him about Léa, who was waiting for me outside, about his possessions, which had been put away safely and which he would get back when he was discharged from hospital. . . . He seemed pleased at that.

'I also told him that he need not see his wife again if he didn't want to, that she had offered to pay for a private room for him but there was none available.

'I must have looked, from a distance, as though I were reciting my prayers. . . .

'"I assume you'd rather stay here than go into a nursing home?"'

'And did he still give no answer?'

Maigret looked embarrassed.

'I know it's silly, but I'm sure that he agreed with me, that we understood one another. . . . I tried to return to the subject of the assault. . . .

'"Were you asleep?"'

'We seemed to be playing cat and mouse. . . . I'm convinced that he has made up his mind once and for all to say nothing. And a man who has been capable of living rough for so long is capable of holding his tongue. . . .'

'Why should he hold his tongue?'

'I don't know.'

'To avoid accusing somebody?'

'Possibly.'

'Whom?'

234

Maigret stood up, shrugging his broad shoulders.

'If I knew that, I should be the Lord Almighty. . . . I feel like giving you Professor Magnin's answer: I don't work miracles either.'

'So, all in all, you've learnt nothing new?'

'No.'

That was not strictly true. He was convinced that he had learnt a great deal about the Doc. Even though he had not yet begun to know him really, certain secret and somewhat mysterious contacts seemed to have been made between them.

'At one point . . .'

He seemed reluctant to continue, as though he was afraid of being accused of childishness. Well, it couldn't be helped; he needed to talk.

'At one point, I took the marble out of my pocket. . . . Actually I didn't do so consciously. . . . I felt it in my hand and it occurred to me to slip it into his. . . . I must probably have appeared rather ridiculous. . . . But he didn't need to look at it. He recognized it by the feel. . . . I'm sure, whatever the Sister may say, that his face lit up and that there was a sparkle of joy and mischief in his eyes. . . .'

'And yet he never spoke?'

'That's another matter. He's not going to help me. . . . He's made up his mind not to help me, not to tell me anything, and I shall have to find out the truth by myself. . . .'

Was it the challenge that excited him? His wife had seldom seen him show such passionate and lively interest in a case.

'Downstairs, Léa was waiting for me on the pavement, chewing my tobacco, and I gave her what was left in my pouch.'

'D'you suppose she knows anything?'

'If she did she would tell me. . . . There's a greater solidarity between these people than between those who live in the normal way, in houses. I'm convinced that at this very moment they'll be discussing it amongst themselves, conducting their own investigation on the side of mine. . . .

'I learned just one fact from her which might be of interest: that Keller hasn't always slept under the Pont Marie and has belonged to that district, so to speak, only for the past two years. . . .'

'Where did he live before that?'

'On another part of the river bank, higher up, on the Quai de la Rapée, under the Pont de Bercy. . . .'

'Do they often change their quarters?'

'No. It's as much a business as moving house for us. . . . Each of them chooses his own corner and sticks to it, more or less.'

Finally, as though to reward himself or to maintain his good humour, he poured himself a small glass of sloe brandy. After which he picked up his hat and kissed Madame Maigret.

'See you this evening.'

'D'you expect to be back for dinner?'

He did not know, any more than she did. To tell the truth, he had not the slightest idea what he was going to do.

Since that morning, Torrence had been checking the statements of the insurance agent and his stuttering friend. He must already have questioned the concierge in the Rue de Turenne and the wine merchant at the corner of the Rue des Francs-Bourgeois.

They would soon know whether the story of the dog Nestor was true or a complete invention. And even if it was true, that would not prove that the two men had not attacked the Doc.

For what reason? At this stage of the inquiry Maigret could see none.

What reason might Madame Keller have had, for instance, for having her husband thrown into the Seine? And by whom?

One day when a penniless and insignificant fellow had been killed in equally mysterious circumstances, Maigret had said to the examining magistrate:

'Poor chaps don't get murdered.'

Down-and-outs don't get murdered, either. But somebody had in fact tried to get rid of François Keller.

Maigret stood on the platform of the bus, absentmindedly listening to the whispered conversation of two lovers beside him, when a hypothesis occurred to him. It was the expression 'poor chaps' that had suggested it.

As soon as he was back in his office he rang up Madame Keller. She was not at home. The maid informed him that she was lunching in town with a friend, but didn't know in which restaurant. Then he rang up Jacqueline Rousselet.

'I gather you've seen Mother. . . . She telephoned me last night, after your visit. She's just called me again, less than an hour ago. . . . So it really is my father. . . .'

'There appears to be no doubt about his identity.'

'And you've still no idea why he was attacked? Could there have been a fight?'

'Was your father given to fighting?'

'He was the gentlest creature on earth, at least at the time when I was living with him, and I think he'd have let himself be struck without hitting back. . . .'

'Are you acquainted with your mother's business affairs?'

'What business affairs?'

'When she married, she was not rich, and she had no idea that she would become rich one day. Nor had your father. . . . I wonder, under the circumstances, whether they thought of drawing up a marriage settlement. If not, they must have been married under the system of joint property holding, in which case your father could claim his half of the fortune. . . .'

'That's not the case,' she replied unhesitatingly.

'You're quite sure of that?'

'Mother will confirm it. . . . The lawyers raised the question at the time of my own marriage. My father and mother retained control of their separate properties. . . .'

'Would it be indiscreet to inquire your lawyer's name?'

'Maître Prijean, Rue de Bassano.'

'Many thanks.'

'Do you want me to go to the hospital?'

'Do you want to yourself?'

'I'm not sure that he would like a visit from me. He said nothing to my mother. Apparently he pretended not to recognize her. . . .'

'Perhaps, indeed, it would be better not to go. . . .'

He needed to feel that he was doing something, and he promptly rang up Maître Prijean. There was a lengthy argument, and he even had to produce the threat of a rogatory warrant signed by the examining magistrate, for the lawyer objected on grounds of professional secrecy.

'I am just asking you to tell me whether Monsieur and Madame Keller, of Mulhouse, were married under the system of separate property holding, and if you handled the settlement. . . .'

At last there was a curt 'yes'. The lawyer rang off.

In other words, François Keller actually was a poor chap, who had no claims on the fortune amassed by the scrap-metal merchant, which had eventually come down to his wife.

The switchboard operator was somewhat surprised when the Superintendent demanded:

'Put me through to the Suresnes lock.'

'The lock?'

'Yes, the lock. They must be on the phone, aren't they?'

'O.K., Chief.'

Eventually he got through to the head lock-keeper and introduced himself.

'I suppose you make a note of the boats that pass from one reach to another? . . . I want to know where I can find a motor barge which must have gone through your lock late yesterday afternoon. . . . A Flemish name, *De Zwarte Zwaan*. . . .'

'Yes, I know it. . . . Two brothers, a little fair-haired woman and a baby. They went through on the last opening, and spent the night just below the gates.'

'Have you any idea where they are now?'

'Wait a minute. . . . They've got a good diesel and the stream is still pretty fast . . .'

Maigret could hear him calculating, muttering the names of towns and villages to himself.

'If I'm not mistaken they must have covered about a hundred kilometres, which would bring them somewhere around Juziers . . . . In any case they're likely to have gone beyond Poissy. . . . It depends how long they had to wait at the locks at Bougival and Carrière. . . .'

A few minutes later the Superintendent was in the inspectors' room.

'Does anyone here know the Seine well?'

A voice asked: 'Upstream or downstream?'

'Downstream. Somewhere near Poissy. . . . Probably a bit beyond. . . .'

'I do! I've got a small boat and I go down to Le Havre every year in the summer holidays. . . . I know the neighbourhood of Poissy particularly well because that's where I dock my boat. . . .'

The speaker was Neveu, a detective of undistinguished

petty-bourgeois appearance whom Maigret had not suspected of such sporting proclivities.

'Take one of the cars in the yard. . . . You can drive me. . . .'

The Superintendent kept Neveu waiting, for Torrence had just come back to report on the result of his inquiry.

'It's quite true that the dog died on Monday night,' he declared. 'Madame Guillot is still in tears when she talks about it. . . . The two men put the body into the boot of the car and went to throw it into the Seine. The people in the café in the Rue de Turenne remember them. They came in a little before closing time. . . .'

'What time was that?'

'Shortly after half-past eleven. . . . Some card-players were just finishing a game of *belote*, and the landlord was waiting to pull down his shutters. . . . Madame Guillot also admitted shamefacedly that her husband had come home late, she didn't know how late for she'd fallen asleep, and that he was half drunk. She felt obliged to assure me that this was most unusual, that it was because he'd been so upset.'

Eventually Maigret took his seat beside Neveu in the car, which threaded its way towards the Porte d'Asnières.

'We can't follow the Seine all the way,' the detective explained.

'You're sure the barge has gone beyond Poissy?'

'So the head lock-keeper says. . . .'

They began to see open cars along the road, and sometimes the driver had a girl's arm round his waist. People were planting flowers in their gardens. Somewhere they saw a woman in a light blue dress feeding her hens.

Maigret sat drowsing with his eyes half closed, apparently uninterested in the landscape, and every time the Seine came into view Neveu would tell him where they had got to.

Thus they saw a number of boats peacefully travelling up or down the river. On one, a woman was washing her linen on deck; on a second, another woman held the tiller, with a child of three or four years old sitting at her feet.

The car stopped at Meulan, where several barges were moored.

'What name did you say, Chief?'

'*De Zwarte Zwaan* . . . means The Black Swan.'

The inspector got out of the car, walked across the quayside and began a conversation with some bargees; Maigret, from a distance, watched them gesticulating.

'They came past half an hour ago,' Neveu announced, resuming his seat at the wheel. 'As they're doing a good ten kilometres an hour or more, they can't be far from Juziers now. . . .'

It was a little way beyond that village, by the island of Montalet, that they caught sight of the Belgian barge travelling downstream.

They drove two or three hundred yards past it and Maigret took up his position on the bank. Here, unconcerned lest he appear ridiculous, he started making great gestures.

Hubert, the younger of the two brothers, was at the wheel, a cigarette between his lips. He recognized the Superintendent, went to lean over the hatchway and slowed down the engine. A moment later Jef Van Houtte, tall and thin, appeared on deck, head first, then shoulders, finally his whole long gangling body.

'I've got to talk to you,' the Superintendent shouted, using his hands as a megaphone.

Jef made signs to show that he could hear nothing on account of the engine, and Maigret tried to explain that he must stop.

They were in the open countryside. About one mile away they could see red and grey roofs, white walls, a petrol pump and a gilt inn sign. Hubert Van Houtte reversed the engine. The young woman had now put her head through the hatchway and was evidently asking her husband what was happening.

A somewhat confused manœuvre followed. From a distance it looked as if the two men were not in agreement. Jef, the elder, was pointing to the village, as though ordering his brother to make for it, while Hubert, at the tiller, was already proceeding towards the bank.

Since there was no alternative, Jef finally flung out a mooring rope and Inspector Neveu, as an experienced sailor, caught hold of it with a certain pride. There were some bollards on the bank and a few moments later the barge had come to a halt in the stream.

'What d'you want now?' shouted Jef, who looked furious.

The barge lay several yards from the bank and he made no attempt to put down the landing-plank.

'What's the idea, stopping the boat like that? It's the right way to have an accident, I can tell you that.'

'I need to talk to you . . .' Maigret retorted.

'You talked to me as much as you wanted to in Paris. I've got nothing further to tell you.'

'In that case I shall be obliged to summon you to my office . . .'

'What's that? . . . Me go back to Paris without unloading my slates?'

Hubert, more accommodating, was motioning his brother to calm down. Eventually he flung the landing-plank over to the bank and crossed it like an acrobat to make it safe.

'Don't mind him, monsieur. It's quite true what he says. You can't stop a boat just anywhere. . . .'

Maigret went on deck, feeling somewhat uneasy, since he did not know exactly what questions he was going to ask. Moreover, he was in the department of Seine-et-Oise, and according to regulations it was up to the Versailles police to get a rogatory warrant and question the Flemings.

'Say, are you going to keep us a long time?'

'I don't know.'

'Because we're not going to spend the night here, you know. We've just time to get to Mantes before sunset.'

'In that case, carry on with your journey.'

'D'you want to come with us?'

'Why not? . . .'

'Well this is something new!'

'Do you hear, Neveu? . . . Go on to Mantes with the car. . . .'

'What d'you think of this Hubert?'

'There's nothing to be done, Jef. With the police, it's no use getting angry.'

The young woman's blonde head could still be seen on a level with the deck, and the babble of a child sounded down below. As on the previous day, a good smell of cooking rose from the living quarters.

The plank which served as a footbridge was withdrawn. Neveu, before getting back into the car, unfastened the mooring rope, which sent up a glittering shower as it splashed into the water.

'If you've got more questions to ask, I'm ready. . . .'

Once again the chugging of the diesel could be heard, and the lapping of water against the hull.

Maigret, standing at the stern of the barge, was slowly filling his pipe and wondering what he was going to say.

CHAPTER SIX

'YOU DID TELL ME YESTERDAY, didn't you, that the car was a red one?'

'Yes, monsieur' (he pronounced the word *mossieu*, as circus clowns do). 'It was as red as the red on that flag. . . .'

He pointed to the Belgian flag, red, yellow and black, waving above the stern of the boat.

Hubert was at the tiller and the blonde young woman had gone back to her child down below. As for Jef, his face betrayed two conflicting feelings, between which he seemed torn. On the one hand, Flemish hospitality required him to give a decent welcome to the Superintendent, as to any other visitor, and even to offer him a small glass of gin; on the other hand, he was still annoyed at having been stopped in mid-journey and he considered this further interrogation as an insult to his dignity.

He cast a crafty look at the intruder, whose town suit and black hat looked out of place on board the boat.

As for Maigret, he felt somewhat ill at ease and still uncertain how to tackle his difficult interlocutor. He had a long acquaintance with men of this sort, simple and rather stupid, who assume that one wants to take advantage of their naïvety, and because they are mistrustful, quickly become aggressive, or else withdraw into stubborn mutism.

This was not the first time the Superintendent had conducted an inquiry on board a barge, although he had not done so for a long time. He remembered, in particular, what used to be called a 'stable-boat', drawn along canals by a horse that spent the night on board with its master.

Those boats were built of wood and had a pleasant smell, due to the resin with which they were periodically coated. Inside they were as neat as any suburban bungalow.

Here, through the open door, he observed a more bourgeois interior, with heavy oak furniture, rugs, vases on embroidered mats and a profusion of gleaming brass.

'Where were you when you heard a noise on the quayside? You were busy working on the engine, I believe?'

Jef's pale eyes were fixed on Maigret and he seemed to be still undecided what attitude to adopt, fighting down his anger.

'See here, monsieur. . . . Yesterday morning you were there when the magistrate asked me all those questions. You asked me some yourself. . . . And the little fellow who was with the magistrate wrote it all down on paper. He came back in the afternoon to make me sign my statement. Isn't that right?'

'Quite correct.'

'Well, now you're asking me the same things. And I tell you it's not right . . . because, if I make any mistake, you'll think I've been telling you lies. . . . I'm not an educated man, monsieur. I didn't hardly go to school . . . nor did Hubert. . . . But we're both workers and Anneke's a working woman too . . .'

'I'm only trying to check up.'

'Check up on nothing. . . . I was quietly in my boat, as you were at home. . . . A man was thrown into the water and I jumped into the punt to fish him out. I'm not asking for a reward nor for congratulations. But that's no reason to come bothering me with questions. . . . That's the way it seems to me, monsieur. . . .'

'We've found the two men who were in the red car. . . .'

Did Jef's brow really darken, or was it just an impression of Maigret's?

'Well, you've only got to ask them. . . .'

'They declare that it was not midnight, but half past eleven, when they drove down on to the bank.'

'Perhaps their watches were slow, eh?'

'We checked their evidence. . . . They went on to a café in the Rue de Turenne and got there at twenty minutes to twelve. . . .'

Jef looked at his brother, who had turned a quick glance towards him.

'We might go and sit inside?'

The big cabin served both as kitchen and living-room, and a stew was simmering on the white enamel stove. Madame Van Houtte, who was nursing her baby, hurried into a bedroom where the superintendent glimpsed a bed covered with a quilt.

'Sit down, won't you?'

Still hesitant, with apparent reluctance he opened the glass-fronted sideboard and took out a brown earthenware jug of gin and two thick-bottomed glasses.

Through the square windows they could see the trees along the bank, and occasionally the red roof of a villa. There was a longish silence during which Jef remained standing, his glass in his hand. Finally he drank a mouthful, holding it for some time in his mouth before swallowing it.

'Is he dead?' he asked at last.

'No. He's recovered consciousness.'

'What does he say?'

It was Maigret's turn, now, to remain silent. He looked round at the embroidered curtains on the windows, the brass containers holding green pot-plants, a photograph on the wall, in a gilt frame, showing a stout middle-aged man in a sailor's sweater and cap.

This was the kind of figure one often saw on boats, thick-set and broad-shouldered, with a walrus moustache.

'Is that your father?'

'No, monsieur. It's Anneke's father. . . .'

'Was your father a bargee too?'

'My father was a docker, monsieur, at Antwerp. . . . And that's not a job for a Christian, you know. . . .'

'That was why you became a bargee?'

'I've been working on barges since I was thirteen and nobody's ever had any complaints to make about me.'

'Last night . . .'

Maigret thought he had disarmed him by these indirect questions, but the man shook his head.

'No, monsieur. . . . It's not on. . . . You've only got to look at that paper again. . . .'

'And what if I should discover that your answers were untrue?'

'Then you can do what you like. . . .'

'Did you see the two men from the car come out from under the Pont Marie?'

'Read the statement. . . .'

'They declare that they never went past your barge. . . .'

'People can say what they like, can't they?'

'They also assert that they saw nobody on the quayside and that they only threw a dead dog into the Seine. . . .'

'It's not my fault if they say it was a dog.'

The young woman came back without the child, which she must have put to bed. She spoke a few words in Flemish to her husband, who nodded, and she began to sieve the soup.

The boat was slowing down. Maigret wondered if they had reached Mantes already, but through the window he presently caught sight of a tug followed by three barges, slowly travelling upstream. They were passing under a bridge.

'Does the boat belong to you?'

'It's mine and Anneke's, yes.'

247

'Your brother is not co-owner?'

'What's that mean?'

'He doesn't own part of it?'

'No, monsieur. The boat's mine and Anneke's. . . .'

'So your brother works for you?'

'Yes, monsieur.'

Maigret was getting used to his accent, his repeated *monsieurs* and *n'est-ce-pas*. It was clear from the young woman's expression that she understood only a few words of French and was wondering what the two men could possibly be saying.

'How long has he been doing so?'

'About a couple of years. . . .'

'Before that, did he work on another boat? In France?'

'He worked like we do, sometimes in Belgium, sometimes in France. It depends on the cargoes. . . .'

'Why did you send for him?'

'Because I needed somebody, you see. It's a big boat, you know. . . .'

'And before?'

'Before what?'

'Before you sent for your brother?'

Maigret was moving cautiously, choosing the most innocuous questions lest his interlocutor should jib again.

'I don't follow. . . .'

'Was there somebody else to help you?'

'Sure. . . .'

Before replying, he had glanced at his wife as though to make certain that she had not understood.

'Who was it?'

Jef filled the glasses so as to give himself time to think.

'It was me,' he finally declared.

'You were the crew?'

'I was the mechanic.'

'Who was the skipper?'

'I wonder if you've really got the right to ask me all these questions. . . . A man's private life is his own business. And I'm a Belgian, monsieur. . . .'

As he began to lose his temper his accent became more marked.

'That's no way to behave, I must say. My business doesn't concern anybody else and just because I'm a Fleming isn't a reason to go meddle with my belongings. . . .'

Maigret took a few moments to understand the expression and could not restrain a smile.

'I might come back with an interpreter and question your wife.'

'I won't have Anneke bothered. . . .'

'You may have to, if I bring a warrant from the magistrate. . . . I wonder now if it would not be simpler to take you all three back to Paris. . . .'

'And then what would become of the boat? . . . That you've no right to do, I'm sure. . . .'

'Why don't you just answer my questions?'

Van Houtte, with lowered head, glanced furtively at Maigret, like a schoolboy planning mischief.

'Because it's my own business. . . .'

So far, he was quite right. Maigret had no serious pretext for worrying him in this way. He was acting on intuition. He had been struck by the attitude of the bargee when he went on board near Juziers.

Jef was not quite the same man as he had been in Paris. He had been surprised to see the Superintendent on the river bank and had reacted sharply. Since then he had remained suspicious and withdrawn, without that glint in the eyes, that touch of humour he had displayed on the Quai des Célestins.

'Well, am I to take you along?'

'You'll have to have a reason. We've got laws. . . .'

'The reason is that you refuse to answer ordinary routine questions.'

The diesel was still chugging away and Hubert's long legs could be glimpsed as he stood beside the tiller.

'Because you're trying to confuse me. . . .'

'I'm not trying to confuse you but to establish the truth.'

'What truth?'

He seemed of two minds, now sure of his rights and now, on the contrary, obviously ill at ease.

'When did you buy this boat?'

'I didn't buy it.'

'But yet it belongs to you?'

'Yes, monsieur, it belongs to me and it belongs to my wife. . . .'

'In other words, it was when you married her that you became owner of it. . . . Did the boat belong to her?'

'What's so odd about that? We got married quite legally, in front of the burgomaster and the priest. . . .'

'Until then her father had been skipper of the *Zwarte Zwaan*?'

'Yes, monsieur. . . . It was old Willems. . . .'

'He had no other children?'

'No, monsieur.'

'What happened to his wife?'

'She'd been dead a year already. . . .'

'Were you working on the boat by then?'

'Yes, monsieur.'

'Since when?'

'Old Willems took me on when his wife died. . . . It was at Oudenarde. . . .'

'Were you working on another boat at the time?'

'Yes, monsieur. The *Drie Gebrouders*. . . .'

'Why did you change?'

'Because the *Drie Gebrouders* was an old barge that scarcely ever came to France and mostly carried coal. . . .'

250

'You dislike carrying coal?'

'It's dirty. . . .'

'So you came aboard this boat about three years ago.
. . . How old was Anneke at that time?'

On hearing her name, she glanced at them with
curiosity.

'Eighteen, *n'est-ce-pas*?'

'Her mother had just died . . .'

'Yes, monsieur. At Oudenarde, as I've already told
you . . .'

He was listening to the sound of the engine, and looking
at the river bank; then he went up to say a word to his
brother, who slowed down to pass underneath a railway
bridge.

Maigret patiently picked up his tangled skein, trying
to follow a very slender thread.

'Until then, they had run the boat as a family . . .
when the mother died they needed somebody. . . . Is that
right?'

'That's right.'

'You looked after the engine. . . .'

'The engine and all the rest. On board you've got to
do a bit of everything. . . .'

'Did you fall in love with Anneke right away?'

'That's a personal matter, monsieur, *n'est-ce-pas*? . . .
That's my business and her business. . . .'

'When did you get married?'

'It'll be two years come next month. . . .'

'When did Willems die? Is that his portrait on the
wall?'

'That's him.'

'When did he die?'

'Six weeks before our wedding. . . .'

More and more, Maigret had the feeling that his
progress was discouragingly slow, and he summoned up

all his patience, moving round in ever narrowing circles so as not to scare the Fleming.

'Had the banns been published when Willems died?'

'In our country they publish the banns three weeks before the wedding . . . I don't know what they do in France.'

'But the marriage had been arranged?'

'Must have been, since we got married. . . .'

'Would you put that question to your wife?'

'Why should I put a question like that to her?'

'Otherwise I shall be obliged to have an interpreter do so. . . .'

'Well . . .'

He was about to say: 'You do that!'

And Maigret would have been most embarrassed. They were in the department of Seine-et-Oise now, and the Superintendent was not entitled to carry on such an inquiry.

By chance, Van Houtte changed his mind, and spoke to his wife in their own language. She blushed in surprise, looked at her husband, and then at their guest, saying something with a slight smile.

'Would you translate?'

'Well, she says, you see, that we'd loved each other for a long time . . .'

'For nearly a year, by then?'

'Almost right away. . . .'

'In other words, it began as soon as you came on board.'

'What's wrong . . .'

Maigret interrupted. 'What I'm wondering is whether Willems knew about it. . . .'

Jef did not answer.

'I suppose that to begin with, at all events, like most other lovers, you kept out of his way? . . .'

Once more the bargee was staring out of the window.

'We're nearly there now. My brother needs me on deck. . . .'

Maigret followed him up, and there, in fact, were the wharfs of Mantes-la-Jolie, the bridge, and a dozen barges moored in the river port.

The engine had slowed down. When it reversed, a wash of great bubbles broke around the stern. There were people watching, there were other boats; a boy of about twelve years old caught hold of the mooring rope.

It was obvious that the presence of Maigret in his town suit and felt hat aroused some curiosity.

From one of the barges, somebody hailed Jef in Flemish and he replied in the same tongue, carefully manœuvring his boat meanwhile.

Inspector Neveu was standing on the quay, a cigarette between his lips, beside the little black car, and not far from an enormous pile of bricks.

'I hope you're going to leave us alone now? It's time for us to eat. People like us get up at five in the morning. . . .'

'You haven't answered my question.'

'Which question?'

'You haven't told me whether Willems was aware of your relations with his daughter.'

'Did I marry her or didn't I?'

'You married her after he died. . . .'

'Was it my fault that he died?'

'Had he been ill for a long time?'

Once again they were standing in the stern of the boat and Hubert was listening to them, with a puzzled frown.

'He was never ill in his life, unless being drunk every night is an illness. . . .'

Maigret might have been mistaken, but it seemed to him that Hubert was surprised by the turn their talk had taken, and was watching his brother with a peculiar expression.

253

'Did he die of delirium tremens?'

'What's that?'

'The way drunkards usually end up. . . . They have an attack which . . .'

'He didn't have any attack. . . . He was so tight that he fell. . . .'

'Into the water?'

Jef did not seem to welcome the presence of his brother, who was still listening.

'Into the water, yes. . . .'

'Was it in France that this happened?'

He nodded again.

'In Paris?'

'Paris was where he used to drink most. . . .'

'Why?'

'Because he used to meet some woman, I don't know where, and they spent part of the night getting drunk together. . . .'

'D'you know the woman?'

'I don't know her name.'

'Nor where she lives?'

'No.'

'But you saw her with him?'

'I met them together and once I saw them go into a hotel. . . . There's no point in telling Anneke. . . .'

'Doesn't she know how her father died?'

'She knows how he died, but she was never told about the woman. . . .'

'Would you recognize her?'

'Maybe . . . I'm not sure. . . .'

'Was she with him at the time of the accident?'

'I don't know.'

'How did it happen?'

'I can't tell you, for I wasn't there. . . .'

'Where were you?'

'In my bunk. . . .'

'And Anneke?'

'In her bunk. . . .'

'What time was it?'

His answers came unwillingly, but they came none the less.

'After two in the morning. . . .'

'Was it usual for Willems to come back so late?'

'In Paris, yes, on account of that woman. . . .'

'What happened?'

'I've told you. He fell in.'

'While he was crossing the gangway?'

'I suppose so.'

'Was it in summer?'

'In December. . . .'

'Did you hear a noise when he fell?'

'I heard something bumping against the hull.'

'And cries?'

'He didn't call out.'

'Did you hurry to help him?'

'Of course.'

'Without bothering to get dressed?'

'I pulled on my trousers. . . .'

'Did Anneke hear too?'

'Not immediately. . . . She woke up when I went on deck.'

'While you were going up, or after you were already there?'

There was something very like hatred in Jef's look.

'Ask her. . . . If you think I can remember . . .'

'You saw Willems in the water?'

'I saw nothing at all. . . . I could only hear something moving. . . .'

'Couldn't he swim?'

'He could swim. I suppose he wasn't able to . . .'

'Did you jump into the punt, as you did on Monday night?'

'Yes, monsieur.'

'Did you succeed in pulling him out of the water?'

'Not for a good ten minutes, because each time I tried to catch hold of him he disappeared. . . .'

'Was Anneke standing on deck?'

'Yes, monsieur.'

'Was the man dead when you eventually brought him out?'

'I didn't know as yet that he was dead. . . . I know he was purple in the face, that's all.'

'Did the doctor come? The police?'

'Yes, monsieur. Are you going to ask me any more questions?'

'Where did this take place?'

'In Paris, I told you.'

'Whereabouts in Paris?'

'We had taken on some wine at Macon and we were unloading it on the Quai de la Rapée. . . .'

Maigret managed to betray no surprise, no satisfaction. He suddenly seemed to have become more good-humoured, as though his nerves were relaxed.

'I think I've nearly done. . . . Willems was drowned one night by the Quai de la Rapée, while you were asleep on board and his daughter was asleep too. . . . Is that correct?'

Jef blinked.

'About a month later you married Anneke. . . .'

'It wouldn't have been proper to live on the boat together without being married. . . .'

'At what point did you send for your brother?'

'Right away. . . . Three or four days after.'

'After your marriage?'

'No. After the accident. . . .'

256

The sun had disappeared behind the rosy roofs, but a strangely unreal, disturbing light still lingered.

Hubert, standing motionless at the tiller, seemed to be brooding.

'I suppose *you* don't know anything about it?'

'About what?'

'About what happened on Monday night?'

'I was out dancing in the Rue de Lappe. . . .'

'And about Willems's death?'

'I was in Belgium when I got the telegram. . . .'

'Well, is that all?' asked Jef Van Houtte impatiently. 'Are we going to be able to eat our soup?'

And Maigret replied unconcernedly, with the utmost calm:

'I'm afraid not.'

This produced a shock. Hubert looked up sharply and stared, not at the Superintendent but at his brother. As for Jef, he demanded with an even more aggressive look in his eyes:

'And will you tell me why I mayn't eat my soup?'

'Because I intend to take you back to Paris.'

'You've no right to do that. . . .'

'In an hour's time I can procure a summons signed by the examining magistrate. . . .'

'And what for, may I ask?'

'So that we can carry on this interrogation somewhere else. . . .'

'I've said all that I had to say.'

'And in order to bring you face to face with the tramp that you pulled out of the Seine on Monday night. . . .'

Jef turned to his brother as though appealing for help.

'Hubert, do you believe the Superintendent has the right . . .'

But Hubert kept silent.

'Do you want to take me in your car?'

He had recognized it on the quayside, near to where Neveu was standing, and he pointed to it.

'And when shall I be allowed to come back to my boat?'

'Maybe tomorrow.'

'And if not tomorrow?'

'In that case, it's possible that you might never come back to it. . . .'

'What's that you're saying?'

He had clenched his fists and for a moment seemed about to rush at Maigret.

'And what about my wife? . . . And my child? . . . What's it all about, what are these stories you've made up? . . . I'm going to tell my consul. . . .'

'You're entitled to do so.'

'You're joking, aren't you?'

He still could not believe it.

'A man who's done nothing can't be arrested on his own boat. . . .'

'I'm not arresting you.'

'What d'you think you're doing, then?'

'I'm going to take you to Paris to confront you with a witness who cannot travel.'

'I don't even know the man, I don't . . . I pulled him out of the water because he was calling for help. . . . If I'd known . . .'

His wife emerged and put a question to him in Flemish. He replied volubly. She looked up at the three men in turn, then she spoke again and Maigret could have sworn she was advising her husband to go along with the Superintendent.

'And where am I going to sleep?'

'You'll be given a bed at the Quai des Orfèvres.'

'In jail?'

'No. At Police Headquarters.'

'Am I allowed to change my clothes?'

The Superintendent gave permission, and Jef disappeared with his wife. Hubert, left face to face with Maigret, said nothing, staring blankly at the passers-by and the cars on the bank. Maigret said nothing either, and he felt exhausted by that desultory interrogation, during which he had repeatedly been so disheartened as to believe he would never get anywhere.

Hubert broke the silence first, in a conciliatory tone.

'You mustn't mind him. . . . He's hot-tempered, but he doesn't mean any harm. . . .'

'Was Willems aware of Jef's relations with his daughter?'

'On board a boat it's not easy to hide things. . . .'

'Do you think he approved of the marriage?'

'I wasn't there. . . .'

'And do you believe he fell into the water while crossing the gangway, one night when he was drunk?'

'That often happens, you know. A lot of boatmen die that way. . . .'

Downstairs an argument was going on in Flemish, and Anneke's voice had a pleading note whereas her husband's sounded angry. Could he yet again be threatening to refuse to go with the Superintendent?

She must have won the day, for Jef eventually emerged on deck, his hair sleek and still damp. He was wearing a white shirt that showed off his tanned skin, a blue suit that was almost new, a striped tie and black shoes, as though he was going to Sunday mass.

He spoke to his brother again in Flemish, without a look at Maigret, then left the boat and made his way to the black car, where he stood waiting.

The Superintendent opened the door, while Neveu watched them both in astonishment.

'Where to, Chief?'

'Quai des Orfèvres.'

They completed the journey in darkness, the headlamps shining now on trees, now on village houses, finally on the grey streets of the outer suburbs.

Maigret did not utter a word, but smoked his pipe in one corner. Jef Van Houtte was equally mute, and Neveu, impressed by this unusual silence, wondered what could have happened.

He ventured to ask: 'Any luck, Chief?'

Receiving no reply, he just kept on driving the car.

It was eight o'clock at night when they entered the courtyard of Police Headquarters. Only a few windows still showed lights, but old Joseph was there at his post.

In the inspectors' room, there were only three or four men, among them Lapointe busy at his typewriter.

'Get them to send up some sandwiches and beer.'

'For how many?'

'For two. . . . No, three, for I might need you. Are you free?'

'Yes, Chief.'

Standing in the middle of Maigret's office the bargee seemed even taller and thinner, and his features more strongly marked.

'You may sit down, Monsieur Van Houtte.'

Jef scowled at the word 'monsieur', interpreting it as a sort of threat.

'They're going to bring us sandwiches. . . .'

'And when can I see the consul?'

'Tomorrow morning.'

Sitting at his desk, Maigret rang up his wife.

'I shan't be back for dinner. . . . No . . . I might have to stay here part of the night. . . .'

She must have been longing to ask him heaps of questions, but she confined herself to one, knowing her husband's interest in the dosser.

'He's not dead?'

'No.'

She did not ask him if he had arrested anyone. Since he had telephoned from his office and was planning to stay there part of the night, that meant that a cross-examination was taking place, or was about to begin.

'Good night . . .'

He looked up at Jef in some annoyance.

'I asked you to sit down. . . .'

It worried him to see that tall figure motionless in the middle of the room.

'And suppose I don't want to sit down? I've a right to stand up, haven't I?'

Maigret merely heaved a sigh, and sat waiting patiently for the beer and sandwiches to be brought up from the Brasserie Dauphine.

CHAPTER SEVEN

SUCH NIGHTS, which eight times out of ten ended with a confession, had in course of time acquired their own rules, their traditions as it were, like stage plays which have been performed hundreds of times.

The inspectors on duty in the various departments had immediately understood what was happening, as had the waiter from the Brasserie Dauphine who brought up sandwiches and beer.

His bad temper, his ill-repressed anger did not prevent the Fleming from eating heartily and tossing off his first glass of beer at one go, meanwhile watching Maigret out of the corner of his eye.

Deliberately, by way of defiance or protest, he ate in a disgusting way, munching noisily with his mouth open and spitting out a hard morsel of ham on to the floor as he might have spat it into the water.

The Superintendent, seemingly calm and bland, ignored this provocative behaviour and let the man pace to and fro about the room like a caged animal.

Had he been right? Had he been wrong? The most difficult thing in an investigation is to know at what point to play high. Now there are no established rules. It depends on no particular factor; it's a matter of intuition.

On certain occasions he had attacked without any solid evidence to go on, and had succeeded in a few hours. At other times, on the contrary, with all the trumps in his hand and a dozen witnesses, it had taken him the whole night.

It was important, too, to find the right tone, which was different for each interlocutor, and this was what he was hunting for as he finished eating, with his eye still on the bargee.

'Do you want any more sandwiches?'

'All I want is to go back to my boat and my little wife!'

He was bound, in the end, to get tired of walking round and round, and would sit down. It was useless trying to rush that sort of man; and the way to deal with him was probably by the 'wheedling' method, starting gently, without accusing him, making him admit to one important inconsistency, then another, some trivial mistake, so as little by little to get him caught up in the wheels.

The two men were alone. Maigret had sent Lapointe on an errand.

'Listen to me, Van Houtte. . . .'

'I've been listening to you for hours, haven't I?'

'If it's gone on so long, it's perhaps because you've not been answering me frankly. . . .'

'You're going to call me a liar, maybe?'

'I'm not accusing you of lying, but of not telling me everything. . . .'

'And suppose I were to begin asking *you* questions about your wife or your children. . . .'

'You had a difficult childhood. . . . Did your mother take much care of you?'

'So it's my mother's turn now, is it? . . . I'd have you know that my mother died when I was only five. . . . And she was a decent woman, a saintly woman, and if she's looking down at me from Heaven at this moment . . .'

Maigret kept a straight face.

'Did your father not remarry?'

'That's another matter. My father drank too much.'

'At what age did you begin to earn your living?'

'I worked on a barge when I was thirteen, I told you that. . . .'

'Have you other brothers besides Hubert? A sister?'

'I've got a sister. And so what?'

'Nothing. We're becoming acquainted. . . .'

'Well then, if we're to become acquainted, I ought to be putting questions to you, too. . . .'

'I should raise no objection. . . .'

'You say that because you're in your own office and you think yourself almighty. . . .'

Maigret had known from the start that it would be a lengthy, difficult business, because Van Houtte was not intelligent.

Almost invariably, it was stupid people that gave him the most trouble, because they stubbornly refuse to answer, and have no hesitation about denying what they have asserted an hour before, without worrying when their contradictions are pointed out.

Often, with an intelligent suspect, one merely has to disclose the flaw in his line of argument, in his system, and before long everything collapses.

'I think I'm right in assuming that you're a good worker. . . .'

A suspicious sideways glance.

'Sure, I've always worked hard.'

'Some bosses must have taken an unfair advantage of your youth and willingness. . . . One day you met Louis Willems, who drank as your father used to.'

Standing motionless in the middle of the room, Jef was watching him like an animal scenting danger but still uncertain how the attack will come.

'I'm convinced that but for Anneke you'd not have stayed on board the *Zwarte Zwaan*, but moved to another boat. . . .'

'Madame Willems was a decent woman, too.'

'And she was not proud or domineering like her husband. . . .'

'Who told you he was proud?'

'Wasn't he?'

'He was the boss, and he wanted everyone to know it.'

'I'd wager that Madame Willems, if she had lived, would not have been opposed to your marrying her daughter. . . .'

He might have been an idiot, but he had a wild creature's instinct, and this time Maigret had gone too fast.

'That's your story, isn't it? Well, can't I invent stories too?'

'It's your story, such as I imagine it, though I may be mistaken.'

'And it's bad luck on me if I get stuck in jail because of your mistake. . . .'

'Let me finish. . . . You had a difficult childhood. . . . When you were still a boy you worked as hard as a man. . . . Then you met Anneke and she looked at you in a way you'd never been looked at before. She considered you as a human being, not just as somebody who did all the chores on the boat and got all the abuse. Naturally you fell in love with her. . . . No doubt her mother, if she'd been alive, would have encouraged your relations. . . .'

Phew! The man had sat down at last; true, he was only perching on the arm of a chair, but that was progress already.

'And what next? It's a good story, you know. . . .'

'Unfortunately Madame Willems was dead. You were alone on board the boat with her husband and Anneke, you were in contact with Anneke all day and I bet Willems kept an eye on you. . . .'

'That's what you say. . . .'

'As the owner of a fine boat, he didn't want his daughter to marry a penniless fellow. . . . When he'd had a drink he turned rough and unpleasant. . . .'

265

Maigret had recovered his prudence and was observing Jef's eyes relentlessly.

'D'you think I'd let any man lay a hand on me?'

'I'm sure not. Only it wasn't on you that he laid a hand . . . it was on his daughter. . . . I wonder whether perhaps he didn't catch you together. . . .'

It was wiser to let a few moments elapse, and the silence hung heavy while the smoke rose gently from Maigret's pipe.

'You provided me with an interesting detail just now. . . . It was chiefly in Paris that Willems went out at night, because he met his woman friend and they got drunk together. . . .

'Elsewhere he drank on board the boat or in a pub near the quayside. Like all boatmen who, as you told me, got up before dawn, he must have gone early to bed. . . .

'In Paris you and Anneke had the opportunity to be alone together. . . .'

There was a sound of footsteps and voices from the next room. Lapointe half opened the door.

'Job's done, Chief.'

'Presently . . .'

And the 'wheedling' went on in Maigret's smoke-filled office.

'It's possible that one night he may have come back earlier than usual and found you in one another's arms. . . . If that's what happened he must certainly have flown into a rage. . . . And his rages must have been terrible. . . . He may have threatened to fling you out . . . and struck his daughter. . . .'

'That's your story,' Jef repeated in an ironical tone.

'It's the story I should choose if I were in your shoes. . . . For in that case Willems's death would have been almost an accident. . . .'

'It was an accident.'

'I said almost. . . . I'm not even suggesting that you helped him fall into the water. . . . He was drunk . . . walking unsteadily. . . . Was it raining that night?'

'Yes.'

'You see! . . . So the plank was slippery. . . . What you did wrong was not to go to his rescue immediately. . . . Unless it was something more serious, and you pushed him. . . . All this happened two years ago and the police report mentions an accident, not a murder. . . .'

'Well then? Why do you persist in blaming me for it?'

'I'm only trying to explain it. . . . Suppose, now, that somebody had seen you push Willems into the water. Somebody who was on the embankment, unseen by you. . . . He could have told the police that you had waited on deck a longish time before jumping into the punt, so as to give your boss time to drown. . . .'

'And what about Anneke? Did she stand there watching without saying a word?'

'At two in the morning, she was probably asleep. In any case the man who saw you, and who at that time used to sleep under the Pont de Bercy, said nothing to the police. . . . Down-and-outs aren't keen on meddling in other people's business. They don't look at things the way other people do, and they have their own ideas about justice. . . .

'You were able to marry Anneke, and as you needed somebody with you to sail the boat you sent for your brother from Belgium. . . . You had found happiness at last. You were your own boss now. . . .

'Since then, you've passed through Paris several times and I'll bet you've avoided mooring by the Pont de Bercy. . . .'

'No, monsieur! I've moored there at least three times.'

'Because the dosser was no longer there. . . . Dossers

move around, too, and yours had settled underneath the Pont Marie. . . .

'On Monday, he recognized the *Zwarte Zwaan*. . . . He recognized you. . . . I wonder . . .'

He appeared to be following out a fresh idea.

'You wonder what?'

'I wonder if on the Quai de la Rapée, when Willems was pulled out of the water, you didn't catch sight of him. . . . Yes, you must almost certainly have seen him. . . . He came close, but he said nothing. . . .

'On Monday, when he began prowling round near your boat, you realized that he might talk. . . . He may quite possibly have threatened to do so. . . .'

Maigret did not believe that. The Doc was not that sort. But for the time being his story required it.

'And then I threw him into the water, eh?'

'Let's say you jostled him. . . .'

Once again Jef was on his feet, calmer and more resolute than ever.

'No, monsieur! You'll never make me admit such a thing. It's not the truth.'

'Then if I've been mistaken in any detail, tell me.'

'I've told it all already.'

'What?'

'It's been written down in black and white by the little man who came with the magistrate.'

'You stated that towards midnight you heard a noise. . . .'

'If I said so, it's true.'

'You added that two men, one of whom wore a light-coloured raincoat, were just coming out from under the Pont Marie and hurrying towards a red car. . . .'

'It was red. . . .'

'They must have passed alongside your barge. . . .'

Van Houtte did not stir a muscle. Maigret went to the door and opened it.

'Come in, messieurs.'

Lapointe had gone to fetch the insurance agent and his stuttering friend from their homes. He had found them playing a three-handed game of *belote* with Madame Guillot, and they had followed him without demur. Guillot was wearing the same yellowish raincoat as on Monday night.

'Are these the two men who went off in the red car?'

'It's a different matter seeing people at night on a dark quayside and seeing them in an office. . . .'

'They answer to the description you gave. . . .'

Jef shook his head, still refusing to commit himself.

'They were, in fact, at the Port des Célestins that night. Monsieur Guillot, would you tell us what you did there?'

'We drove down the ramp.'

'How far from the bridge was this ramp?'

'More than a hundred metres.'

'Did you stop the car just at the foot of the ramp?'

'Yes.'

'And then?'

'We took the dog out of the boot of the car.'

'Was it heavy?'

'Nestor weighed more than I do. Seventy-two kilos two months ago, last time we weighed him on the butcher's scales. . . .'

'Was there a barge beside the embankment?'

'Yes.'

'Did you then both go towards the Pont Marie, carrying your burden?'

Hardoin had opened his mouth to protest, but fortunately his friend broke in first.

'Why should we have gone to the Pont Marie?'

'Because this gentleman asserts that you did.'

'He saw us go towards the Pont Marie?'

'Not exactly. He saw you coming back from it . . .'

The two men stared at one another.

'He can't have seen us walking alongside the barge, because we threw the dog into the river astern of it. . . . I was even afraid the sack might get caught in the rudder. . . . I waited a moment to make sure that the current was carrying him out into midstream. . . .'

'Do you hear, Jef?'

And Jef, quite untroubled, replied: 'That's his story, isn't it? . . . And you've told your story, too. . . . And perhaps there'll be still more stories. . . . It's none of my fault.'

'What time was it, Monsieur Guillot?'

But Hardoin could not resign himself to playing a silent role, and began:

'Half pa . . . pa . . . past ele . . . le . . .'

'Half past eleven,' his friend interrupted. 'The proof is that we were in the café of the Rue de Turenne at twenty to twelve. . . .'

'Is your car a red one?'

'A red 403, yes.'

'Does the number plate include two nines?'

'7949 LF 75. . . . If you want to see the licence . . .'

'Monsieur Van Houtte, do you want to go down into the courtyard to identify the car?'

'I don't want anything except to go back to my wife.'

'How do you explain these contradictions?'

'It's up to you to explain things. . . . It's not my job.'

'You know where you went wrong?'

'Yes. In pulling the man out of the water. . . .'

'That, to begin with . . . but you didn't do it on purpose. . . .'

'What d'you mean, I didn't do it on purpose? . . . Was I walking in my sleep when I untied the punt and took the boathook to try and . . .'

'You're forgetting that somebody else had heard the

270

dosser's shouts. . . . Willems had not called out, probably, owing to shock at contact with the cold water. . . .

'In the case of the Doc, you took care to knock him out beforehand. You thought he was dead, or as good as dead, and that in any case he would be unable to resist he current and the eddies. . . .

t 'You were unpleasantly surprised when you heard him shouting for help. . . . And you'd have let him go on shouting if you had not heard another voice, that of the skipper of the *Poitou*. He could see you standing on the deck of your barge. . . .

'Then you thought it would be clever to play the rescuer. . . .'

Jef merely shrugged his shoulders.

'When I told you a moment ago that you'd gone wrong, this is not what I was referring to. . . . I was thinking of your story. . . . For you chose to tell a story in order to avert any suspicion. . . . And you worked it out elaborately. . . .'

The insurance agent and his friend, much impressed, looked at the Superintendent and the bargee in turn, realizing at last that a man's life was at stake.

'At half past eleven you were not busy working at your engine, as you claimed, but you were at some spot from which you could see the embankment, either in the cabin or somewhere on deck. . . . Otherwise you could not have seen the red car. . . .

'You witnessed the dog being thrown into the water. You remembered that, when the police asked you what had happened. . . .

'You felt sure the car would not be traced and you spoke of two men coming back from under the Pont Marie.'

'I'm not stopping you talking, am I? They tell what stories they like and you can tell what stories you like.'

Maigret went to the door again.

'Come in, Monsieur Goulet.'

This was the skipper of the *Poitou*, which was still unloading sand on the Quai des Célestins; he, too, had been brought in by Lapointe.

'What time was it when you heard someone calling out from the river?'

'About midnight.'

'You can't be more specific?'

'No.'

'It was later than half past eleven?'

'It must have been. When it was all over, I mean when we'd hoisted the body on to the bank and the policeman had come, it was half past twelve. . . . I believe the officer noted the time in his book. . . . And not more than half an hour had gone by since.'

'What d'you say to that, Van Houtte?'

'Me? Nothing, see? He's telling a story. . . .'

'And the policeman?'

'The policeman's telling a story, too. . . .'

By ten p.m. the three witnesses had left and a new tray of sandwiches and beer had been sent up from the Brasserie Dauphine. Maigret went into the next room and told Lapointe:

'It's your turn now. . . .'

'What am I to ask him?'

'Anything you like. . . .'

This was a routine practice. Sometimes three or four of them would take it on in relays during the night, putting roughly the same questions in a fresh way so as gradually to wear down the suspect's resistance.

'Hullo! Put me through to my wife, would you?'

Madame Maigret had not yet gone to bed.

'You'd better not wait up for me.'

'You sound tired. Is it being difficult?'

She had sensed discouragement in his voice.

'He'll go on denying to the end, without giving us the least handle. . . . He's the finest specimen of an obstinate idiot that I've ever been confronted with.'

'And the Doc?'

'I'm going to inquire about him.'

He next rang the Hôtel-Dieu and spoke to the nurse on night duty in the surgical ward.

'He's asleep. . . . No, he's in no pain. . . . The Professor came to see him after dinner and considers him to be out of danger '

'Has he spoken?'

'Before going to sleep he asked me for a drink.'

'He's said nothing else?'

'No. He took his sedative and closed his eyes.'

Maigret paced up and down the passage for half an hour, giving Lapointe his opportunity; he could hear the murmur of the Inspector's voice behind the closed door. Then he went back into his office, to find Jef Van Houtte seated on a chair at last, with his big hands folded on his knees.

The inspector's expression told him clearly enough that he had got no results, while there was a look of mockery on the face of the bargee.

'Is it going on much longer?' he inquired, watching Maigret resume his seat. 'Don't forget that you promised me you'd send for the consul. I shall tell him everything that you've done, and it'll be in all the Belgian newspapers. . . .'

'Listen to me, Van Houtte . . .'

'I've been listening to you for hours and you've kept on repeating the same thing. . . .'

He pointed to Lapointe: 'So has he. . . . Are there some more of them, behind that door, coming to ask me questions?'

'Perhaps there are.'

'I shall give them the same answers.'

'You've contradicted yourself several times. . . .'

'And what if I did contradict myself? Wouldn't you contradict yourself, if you were in my shoes?'

'You've heard the witnesses. . . .'

'The witnesses say one thing . . . I say another. . . . That doesn't mean that it's me that's lying. . . . I've worked hard all my life. . . . Ask any bargee what he thinks of Jef Van Houtte. Not one of them'll have a thing to say against me. . . .'

And Maigret started again from the beginning, determined to keep on trying, remembering one case where the man sitting opposite him, as tough as the Fleming, had suddenly yielded after sixteen hours, just as the Superintendent had been about to give up.

It was one of the most exhausting nights he had ever spent. Twice he withdrew into the next room and let Lapointe take over. By the end there were no more sandwiches, no more beer, and they felt as if the three of them were alone, like ghosts, in the deserted buildings of Police Headquarters, where charwomen had begun sweeping the corridors.

'It's impossible that you should have seen the two men walking alongside the barge. . . .'

'The difference between us is that I was there and you weren't.'

'You heard what they said. . . .'

'Anyone can say anything.'

'Note that I'm not accusing you of premeditation.'

'What does that mean?'

'I'm not saying that you knew beforehand that you were going to kill him. . . .'

'Who? Willems or the fellow I pulled out of the water? Because by now there are two of them, aren't there?

And by tomorrow there may be three, or four, or five. . . .
It's easy enough for you to add some more. . . .'

By three o'clock Maigret, exhausted, decided to call a
halt. For once it was he, and not his interlocutor who had
had enough of it. He got up.

'That'll do for today,' he muttered.

'Can I go back to my wife, then?'

'Not yet.'

'Are you going to make me spend the night in jail?'

'You can go to bed here, in a room where there's a
camp bed.'

Lapointe took him there. Maigret, meanwhile, left
Police Headquarters and walked, his hands in his pockets,
through the deserted streets. It was only at Châtelet that
he found a taxi.

He entered the bedroom noiselessly. Madame Maigret
stirred in her bed and muttered sleepily: 'Is that you?'

As though it could have been anyone else!

'What time is it?'

'Four o'clock.'

'Has he confessed?'

'No.'

'You believe it's him?'

'I'm morally convinced of it. . . .'

'Have you had to let him go?'

'Not yet.'

'Wouldn't you like me to get you something to eat?'

He was not hungry, but he poured himself a glass of
spirits before going to bed, which did not prevent him
from lying awake for a good half-hour more.

He would not forget that Belgian boatman in a hurry!

CHAPTER EIGHT

TORRENCE WENT ALONG with them that morning, for
Lapointe had spent the night at Headquarters. Maigret
had had a longish telephone conversation beforehand
with Professor Magnin.

'I'm convinced that he has been fully conscious since
yesterday evening,' the Professor had declared. 'I must
just ask you not to tire him. Don't forget that he's had a
severe shock and it'll take him some weeks to recover
from it completely.'

The three of them walked along the embankment in
the sunshine, Van Houtte between the Superintendent
and Torrence, and they might well have been mistaken
for strollers enjoying a fine spring morning.

Van Houtte had not shaved, for lack of a razor, and the
fair bristles on his face glistened in the sunlight.

Opposite the Palais de Justice they had stopped in a
bar to drink coffee and eat croissants. The Fleming had
devoured seven with the utmost calm.

He must have thought they were taking him to the
Pont Marie for some sort of reconstruction, and was sur-
prised at being led into the grey courtyard of the Hôtel-
Dieu, and then into the hospital corridors.

Although he gave a slight frown, he seemed unper-
turbed.

'May we go in?' Maigret asked the Ward Sister.

She scrutinized his companion with some curiosity, and
eventually shrugged her shoulders. It was beyond her; she
gave up trying to understand.

This, the Superintendent thought, was his last chance.
He led the way into the ward, where, as on the previous

day, the patients stared at him; Jef followed, partially concealed by Maigret, while Torrence brought up the rear.

The Doc watched him coming without apparent curiosity, and when he noticed the bargee his attitude did not change.

As for Jef, he remained as unconcerned as he had been during the night. With dangling arms and an expression of indifference on his face, he surveyed the unfamiliar scene of a hospital ward.

The hoped-for shock did not occur.

'Come forward, Jef.'

'What have I got to do now?'

'Come here. . . .'

'All right . . . what next?'

'Do you recognize him?'

'I suppose he's the chap that was in the water, isn't he? Only that night he had a beard. . . .'

'You recognize him all the same?'

'I think so. . . .'

'And you, Monsieur Keller?'

Maigret almost held his breath, and kept his eyes fixed on the dosser, who was gazing at him and who, slowly, made up his mind to look at the bargee.

'Do you recognize him?'

Did Keller hesitate? The Superintendent could have sworn to it. There was a long, expectant pause, until the doctor from Mulhouse turned his gaze on Maigret again without any sign of emotion.

'Do you recognize him?'

He had to control himself, suddenly feeling an almost furious resentment against the man who, as he now knew, had decided to say nothing.

The proof was that the ghost of a smile flitted over the dosser's face and a mischievous gleam came into his eyes.

His lips parted and he muttered: 'No.'

'This is one of the two boatmen who pulled you out of the Seine. . . .'

'Thank you,' whispered a barely audible voice.

'And it's also he, I'm practically certain, who gave you a knock on the head before throwing you into the water. . . .'

Silence. The Doc remained quite still, only his eyes showing any sign of life.

'Do you still not recognize him?'

What made the scene particularly impressive was that everything was said in hushed tones, while the two rows of patients, lying in their beds, watched and listened intently.

'Aren't you going to say anything?'

Keller still did not move.

'And yet you know why he attacked you. . . .'

The man's gaze betrayed a certain curiosity. He seemed surprised that Maigret had found out so much.

'It goes back to two years ago, when you were still living under the Pont de Bercy. . . . One night. . . . Can you hear me?'

He nodded.

'One night in December you witnessed a scene in which this man was involved. . . .'

Keller seemed, once again, to be wondering what decision to take.

'Another man, the skipper of the barge close to which you were lying, was pushed into the river . . . and *he* did not survive. . . .'

There was still the same silence, and finally a look of complete indifference came over the injured man's face.

'Isn't that true? . . . On seeing you again on Monday on the Quai des Célestins, the murderer was afraid of your speaking. . . .'

The head moved slightly, with an effort, just enough to enable Keller to catch sight of Jef Van Houtte.

There was no hatred or resentment in his gaze, nothing but a certain curiosity.

Maigret realized that he would extract nothing further from the dosser, and when the Ward Sister came to tell them they had stayed long enough, he did not protest.

In the corridor, the bargee held his head high.

'You're none the wiser, are you?'

He was quite right. It was he who had won the game.

'I can make up stories, too,' he remarked triumphantly.

And Maigret could not resist muttering between his teeth:

'To hell with you!'

While Jef waited at Police Headquarters with Torrence, Maigret spent nearly two hours in Judge Dantziger's chambers. The latter had rung up Deputy Public Prosecutor Parrain and asked him to join them, and the Superintendent told his story from beginning to end, down to the smallest detail.

The magistrate made notes in pencil, and when the story was ended he sighed:

'In a few words, we haven't the least proof against him. . . .'

'No proof, no. . . .'

'Apart from the question of the times which don't tally. . . . Any good lawyer would tear that argument to shreds.'

'I know.'

'Have you still any hope of getting a confession?'

'None at all,' admitted the Superintendent.

'Will the vagrant persist in keeping silent?'

'I'm convinced of it.'

'What reason can you suggest for his attitude?'

That was harder to explain, particularly to people who were unacquainted with that small social group that lives under bridges.

'Yes, what reason?' put in the Deputy Public Prosecutor. 'After all, it was nearly the end of him. . . . In my opinion, he ought to . . .'

In the opinion of a Deputy Public Prosecutor, of course, who lived in a flat in Passy with his wife and children, held weekly bridge-parties and was concerned with his own promotion and the scale of salaries.

But not in the opinion of a dosser.

'There's such a thing as justice, after all. . . .'

Yes, indeed. But in fact people who were not afraid of sleeping under bridges in midwinter, wrapped in old newspapers to keep themselves warm, were not interested in that sort of justice.

'Can you understand, yourself?'

Maigret was reluctant to say yes, for they would certainly have looked askance at him.

'You see, he doesn't think that a trial in the Assize Court, or counsels' speeches, or juries' decisions, or prisons are terribly important things.'

What would these two have said if he had told them how he had slipped that marble into the injured man's hand? And indeed if he had told them that Keller, sometime doctor, whose wife lived on the Ile Saint-Louis and whose daughter had married an important manufacturer of pharmaceutical products kept glass marbles in his pocket like a ten-year-old schoolboy?

'Is he still asking to see his consul?'

They were talking about Jef now.

And the magistrate, after a glance at the Deputy Public Prosecutor, muttered with some hesitation:

'In the present state of the inquiry, I don't think I can sign a warrant for his arrest. From what you tell me, there would be no point in my having a turn at questioning him. . . .'

It was certainly unlikely that the magistrate would succeed where Maigret had failed.

'Well then?'

Well then, as Maigret had already known when he got there, the game was lost. There was nothing for it but to release Van Houtte, who might perhaps demand an apology.

'I'm sorry, Maigret. But as things now stand . . .'

'I know. . . .'

It was always a difficult moment to live through. This was not the first time it had happened to him—and always with half-wits.

'I apologize, gentlemen,' he muttered as he left them.

Back in his office, a little later, he had to say the same thing:

'I apologize, Monsieur Van Houtte. . . . That's to say I apologize formally. . . . I'd have you know, however, that I've not changed my mind, that I'm still convinced that you killed your skipper, Louis Willems, and that you did all you could to get rid of the tramp, who was an awkward witness. . . .

'Having said this, I'll add that there's nothing to prevent you from returning to your barge and getting back to your wife and child. . . . Goodbye, Monsieur Van Houtte. . . .'

What happened next, however, was that the bargee made no protest, but merely looked at the Superintendent in some surprise, and as he stood in the doorway stretched out his long arm and offered his hand, mumbling:

'Anyone can make a mistake, *n'est-ce pas*?'

Maigret avoided looking at the hand, and five minutes

later he had immersed himself frenziedly in current problems.

During the weeks that followed, an arduous series of checks were carried out both in the neighbourhood of the Quai de Bercy and in that of the Pont Marie, and numbers of people were questioned, while the Belgian police sent reports which were added, all in vain, to other reports.

As for the Superintendent, for three months he was often to be seen hanging about near the Port des Célestins, with his pipe between his teeth and his hands in his pockets, as if he had nothing better to do. The Doc had finally been discharged from hospital. He had gone back to his nook under the bridge and his belongings had been restored to him.

Sometimes Maigret would stop beside him, as though by chance. Their conversation was always brief.

'You all right?'

'I'm all right.'

'None the worse for your injury?'

'Just a touch of dizziness from time to time. . . .'

Although they avoided talking about the matter, Keller knew quite well what Maigret was after and Maigret knew that Keller knew. It had become a sort of game they played together.

A little game that went on until one morning in the full heat of summer, when the Superintendent halted beside the dosser, who was eating a chunk of bread and drinking some red wine.

'You all right?'

'I'm all right!'

Had François Keller decided that his interlocutor had waited long enough? He was watching a barge moored nearby, a Belgian barge which was not the *Zwarte Zwaan*, but which looked like it.

'Those people have a good life,' he commented.

And pointing to two fair-haired children playing on the deck, he added:

'Particularly those. . . .'

Maigret looked him in the eyes, gravely, with a presentiment that there was something more to come.

'Life's not easy for anyone . . .' the dosser went on.

'Nor is death.'

'What's impossible is to pass judgement.'

They understood one another.

'Thank you,' murmured the Superintendent, who knew the truth at last.

'For nothing. . . . I've said nothing. . . .'

And the Doc added, like the Fleming: '*N'est-ce pas?*'

And indeed he had said nothing. He refused to pass judgement. He would not give evidence.

Nevertheless Maigret felt able to announce to his wife, casually, while they were having lunch:

'You remember the barge and the dosser?'

'Yes. Anything new?'

'I wasn't mistaken. . . .'

'Have you arrested the man, then?'

He shook his head.

'No! Unless he does something rash, which would surprise me in his case, he'll never be arrested.'

'Has the Doc spoken to you?'

'In a sort of way, yes. . . .'

With his eyes, rather than with words. They had understood one another, and Maigret smiled on remembering the sort of understanding that had been established between them, for a brief moment, under the Pont Marie.

Noland, May 2, 1962